COMFORT

COMFORT

Joyce Moyer Hostetter

CALKINS CREEK
Honesdale, Pennsylvania

Front jacket photograph:
Campus Pool at Georgia Warm Springs Foundation, 1940s
Title page:
Wooden sculpture carved by Michael Martin

Library of Congress Cataloging-in-Publication Data

Hostetter, Joyce.
Comfort / Joyce Moyer Hostetter. — 1st ed.
p. cm.
Summary: In 1945 Hickory, North Carolina, Ann Fay's father is back from the
war but she must still rely on her own strength and determination as she faces
the problems of her polio-induced disability and her father's failure to get a job.
Includes facts about the disability rights movement.
ISBN 978-1-59078-606-2 (hardcover : alk. paper)
[1. People with disabilities—Fiction. 2. Family problems—Fiction.
3. Emotional problems—Fiction. 4. Poliomyelitis—Fiction.
5. North Carolina—History—20th century—Fiction.] I. Title.
PZ7.H81125Com 2009
[Fic]—dc22
2008043664

jFie

CALKINS CREEK
An Imprint of Boyds Mills Press, Inc.
815 Church Street
Honesdale, Pennsylvania 18431

To Shirley Cunningham,
the eighth grade teacher who convinced me
that I am a writer

Contents

Prologue

It was my friends and neighbors and the singing of Imogene's people that got me through that first year after the war.

But to tell you the truth,

I never thought it would be a matter of just getting through.

For some reason, I thought that when my daddy come home from fighting, my world would be put back right again.

Not perfect right, of course, on account of Bobby dying of polio while Daddy was gone.

And me catching it too and coming home from the hospital on crutches.

Still, I thought Daddy and me both coming home would be like putting the last piece in a puzzle and sitting back to enjoy the pretty picture.

But hard as I tried, I couldn't make things be the way I wanted them with Daddy.

I learned quick enough that when someone drops a bomb in one small place on this planet, it shatters the whole universe.

And not just for a little while either.

The breaking goes on forever...

1

After the War

July 1945

Daddy was snuggling with Momma on the sofa and I was pretending to read the newspaper. But really, I was listening in on the two of them. Momma run her fingers through his black hair and played with the gray around his ears.

"Oh, it never felt so good," said Daddy.

At first when Daddy come home I didn't even notice the gray hairs. But soon I saw that me and him were starting to show some differences. Of course, my eyes was still blue like his and we had both lost weight, what with polio hitting me and the war taking so much out of him. But my hair was still as black as Daddy's on the day he went off to fight.

Momma smoothed the gray hairs with her thumb. "You look so distinguished," she teased. Her happy brown eyes crinkled into pretty comma shapes when she smiled.

"I have an idea," said Daddy. "Why don't you and me go out on the porch where we can get some peace and quiet?" He gave a little nod in the direction of my eight-year-old twin sisters. They were sitting on the floor, dressing their paper dolls. But the dolls seemed to be fighting over the same outfit.

Daddy pulled Momma to her feet and the two of them went outside. He let the screen door close real soft. But it seemed like every time he left the room we all felt it. Just as soon as they were gone, Ida looked up and said, "Where's Daddy?"

"Yeah," said Ellie. "Where'd he go?" She started gathering up the paper dolls.

"You leave them be," I said. "Momma and Daddy got lots of catching up to do."

To be honest, I wanted to follow them too. I wanted Daddy to pull *me* up and take *me* out on the porch. But I stayed in the armchair, reading the front page of the *Hickory Daily Record*. It said how hard we were bombing the Japanese and how we thought they would surrender any minute now—the same thing it said every day.

Sometimes my daddy was real interested in those stories, to hear if the war was about to end. But other times when I read the paper to him, he would change the subject or get up and leave. And I hated when he moved away from me.

I couldn't keep my mind on the newspaper, so I folded it, stuffed it under my armpit, and reached for my crutches. I locked my leg brace and hoisted myself to my feet. Once I got to the sofa, I sat on the end closest to the window. I could hear a rocking chair going out there. Just one, so I knew Momma was sitting on Daddy's lap, her head so close to his that her shiny brown hairs was mixed in with his darker ones. And I knew he was holding on to her like he thought she might leave him.

I knew just what they'd be seeing out there too, if they wasn't so busy looking at each other. They'd see the dark outlines of trees in the yard, the mailbox at the end of our lane, and the deep blue shape of Bakers Mountain beyond that.

Suddenly the rocking stopped. "Listen," Daddy said.

There was silence for a minute. Then Momma said, "I don't hear anything."

"I do," said Daddy. "It's so quiet I can hear the stars sparkle." Momma giggled, and I heard him say again, real slow, "It never felt so good."

I closed my eyes and thought how ever since I was a little girl it made me feel safe to see how my momma and daddy loved each other. Now, after more than a year of them being apart, I figured this was as perfect as it was going to get.

Ida and Ellie's paper dolls were getting along again. They'd finally agreed on who got to wear that red party dress.

I wished I had a good book to read. But I stared at the pictures on the wall, the ones my brother Bobby had made before he got polio and went to Hickory's emergency hospital. Bobby was four years old when Daddy went off to the war. He used to draw Daddy pictures of wild animals with his crayons. At the bottom of every one, in my handwriting, were these words: *Good night. Sleep tight. Don't let the bedbugs bite.*

I just wrote what Bobby told me.

Now he was the one sleeping tight, down there in his grave under the mimosa tree in our side yard. Or maybe not. Probably he was up in heaven making those stars sparkle. Trying to bring some comfort to Daddy.

Ever since the war, comfort was something my daddy seemed to hanker after. He had a shoulder wound that brung him home earlier than we expected. But he never talked about it, and anyway I could tell he was looking for a different kind of comfort. The kind that made you feel safe on the inside, instead of sad or worried. The kind that reminded you of how life was before some disaster snuck up and knocked you off your feet.

I felt the same way. When Daddy was driving me home

from the polio hospital he offered to celebrate by going to a diner. Any other time, I would've begged to eat in a restaurant. But I just wanted to get home. I needed home-cooked foods, and the sight of my momma's wood cookstove, and our table set with chipped dishes.

I noticed right off that whenever Momma asked Daddy what he was hungry for, he'd say the same things every time. If it was morning he wanted biscuits and white gravy. Evenings he'd ask for mashed potatoes and brown gravy. And corn on the cob every chance he got.

And blackberries. My daddy was so happy for the taste of them. Naturally, I wanted to be wherever he was, so the first day he took a notion to pick I followed him across the dirt road that runs by our house. But I learned real quick that when you're on crutches, picking blackberries is more than a notion. While he tramped through the field I sat in the side ditch and picked whatever I could reach.

Daddy wouldn't let me work for more than thirty minutes because Dr. Gaul had said to save my best energy for my therapy. I had to do exercises every day to strengthen my muscles. And go to a clinic once a week so my doctor could check my progress. Polio had made my left leg real weak, and my left arm was weak too. Some of the muscles just didn't want to work, so I practiced using other muscles to do their jobs.

I thought about Imogene Wilfong, my friend from the polio hospital. I wished I could see her at the clinic. But she lived in Greensboro, and anyhow she was colored. She'd probably have to go to her own doctor. They had broke the rules about segregation during the polio epidemic—as long as we was in contagious—but that didn't mean they would keep on breaking them.

I'd got just one letter from her since I come home from the hospital a few weeks earlier. And it was in my pocket. I pulled it out.

Dear Ann Fay,

I got your letter about leaving the Charlotte hospital and your daddy coming home from the war. I know you're happy!

I'm glad to be home, but I'm bored already. It wouldn't be so bad if I could play ball with my brothers and sisters in the backyard. But I'm tired of being the referee. I'm counting the weeks until school starts.

Have you read any good books? I'm reading Blue Willow. It's easy but I like it. It's about a girl. Her family loses everything valuable except one blue plate with pictures that tell a story. The plate helps her believe that someday her family will have a real home again.

We got to have our dreams, don't we?

Your friend,

Imogene

I folded the letter up and then took it back out and read it again. I thought about what Imogene said about dreams. Once, since I come home from the hospital, I dreamed about seeing her again. But then I woke up.

In real life I dreamed the same thing. So I asked my daddy about going to see Imogene. But his answer hadn't changed since the last time I asked him. *It's best if folks stick with their own kind.*

I sat there thinking how our polio hospital was willing to break the rules and put blacks and whites side by side during an emergency. And how the minute the crisis was over they thought it was so important to put everybody back in their places. You would think they would learn a thing or two from how good we got along. Not just me and Imogene, but others in the hospital too. We could do it again if they give us a chance!

All of a sudden, right in the middle of my Imogene thoughts, I heard the call of a bobwhite. I knew right off it was Junior Bledsoe asking for me. Junior is our neighbor—he's eighteen years old. His daddy is dead, so it's just him and his momma now. He done his best to look after us while Daddy was gone, even though I was almost fourteen then and Daddy had told *me* to be the man of the house.

I couldn't leave the room without the girls noticing because my brace clicked every time I made a move. So I nudged Ida with my crutch. "I'm going out for some fresh air," I said. "You keep right on doing what you're doing."

"We're having a party," Ida said.

"And I'm wearing the red dress," said Ellie. She held her doll up for me to see.

"Well, aren't you looking pretty!" I was already on my way out of the room.

The kitchen was dark, but I worked my way around the white shape of the table, the wood cookstove, and the refrigerator.

When I got to the back porch I answered with my own bobwhite whistle, then sat on the top step and waited for Junior.

2

The Radio

July 1945

The toolshed was just ahead of me. And the johnny house off to the right from that, waiting for company to come to its door. Personally, I'd be thrilled if I never visited johnny again. Not having an indoor bathroom was just one of the things that got extra complicated by polio. I looked past the outhouse to the walnut tree with the tire swing turning slowly in the breeze. It made me wish I was a young'un again.

Then, just like that, Junior was standing in front of me. Seemed like he had got so big while I was in the polio hospital. I'd been home for three weeks already, but I still hadn't got used to his broadness.

"Hey, Ann Fay," he said.

"Hey, yourself."

"I brought you a radio." Junior held out a brown box with a cord hanging from the back. I could see it shining in the moonlight.

"A radio? Whatever for?"

"To listen to, silly." He put it on my lap and sat down on the step beside me. But first he pulled a short black comb out of his back pocket and run it through his hair. That was another change in Junior. Seemed like all of a sudden he was awful concerned about which direction his curly brown hair was going.

"Junior, I can't take this. Radios cost a lot of money."

"Didn't cost me a dime. Ruth Whitener gave it to me for fixing her flat tire. A customer gave it to her when they couldn't pay their bill. She already has one, and you know me and Momma do too. It'll help pass the time of day. Since you don't get around like you used to." Then real quick, Junior added, "And it can be for your daddy for serving his country the way he done."

"Well, if you're sure..." I rubbed my hands over the shiny case and tried to imagine my family listening to war news right in our own home. Used to be we'd have to go over to Junior and Bessie's if we wanted to hear the radio. And to read a newspaper we had to wait for our neighbors, the Hinkle sisters, to share theirs with us.

"Do you think the war's about over?" I asked.

"Of course. Our boys are clobbering the Japs. They can't hold out much longer."

I knew I could count on Junior Bledsoe to have an opinion. If there's anyone that's got an opinion on every subject, it's Junior. "I hope you're right," I said. And I laid my head down on that radio. I sure wished I could listen to Franklin Roosevelt giving one of his fireside chats from the White House. "I still can't believe he's dead."

"Huh?"

"President Roosevelt. I'd give anything to hear him talking to me on the radio again. Junior, it makes me so mad! I was all set on going to his Georgia Warm Springs Foundation for people who had polio. And maybe even seeing him there. Why did he have to die?"

"Well, Ann Fay Honeycutt, it's not like he done it just

to make you mad. He wore out, that's all. Besides, what did you want to go there for anyway—to see the president or to get over polio?"

"Maybe both," I said. "This blasted brace on my leg is dragging me down. And getting rid of these crutches would be like breaking out of jail. I bet if I'd met Franklin Roosevelt I'd have felt so good I'd be walking by now."

"Probably not," said Junior. "I say if you want something bad enough it doesn't matter if you're in Warm Springs, Georgia, or right here at home. It all depends on what's inside of you."

I rolled my eyes, but of course Junior couldn't see it. Like I said before—that boy has an opinion on just about everything. But I didn't argue with him. "Maybe," I said. "You know what else I want?"

"Bet you're gonna tell me."

"I wanna see Imogene Wilfong, my colored friend from the hospital. Too bad you don't have a car. You could take me to Greensboro."

"Yeah," said Junior. "Too bad I *don't* have a car. We could really go places then. Tell ya what. I'll start saving my money."

"Did *you* ever have a colored friend?"

"Huh?"

"What do you think, Junior? Can white people be friends with coloreds or do we have to stick with our own kind?"

Junior shrugged. "Like I said, if you want something bad enough, you can get it." He stood up. "There's a colored man works on the farm during haying season. Jake can throw a bale like nobody's business, and take a tractor apart and put it back together. And he's real good to joke around with. Time flies when I'm working with him."

"Does that make him your friend?"

Junior shrugged. "I only see him during haying season. We're not girls, Ann Fay. We just work together." He stood up. "I better get back. Just wanted you to have the radio."

"Well...thanks a heap."

"Like I said, didn't cost me a dime."

Before I knew it, Junior was halfway across the yard and I was alone on the back porch. Thinking how Momma and Daddy had each other on the front porch and how I should just leave them be. Ida and Ellie too—they and their paper dolls didn't need me hanging around.

I leaned against the porch post and imagined I was in the Hickory polio hospital. In the contagious ward. I remembered how my daddy come to me in my fever, walking on water and holding me so I felt safe.

But that was all in my head. He was actually on the other side of the world, fighting in the war.

I thought about the hard cramping I had in my legs and my arm. And the feel of the hot blankets the nurses wrapped around my muscles to make them relax. How it felt like they was burning my skin off. And how Imogene was right there in the bed beside mine. "It mostly hurts at first," she said real soft when I hollered out. "After a while it starts to feel better."

I could still hear the sound of her voice, playing like a radio show in my head.

As bad as it felt at the time, there was something about that contagious ward that I missed. Something about just resting and letting someone else take care of me...

That first day in the ward was like a dividing line in my life. Kind of like the ditch my daddy dug once between his garden and the wisteria vine that was trying to take it over.

It was a line between being strong one minute and weak the next. It was the beginning of a new kind of fear. Was I going to spend the rest of my life in a bed? Or even die? Those things didn't happen, but now that I was home from the hospital I was learning one thing. I would never fit in again. I was different from everyone I knew.

Except Imogene. But she wasn't around, and I didn't have any way to get to her either.

So I decided to go inside and write her a letter. I set the radio on the porch floor. Daddy could carry it in later.

But I tell you what's the truth—if I'd only known how it would bring the war into the middle of my family, I would've told Junior to give the stupid thing to someone else. Maybe they could've handled the news it brought better than my daddy did.

3

The Bomb
August 1945

I had loved July because it felt so good to be home from the hospital and having Daddy home too. But going into August was like running into a sticky spiderweb. I kept feeling like some furry critter was crawling on me, but I couldn't see it to brush it off.

School was about to start, and I didn't want to go back. I dreaded how other students would stare at my skinny leg and ugly metal brace. And I hated that my best friend, Peggy Sue Rhinehart, would be going to ninth grade without me.

Mountain View School has all twelve grades in one building, so she'd only be one room away. But we wouldn't be able to sit together or meet at the pencil sharpener. And when I saw her at lunch she'd be with her new best friend, Melinda somebody, who moved here from Cherryville while I was in the hospital.

Every day I picked up my crutches and hobbled to the mailbox. And every day Imogene did not write to me. On the way back to the house, the clicking sound of my braces would mock me. *She forgot all about you. She forgot all about you. She forgot...* How could a couple of pieces of metal sound so much like a real person talking?

On top of everything else, Daddy was starting to wear on Momma's nerves. Seemed like no matter how she pushed, he wasn't going to look for a job. He'd been to the American Legion to establish his veteran's benefits. But now that his war wound was healing, Momma wasn't satisfied for him to collect government money.

She had wanted so much for him to come home from the war. But it was starting to feel like now she wanted to push him out of the house.

It wasn't that Daddy was lazy. If Momma asked him to pick tomatoes, he'd head straight for the garden. If she needed him to draw water for doing the wash, he'd be happy to oblige. He just didn't seem to have any get-up-and-go.

Still, on the first Monday in August, he promised Momma he'd go to the manpower office right after dinner. It was a damp gray day.

She fried some squash and I set out light bread, mayonnaise, and tomatoes for making sandwiches. We all sat around the table and held hands—pretty as a picture. Daddy said the blessing and I stared at him the whole time.

I watched the little bone in his cheek moving while he talked in his soft voice, telling God how thankful he was to be home again and how delicious Momma's cooking tasted and how he wished everyone in the world could have the same good things.

Before the war, Daddy hadn't been anywhere much except down in Georgia where he was brought up. And here in North Carolina where he and Momma moved when they got married.

Then he went off to fight Hitler and got attached to other parts of the world. And to the people over there. Sometimes when he sat on the porch the pace of his rocking would slow down and pretty soon it would stop altogether. Daddy would always be staring at something then—a clump of grass in the yard or maybe a mud puddle. But I could tell he wasn't actually noticing them things. He was seeing a field in France or a muddy road in Germany.

And he wouldn't hear us when we talked to him. He was hearing people speaking languages he couldn't understand. He'd told us how they cheered when the American soldiers liberated them from Hitler. "You know what?" he said. "Cheering is the same all over the world."

One day when Ida crawled up on his lap he said, "When I was in Berlin I met a snaggle-toothed girl like you. She held on to my leg and wouldn't let go. So I picked her up and gave her a piece of chewing gum." His voice got real soft and worried then. "Those children didn't need gum. They needed houses. And for their daddies to come home. Alive. All in one piece."

One thing my daddy prayed for at every meal was the end of the war. Listening to him ask for it—so soft and sincere—always made me feel like it would happen. And soon.

Well, when I sat down to dinner that day in August, I just didn't know *how* soon.

Quick as Daddy got done praying, Ellie jumped up and switched on the radio.

At first after Junior give us that radio we mostly listened in the evenings, in the living room. Sometimes me and Momma would fold the wash, and Ida and Ellie would match up the socks. And Daddy would carve little animal shapes out of wood.

But that was before a foggy July morning in New York

City when an American army bomber accidentally crashed into the Empire State Building. Eleven floors caught fire and fourteen people died. It was such big news that Daddy turned on the radio in the middle of the day. And left it on all afternoon.

After that, the rules about listening to the radio didn't apply. Daddy moved it into the kitchen so we could hear it while we canned beans.

So this time, when Ellie switched it on, Daddy didn't tell her not to. He just said, "Ellie, did you ask to get up from the ta—?" He never even finished the question on account of he realized that the regular program had been interrupted for a special announcement from President Truman. In the middle of the day!

The president's spokesman said that the United States had dropped a bomb on the Japanese city of Hiroshima.

Our boys had been dropping bombs on Japan for weeks. But according to the radio, this wasn't any ordinary regular old bomb—it was an atomic bomb with more than two thousand times the power of the British "Grand Slam."

I could see right off that my Daddy knew what a Grand Slam was and that it made him real worried about this new bomb. He had just picked up his knife and was fixing to spread a glob of mayonnaise on his light bread. But when he heard that, his knife clattered to his plate, his face went tight and then slack, and I saw the light go out of his eyes. And all of a sudden I got a real bad feeling, like it was my daddy who had got hit with that bomb.

The man on the radio told us that the Japanese would not be able to withstand another such assault and that the war would likely be over real soon.

Well, Ellie for sure didn't ask could she get up from

the table this time. And Ida didn't either. The two of them jumped up and took each other by the hands and danced around the kitchen like that. They were a-whooping and a-hollering and I felt like doing the same thing—at least until I saw my daddy's face.

Then I was confused. If the war was ending, shouldn't I be on my feet—on my crutches, I mean—dancing and singing? But if I was to go by Daddy's reaction, there wasn't nothing to celebrate.

Momma reached over and put her hand on Daddy's and said real quiet, "Leroy, this is good news—the war is nearly over. It's just a matter of time."

Daddy didn't say a word. He just stared at the glob of mayonnaise on his light bread. I noticed it quivering ever so slightly. But Daddy was so still, I wasn't even sure he was breathing.

I didn't bother reaching for my crutches. I just hung on to the kitchen table and scooted back my chair and pulled myself to my feet. Then I locked my leg brace into place so I wouldn't collapse on the floor. I grabbed onto Daddy. And I hung on like he was the bread and I was the mayonnaise and it had already been spread.

Most times when I hug my Daddy he pulls me up against him and lets me feel his heart beat. But this time he just sat there with his arms resting on the dinner table. It was like he didn't even notice that Momma had took his hand and I had wrapped my arms around the front of his shoulders.

I could feel his Adam's apple working up and down under my hand. And that scared me a little. So I put my head against his.

He just sat there. He didn't turn and hug me. He didn't even squeeze Momma's hand. Or move at all. Not on purpose, anyway. But then I felt him shaking. The day was so warm and humid we were both damp with sweat and I was practically sticking right to him, but still, he was shivering.

I looked at Momma, but she wasn't looking at me. She was staring at him, and I saw a kind of fear in her pretty brown eyes. They should have been crinkled shut with smiling on account of the war being almost over. But she was studying him so hard I could almost see the worry wrinkles being made.

It scared me to see my parents like that. I didn't know what to do, so I just left them be. I worked my way around the corner of the table and sat on my chair so I could pick up my crutches. Then I headed for the back porch.

Ida and Ellie were still dancing and singing some stupid made-up song about the war is over. I couldn't get to the door because of them jumping around.

"Stop it!" I said. "That man did not say the war is over! This is not something to be whooping and hollering about!"

I didn't know why I said it, but I knew it was true.

The man on the radio had said that we had more power than ever to destroy our enemy. He did not say that we were destroying ourselves in the process. But I was watching my daddy when he heard the announcement. Without saying a word or hardly moving a muscle, he had let me know that killing someone you hate isn't the same as living in peace.

4

Nagasaki
August 1945

Three days after they dropped that horrible bomb on Hiroshima, someone come on the radio and said they dropped a worse one on a place called Nagasaki. When Daddy heard that, he dropped his head into his hands. Sometimes I still wonder how he knew to grieve about those bombs.

At first, no one realized how many people they killed. Or how many thousands would die in the weeks afterwards. But my daddy seemed to know. It was like there was a voice inside him saying, *This is much worse than anything you saw while you were fighting in Europe.*

And for some reason my daddy cared about that. He was supposed to hate the Japs, but it was like he just couldn't do it. Like he had already done all the hating he could—which wasn't much to begin with.

When he heard that news about the second bomb, Daddy stared at the worn pattern in the green and white kitchen linoleum and listened for a minute or two more. Or maybe he didn't listen. Maybe he just sat there with his heart in some other part of the world.

The rest of us was hanging on to each other and wondering what to say. Daddy stood up and we stepped back to make room for him. He went onto the back porch and closed the screen door real soft and careful—as if letting it slam would set off something bad in the world. Then he went into the johnny house and stayed for a long time.

Later that night, President Truman come on the radio. He said the reason they started dropping that new, awful kind of bomb was on account of the Japs bombing us at Pearl Harbor and how atrocious they treated our prisoners of war. He said our bomb would save thousands and thousands of American lives.

I looked at my daddy when the president said that. I was thinking it might cheer him up. But I could see that it didn't.

The president went right on talking. He said the bomb had tragic significance but America should gladly bear that burden. "We thank God it has come to us," he said, "instead of to our enemies; and we pray that He will guide us to use it in His ways and for His purposes."

You should have heard my daddy then. "God!" he shouted. I couldn't tell if he was swearing or praying except he don't usually cuss, so I figured it was a prayer. And he was looking up when he said it—like he wanted God to come down there and do something with our president.

But God stayed right where He was and my daddy sure didn't know what to do. So he yanked the cord out of the wall and picked up the radio and threw it at the kitchen window. The radio hit the screen so hard it popped out of place. I heard a clanking sound. And then a rustling noise when the radio landed—smack-dab in the middle of Momma's blue hydrangeas.

5

School
August 1945

About five days later President Truman announced the end of the war.

It was all anyone could talk about after the church service the next Sunday. Except my daddy. He didn't stand under the oak tree in the churchyard and smoke with the rest of the men. Evidently he went off by himself someplace while me and Momma and the girls visited with our friends.

Like always, the young people met behind the church while the adults stood around out front. It was hot and sunny, so we sat in the grass, and of course Junior brought up the subject of that bomb. "Didn't I tell you the war would be over any minute?" he said.

I could see he thought the bombing was a good thing, and of course all the other young people thought so too. "Won't be long until they show us a moving picture of it," said Junior. He was talking about the newsreels they show at the movie theater.

My friend Peggy Sue spoke up then. "Junior," she said, "maybe you could go to the picture show with me and Ann Fay next week."

Well, I just couldn't believe what I was hearing. For

years, Peggy Sue's momma took just the two of us to the movies on Saturday afternoons. But this summer we hadn't hardly gone at all. I guess it was too much to expect that we would pick up right where we left off before the polio epidemic. But still, I was hoping our friendship would get back to normal.

We never let anyone tag along to the movies—not my twin sisters and not Junior Bledsoe either. I gave Peggy Sue's foot a little kick and tried to give her a look that said, *Don't you dare*. But she wasn't looking at me for anything in the world. She had a plan. If there's anybody I know who can get what she wants, it's Peggy Sue Rhinehart.

I'd understand if it was her new friend Melinda she wanted to take along. In fact, I was pretty sure she was already taking Melinda on the Saturdays she didn't ask me. But why in the world would she want *Junior* to go along to the movies? That's what I wanted to know.

I got to wondering if she invited him just in case the two of us ran out of things to talk about. Me and Peggy Sue had been friends since before first grade. But all of a sudden she was thinking about movie stars, boys, and swing dancing. She'd tried dragging me along to a dance. I told her my daddy wouldn't let me. Which was true. But what would *I* want to go to a dance for? I just wanted to get from one place to the next without falling on my backside. Seemed like every move I made was something to calculate beforehand. Such as getting in the car.

The next Saturday, when Mrs. Rhinehart came to take me to the movies, I rode in the front seat with her. It was easier than climbing in the back.

I had my fingers crossed that she would drive right past Junior Bledsoe's lane. But she turned in and drove up to his house. "I hope you don't mind," said Peggy Sue. I couldn't see her from where I was sitting, but I could just imagine the determined look in her blue eyes.

"Well, I'm not crazy about it," I said. "Especially if he wants to see a James Cagney picture."

"Don't worry about that. I told Junior we would see *Lone Texas Ranger.*"

"A cowboy movie?" I'm pretty sure Peggy Sue heard the disgust in my voice. "How'd you let him talk you into that? You hate westerns as much as I do."

"Oh, they're not all that bad," said Peggy Sue.

Then Mrs. Rhinehart spoke up. "Honey," she said, "I was under the impression the three of you had agreed on this."

"Ann Fay, do you mind if we see a western just this once?" pleaded Peggy Sue. "Next time we'll make Junior watch our show."

Next time? I saw Mrs. Rhinehart watching me, waiting for my answer. I thought how many times she'd took me to the movies and bought my ticket even. I sure didn't want to start a squabble between her and Peggy Sue. "All right, then," I said. "Just this once."

By that time Junior had come out of the house. Mrs. Rhinehart bent her seat forward so he could climb in the back with Peggy Sue. I didn't say much on the way to the movies because I was a little bit mad. And I didn't get any happier as the day went on.

At the theater Peggy Sue sat between me and Junior. And all of a sudden she seemed especially interested in gunfights. I might as well have been home by myself. They talked so much I almost wondered if they was even watching the movie.

I didn't see much of it either. For one thing, I wasn't interested, and for another, I was busy worrying about school starting the next week. If my two best friends didn't talk to me, why would the eighth graders at Mountain View School want to?

I fretted over it so much that on the first day of school I woke up with a tummy ache. Momma gave me some pink medicine, but I still had to hurry to the johnny house on account of diarrhea.

On the way back I bumped into Daddy sitting on the steps. He was wearing overalls and I wanted like crazy to put mine on too—the ones he gave me before he went off to war, when he told me to be the man of the house in his place. They were too small by now. But staying home in tight overalls would've felt a lot better than going to school in the brand-new dress Momma had made.

"Come sit for a minute," said Daddy. He pulled me to his lap and leaned my crutches against the porch floor. Then he put my head against his shoulder and started talking. "You can't have a tummy ache every day."

He waited for me to say something. But I didn't. So after a minute he spoke up again.

"It's got to be hard," he said. "Going to school on crutches and being a year behind. But you and I both know—if *anyone* can do hard things, it's Ann Fay Honeycutt."

My daddy has always been like that. So kind and sensitive that if someone else felt pain, he would feel it too. Especially if that someone was me. I wanted to stay there with him all morning, listening to the grasshoppers flicking around in the dry grass.

He shook me real soft and said, "It's the first step that's the hardest. Remember what Franklin Roosevelt said—'The only thing we have to fear is fear itself.'"

I knew it was fear making my tummy hurt and sending

me to the toilet. But I didn't admit it. I just asked, "Do you think President Roosevelt was ever afraid?"

"I think he was. After all, he was a famous politician when polio struck. And I'm sure he wanted to be strong for his family. Then he became president and had to be strong for all of us." Daddy was quiet for a little while and then he said one more thing. "I think polio was the thing that scared him. But he didn't let it make him weak. Maybe polio made him stronger than he already was."

Of all the things my daddy could have said, he picked the perfect thing. *Polio made him stronger than he already was.*

So I hugged him one last time, and when I did, I wiped the tears that were starting to come—right onto the collar of his shirt. I didn't want him to see me crying.

But if I know my daddy, he probably felt my tears anyway.

When I got back inside, Momma handed a paper sack with my lunch to Ellie and said, "Carry this for Ann Fay." She pointed to my notebook on the kitchen table and handed Ida two yellow pencils with a rubber band around them. "Take these for your sister."

Ida and Ellie didn't complain. I think they were proud to be helping *me* for a change. When the school bus stopped by our mailbox they let me get on first.

I hadn't thought about how I'd climb into the bus. So I had to think fast. I laid my crutches on the bus floor one at a time while I held on to the shiny handrail. Then I unlocked my ugly, miserable brace and pulled myself up.

The bus driver waited patiently and greeted me just like she'd always done. "Morning, Ann Fay. You can sit on the front seat. And the twins too."

When the bus started moving, I heard a boy asking how

come *they* had to fill in from the back and we got to sit up front. Someone else said to him, "Can't you see that Ann Fay Honeycutt had polio?"

It made me want to go to the back of the bus. To plop down in my old seat. But I had already called enough attention to myself. So I whispered, *Polio made him stronger than he already was.*

And then another voice popped into my head. It was Imogene Wilfong saying, *It mostly hurts at first. After a while it starts to feel better.*

I have to say, that made me smile.

The bus stopped at Whitener's Store and a bunch of neighborhood children got on. Ruth Whitener, who owned the store, had six children of her own. Her daughter Jean grinned real big when she saw me. "Hey," she said.

After that there was only one more stop and then we were at school.

Even though I had the front seat I waited until last to get off the bus. Jean Whitener and her friend Beckie waited too. They were older than me, but Jean offered to carry my school supplies so Ida and Ellie could go straight to their classroom on the lower hall. "And I'll carry your books in the afternoon," said Beckie.

I hated using crutches on steps. There were only three steps at the side entrance to the school, but they slowed me down. Jean and Beckie waited real patient for me and walked with me down the shiny wooden hallway. I was glad it was them and not my little sisters taking me to my classroom. As it was, people turned and stared when they heard my brace clicking down the hall.

Everyone in the eighth grade stared too. I knew most of them, at least a little bit. But none of them was my friends in the way the ninth graders were. I made the mistake of choosing a desk in front of Rob Walker. It wasn't two seconds later I heard him muttering under his breath, "I'm not sitting next to no cripple." And just like that, he went to a seat across the room.

I felt my ears get hot. "It mostly hurts at first," I told myself.

But Rob didn't let up. Before the morning was out he went by my desk on the way to the pencil sharpener. He made a point of leaving plenty of room between me and him, but he made sure I knew he was there. "How ya doing, Click?" he said in a loud whisper.

Click? It took me a minute to realize he was making fun of my noisy brace. I couldn't believe I hadn't been in school even two hours before polio had earned me a nickname.

Later, when we left the classroom and all the other girls had friends to walk with, I said Imogene's line again. I said it at recess while I was sitting on the wooden bench by the dusty red ball diamond, watching the other students play softball.

After Mrs. Barkley helped the class choose teams she sat on the bench beside me. "How's it going so far?" she asked.

I shrugged. What did she expect me to say—*I'm so excited to be in your class instead of Mrs. Hamrick's*? I liked Mrs. Barkley already, and not just because Peggy Sue had liked her. I could tell she was a good teacher. But I wished I'd had her when I was *supposed* to be in eighth grade.

I didn't know what to say about how things were going. What should it be like? After you have polio, I mean. Were other people supposed to carry your books for you the rest of your life? Did you have to sit at the front of the bus with your little sisters while everyone else sat in the back and talked about you? And warm the bench at recess?

"I used to play softball real good," I said. I don't know why I said that. Maybe I thought Mrs. Barkley would try to understand. I used one of my crutches to write a big A in the soft red dust at my feet.

"I know," she said. "I saw you out here playing when you were in seventh grade. You had a knack for hitting the ball where other players couldn't catch it."

"Really?" I looked at her. "You noticed that?"

Mrs. Barkley laughed. Her gray eyes twinkled. "I've been watching you, Ann Fay. I'm glad you're finally in my class. It won't be the way either of us expected it to be. But you and I are about to have a good year together."

I didn't know what she meant by that. But all of a sudden I thought maybe sitting on the bench wouldn't be so bad. Not if she was there beside me.

When it was almost time for the class to go in, Mrs. Barkley told me to get a head start. "I'm sending everyone to the restroom," she said. "You can go there after you stop by the drinking fountain."

I stood up, locked my brace, and headed by myself toward the big brick school building. The ground was sloped uphill and a little bit stony, so I had to watch where I set the tips of my crutches. I'd fallen plenty of times at the hospital when I was learning to walk. And more after I got home. If I was to fall down at school, I didn't think I would survive the humiliation.

I walked right by Peggy Sue's class on the way to the bathroom. The door was open but I kept my eyes on the floor. I hoped all my old friends were busy working and not looking out the door.

But Peggy Sue must've heard my braces clicking. By the

time I made it to the girls' bathroom she was right behind me. "Hey," she said. "Isn't Mrs. Barkley the best teacher ever?"

"Yes," I said. "So far, anyway." I went into a stall and leaned my crutch against the door. I heard Peggy Sue in the stall beside me.

"Mrs. Hamrick is trying to act strict," she complained. "Junior says she grades really hard. If what he says is true, I'm in trouble for sure."

"Well," I said, "if it came from Junior Bledsoe it's probably exaggerated. He loves to tell a good story."

"I love to listen to him," said Peggy Sue. "Isn't he the cutest thing?"

I just about fell in the toilet when she said that. And it wasn't on account of having polio either—I was in shock.

"Peggy Sue!" I said. "I hope you're not telling me you have a crush on Junior Bledsoe. If you are, I will just throw up in this commode."

6

Disaster
September 1945

After that first day, whenever my class went somewhere, such as the lunchroom or the library, Mrs. Barkley always sent me ahead of the others.

At first it seemed like a good idea because I was so slow. But after a while I began to wonder—how was I supposed to make friends when I had to go everywhere by myself? I didn't exactly like the idea of walking the halls alone for the rest of my life.

Finally, after a few weeks, I worked up my nerve to tell Mrs. Barkley how I felt. "May I go with the rest of the class?" I asked. "It's not much fun being separated from everybody."

"Hmm," she said. "Maybe I could send another student with you."

I thought about that. What if I didn't like the person she picked? Would we get stuck with each other? Or would people have to take turns whether they wanted to or not? Would I get stuck with Rob Walker one day?

Any way I looked at it, her plan just didn't feel right. So I said that if she didn't mind, I would just like to go with the rest of the class.

Mrs. Barkley looked doubtful. "Well, I suppose we can give it a try," she said.

So we did.

Everything went fine all that first day—at least until it was time to go home. Then I made the mistake of not waiting till last. After all, the whole point of it was so I could blend in. Jean and Beckie had just come by for my books, and Charlie Barnes offered to let me go in front of him. So I did. But I should've known that if Rob Walker was behind us, there was going to be problems.

You would think that if a body was in a hurry to get someplace and he got slowed down, he wouldn't run over people like an army tank going into enemy territory.

But some people don't think at all.

I *could* make excuses for Rob, since he wasn't smack-dab behind me. I *could* say he didn't see the crippled girl who was about four people ahead. But then again, you would've had to be just plain blind to miss me.

When I got to the steps going out of the school, I slowed down. Naturally, that held up the people behind me. I heard Rob yell something about some people being slow as ketchup, and evidently he shoved the person in front of him. And just like that, the rest of us went down like a row of books falling off the shelf.

There wasn't nothing I could do to stop myself. There was only three steps, but it still hurt plenty going from the top one to the ground, especially with Charlie Barnes landing half on top of me. Looking back on it, I don't see how I got by without breaking some bones.

I did get my arm skinned up. And I took a hard blow to my hip too. But worst of all is how it hurt my pride. While I was laying there on the ground trying to figure out what hit me, I saw Peggy Sue coming out the school door. And next thing I knew, she was yanking my dress down around my knees. Everything had happened so fast I didn't even realize that my underpants was showing!

Rob Walker thought it was plenty funny. It didn't cross his mind to pick anyone up. He just laughed and ran past us toward his bus. But he wasn't taking into consideration the wrath of Peggy Sue Rhinehart.

Peggy Sue took off yelling Rob's name like it was the nastiest cuss word you ever heard. I was still laying on the ground when she tore into him. First she smacked him across the shoulder with her history book. Then, before he could turn around to see what hit him, she grabbed him by the arm, and she and her friend Melinda dragged him back to me.

She couldn't have kept Rob there on her own, but Peggy Sue had Melinda and Jean Whitener and a few others to back her up. Charlie jumped up and grabbed him by one arm. He twisted it behind Rob's back while Peggy Sue done the talking.

"You *will* apologize to Ann Fay. And you *will* pick her up."

Of course she was trying to help. But it made me feel even worse to have Rob sneering overtop of me. "And risk my life? She's got polio."

"That is just ignorant," said Peggy Sue. "Ann Fay does not have polio anymore."

Charlie twisted Rob's arm a little harder.

Maybe if I wasn't still on the ground I would've smacked Rob Walker upside the head. Maybe. But truthfully, all of a sudden I didn't seem to have any fight in me. I just wanted everyone to go away and leave me alone. I didn't need Rob or anyone else to help me up. And I sure didn't need a crowd watching my humiliation.

A couple of students helped me to my feet. They sat

me on the low wall that runs alongside the school steps. Jean Whitener pressed her clean white handkerchief to my skinned-up elbow. Beckie handed me my crutches. I didn't look at anyone's face, so everything was a blur of hands and elbows.

By this time Mrs. Barkley was there. She insisted that Rob apologize to every one of us he'd knocked down. So he rolled his eyes and mumbled something that sounded like "Sorry" but sure didn't feel like it.

I didn't answer him. I just looked at Mrs. Barkley—hoping she could see in my eyes how much I needed to get out of there. And I guess she did, because she sent Rob to the principal's office and told the rest of the students to get on their buses.

I could swear I heard Rob muttering "Click, Click, Click" under his breath when he went up those steps.

When Mrs. Barkley was sure I hadn't broken any bones, she let Jean and Beckie lead me to my bus. Peggy Sue was fretting. "Are you going to be okay?" she asked. "Want me to ride home with you? Daddy can pick me up later."

"No," I said. "I'll be fine."

But I wasn't fine. I was tired of being a cripple. I wanted my old life back. The one where I could hit a ball and run the bases. And go down steps without stopping to think it through. I wanted to be in ninth grade with people who acted their age. I wanted Peggy Sue to be my friend just because we were as comfortable as biscuits and gravy on the same plate. And *not* because she felt sorry for me.

Right that minute I was wishing like crazy for Imogene. But I didn't even bother telling myself it mostly hurts at first.

When I got on the bus the twins were already there.

They'd seen the whole thing through the bus window. "I'm telling Daddy," said Ida.

"No!"

"Yes," said Ellie. "Daddy will go over to that boy's house and knock some sense in his head."

"Would you sit down and be quiet?" I hissed. In the back of the bus I heard someone talking about Click Honeycutt showing everyone her step-ins. You would think that seeing my underpants was the most exciting thing since the atomic bomb.

7

Comfort
September 1945

When we got off the bus I told the girls to keep their mouths shut. But of course they run into the house to tell Momma and Daddy what happened. I didn't think I could abide one more person feeling sorry for me right then, so I started across the garden.

Just past the garden was the ditch Daddy had dug a long time ago to keep the wisteria vines from growing into our vegetables. And just past the ditch was a path leading to the entrance of Wisteria Mansion. That's mine and Peggy Sue's old playhouse in the pine trees that has wisteria hanging all over it.

I used to love how that vine with its purple flowers grew on everything. But *that* was before I was in charge of Daddy's garden. Before I had to cut it back all by myself because Momma was in a bad way about my brother dying and didn't care two cents about the garden just then. At the time I was so mad at war and polio that I took all my anger out on that vine. And I hadn't been back to Wisteria Mansion since.

But now I didn't know where *else* to go and cry myself a river. So I crawled in under the vines, which had grown thicker than ever. I pulled my crutches in behind me. Then

I collapsed in the pine needles and let it all out. All the sadness about losing the good life my family had before the war. My frustration at not being able to cross the room without crutches. And misery about not having anyone who knew what it felt like to be me!

I thought about Imogene Wilfong. When we were in the hospital she told me that God keeps our tears in a bottle. She said my bottle had to be blue—like them overalls my daddy give me. Like the sky above. The color of truth and faithfulness.

Momma had some blue bottles in her medicine cabinet in the kitchen. I even asked her one day could I have the Bromo-Seltzer bottle when it was empty. Which wasn't going to be long, because lately my daddy was having lots of headaches.

I didn't even hear Daddy crawl in under those wisteria vines. But I felt him pick me up and pull me against his chest. He pulled my hair away from my eyes and patted my cheek with his rough hand. "Let it out, baby," he said. "Let it out."

Who would've thought I had more tears in me? But I started up again—so hard and so long I'm pretty sure God had to go hunting for another bottle. I cried harder than I had in a long time.

When I finally stopped, Daddy said, "How about we go down to the creek? I'll wash your wound and we can clean it up proper when we get back."

He knew I wasn't ready to face my family just yet. So we crawled out under the vines and Daddy knelt and helped me get on his back. When we got to the creek he set me on my favorite rock and took off my clumsy shoe and the steel brace that was weighing me down.

I sat there for a while, enjoying the feel of my feet in the creek. Daddy dipped his handkerchief into the water and blotted at the scrape on my arm. It stung, but I didn't complain because just the fact of him dabbing at it so gentle made even the hurting feel good.

I thought how me and Peggy Sue used to come here and catch crawdads in tin cans. And how Junior helped us build rock dams to make deep pools of water. How I could jump from one rock to another.

When Daddy finished cleaning my scrape he sat on the rock beside me. Then he reached behind him and picked up a stick. I seen from the way he studied it that he was fixing to whittle. Seemed like whittling was the only thing he ever done anymore without being asked.

Since he was home from the war Daddy had made a whole collection of little animals. Cats, dogs, and just about any critter you can imagine. When he finished one he'd give it to Ida or Ellie and they'd run off and play with it while he picked up another piece of wood and started on it.

I sat there with my feet in the water and watched how he turned the stick around, figuring out what was in there. "Daddy," I asked, "how do you decide what to carve?"

He held the stick out so I could get a good look at the shape of it. "What does that look like?" he asked.

"A stick," I said.

Daddy smiled. I loved it when he smiled. "Look again," he said. "Look harder. Deeper."

Well, I didn't know how to look deep into a stick, but I took it in my hand and run my fingers over it and for some reason it felt friendly. It was short and stubby and all I could think of was how the green moss on the end reminded me of curly hair. I thought about Imogene who I hadn't seen for months and months. And who I still hadn't got another letter from.

"I see a friend," I said.

"Well then," said Daddy, "I'll make you a friend." And the first thing he did was start peeling the bark and curly moss away.

The friend Daddy whittled for me didn't look like Imogene. She was kind of flat and only three inches high, but she was all there—a whole person from head to toe. Daddy carved little curlicues into her head because I told him how I thought the moss was going to be her hair.

And he even made little eyes, a nose, and a smile. But the best part of all was the crutches he carved into the sides of her. And if you looked real close you could see that she had a brace on one leg. And clumsy shoes.

When he was done Daddy put it in my hand and folded my fingers around it and said, "There now. You got yourself a friend." Then he pulled my feet out of the creek and dried them off with his big red handkerchief and put my brace and shoes back on and carried me back to the house.

It done wonders for me, having that friend curled into my fist like that. I asked Daddy could he put it on a strip of leather to wear around my neck.

"I don't see why not," he said. He had to make a hole in the top of her head first. And scrounge around for some leather. When he couldn't find any, he took a lace out of his work boot and hung her on that. Then he put her over my head.

It felt almost like there was someone close by who had been through polio too.

I named her Comfort.

8

Imogene's Songs
October 1945

I sat on the steps and watched Ida spinning Ellie on the tire swing. She was giggling and Ellie was squealing. Two hound dogs howled off in the distance. Probably Jesse and Butch. They were Junior's dogs.

Momma and Daddy were in the kitchen. I knew from the sound of things that Daddy was whittling. Momma was annoyed by the wood shavings that landed on the floor. "Leroy," she said, "I swept this floor not ten minutes ago. Now look at the mess you're making."

Daddy grunted and kept on whittling.

Momma sighed a loud, drawn-out sigh. She'd been doing a lot of that lately—breathing out her frustration. Here it was October, and whenever she pushed him on the subject of work, Daddy offered some puny reasons not to go looking. "For one thing," he'd say, "jobs are scarce. And for another, I thought you'd be glad for my help around here."

I could hear Momma in the kitchen arguing with Daddy even though he wasn't saying a word. "Leroy," she said. "How do you think I made it around here when you were in Europe? Don't you think the war showed us what a woman can do when her man isn't around?"

Momma was right. We had both learned how strong we were when Daddy wasn't there to do things for us. We could haul buckets and buckets of water out of the well. And fill the wringer washer and do a load of clothes and then empty the tubs and do it all again. We could plant the garden by ourselves. Well, actually Junior Bledsoe had tilled the soil, but only because he took over the tiller before I could start it up.

Strictly speaking, Momma and I could get by without a man in the house. But I didn't for one minute think I could get along without my daddy. And I didn't see how Momma could either.

Sitting on the steps and listening with every muscle to what was going on between them, I could almost feel the despair my momma's words put on him. I knew he didn't want to believe we could make do without him. He was the one that had always give us the courage to go forward. Ever since I was little I'd seen Daddy pull Momma into his arms when she started fretting over the washing machine that broke. Or worrying how they could afford to pay the light bill.

I remembered how he repeated his wedding vows to her on those days. *For richer or poorer*, he would say. *For better or worse. I'm with you and you're with me and together we're gonna make it.*

That rich-or-poor thing always confused me. One night when Daddy was helping me with my homework, I asked him about it. I was having trouble counting money, so he'd pulled some coins out of his pocket to practice with me.

"Daddy," I asked him, "are we richer or poorer?"

I still remember how he laughed. "Well, now," he said, "I reckon it just depends." He scratched at his head, messing his hair in the process. "Seems to me we're richer than some folks and poorer than others."

Well, I already knew we were poorer than Peggy Sue's family. Her daddy owns a hosiery mill and they live in a nice brick house right along the highway. But I didn't think we were one bit rich. "Who are we richer than?" I asked.

"Hmm," said Daddy. "If you ask me, we're richer than just about anybody who don't have what we got. Just look at us." And he motioned to my family there in the kitchen.

Momma was polishing the cookstove, trying to get every smear of grease off it. Ida and Ellie, who were just a few years old then, were sitting in a big washtub on the kitchen floor, putting their faces in the water and blowing soap bubbles. My little brother Bobby wasn't even born yet.

"When I look at my happy family," said Daddy, "I feel downright rich." He got up, went to where Momma was working, and pulled her against him. "As long as I got me a Myrtle, I'm the richest man in the world." He gave my momma a long kiss. For a minute there I thought he forgot all about having an Ann Fay.

But then he come back to me and my homework. He sat at the table and said, "When me and your momma got married, we promised to stick together whether we have money or not. It don't even matter if we like each other or not. We're staying together. And that makes us rich."

Well, it was obvious that my momma and daddy were in love. Even when they was annoyed with each other, I knew it would pass. But since he'd come home from the war, Daddy seemed to be annoying Momma a lot. And it didn't pass as quick as it used to.

I heard the scraping of a chair inside and then Daddy's footsteps coming toward the screen door behind me. It squeaked when he opened it and I turned to look at him. He was taking the broom off the nail just outside the kitchen door.

I watched him go inside and sweep up the wood shavings and push the chair real neat under the kitchen table and head back to the porch with the broom. Then he went past me to the johnny house without saying a word.

When he come back I thought he might sit with me on the steps and finish his whittling—outside, where it wouldn't matter if he made a mess.

"Whatcha working on, Daddy?"

He just grunted, so I felt like a bother for even asking. He went to the shelf at the end of the porch where we keep a bucket of water for washing up. He poured water into a basin and washed his face and hands. When he was done, he threw the dirty water in the yard and went inside. Without saying a word to me.

I heard him shut himself in his and Momma's bedroom. It was quiet then. Except for Momma sighing. Finally I got up and went in. Momma was rearranging her spices in the door of the green Hoosier cupboard.

It seemed to me like she ought to rest once in a while. "Want to play a game of checkers?"

"No. I don't." Momma sounded edgy. "I couldn't sit still right now if you tied me to that chair." That's when I realized she wasn't organizing spices because they needed it. She was just sorting out her agitation.

Then Daddy called out from the bedroom, and *his* voice had an edge to it. "Would you be quiet out there? I'm trying to sleep."

Sleep? It was only seven thirty in the evening. Not even Ida and Ellie's bedtime.

I propped my crutches against the table and reached for the *Blue Willow* book that I'd checked out of the school library. But one of my crutches didn't stay where I put it, and next thing I knew, it was sliding to the floor and taking the other one with it.

Daddy hollered again. "What in tarnation is all that racket?"

I was fixing to be exasperated with my daddy. Why did he think the whole house should be quiet just because he took a notion to go to bed extra early? I sat real still and tried to read, but I couldn't keep my mind on it.

At eight o'clock Momma said it was time to call Ida and Ellie in for bed. When I got outside, the girls had left the tire swing and were playing hopscotch in the dirt. "Bedtime!" I hollered.

I picked up the basin and put it on the porch floor. I used the tin dipper from the bucket to put water in the basin. Then I threw the soap in and called for the girls.

"Ida! Ellie! This is the last time I'm telling you. We've got school tomorrow so you better get in here."

"Last one there's a rotten egg!" yelled Ida and she took off running while Ellie was still balancing on one leg.

Well, Ellie tried to catch up but she couldn't. So she accused Ida of cheating. That started them squabbling real loud, and all of a sudden we heard a banging from the other side of the porch wall.

"Would you be quiet?" I hissed. "Daddy is not in the mood for your nonsense. Now wash your face and hands and then your feet. And don't forget to brush your teeth."

When the girls was clean we went into our room to get their pajamas on. "Listen here," I whispered. "You got to do this real quiet. Daddy is trying to sleep."

"Why?" asked Ellie. "It's not even his bedtime. Is he sick?"

I didn't know the answer to that, but I figured Ellie had come up with as good a reason as any. "He must be," I said.

But of course the girls forgot to be quiet. They was still wound up from playing. They started giggling and making faces and it didn't do any good telling them to hush. They couldn't seem to stop.

But then I heard Daddy loud and angry behind me. I turned and there he was in the doorway. The light from the living room was back of him and we only had a lamp on in our room. So he was mostly just a big dark shape with his belt folded in his hand. He raised it for us to see.

"Do you girls know the meaning of quiet or not?" he asked. "If this racket keeps up I'm gonna give you something to holler about."

Well, the noise went from happy giggles to dead silence.

Daddy just stood there for a minute like he didn't know what to do with all the quiet. "That's better," he growled. "Now keep it like that." And he turned to go, nearly bumping into Momma, who had come up behind him. She stepped back to let him pass. I heard his footsteps going through the kitchen and into their bedroom.

Momma come into the room and put her hand on my shoulder. "I'll put the girls to bed," she said. "You go outside and get some fresh air."

So I did. I went out on the porch and leaned against the post. I wrapped my hand around my little wooden Comfort hanging there on Daddy's shoestring. "What's happening to my daddy?" I whispered.

It wasn't like he'd never spanked us before. But he never done it over a little noise. It was always because of outright disobeying that he would give us a couple of stinging swats with a switch off a bush.

My daddy had never once used his belt to punish us.

Other people at school talked about getting lickings with a belt—the buckle end, even. And Rob Walker said that when he got a licking, he always had to cut his own switch. If he didn't get just the right size, his daddy would send him back for another one. "Get one that will sing while it makes you dance!" his daddy would say.

I couldn't imagine my daddy being that mean. But now, I was scared. I could still see how the light from the living room shone through the square frame of his belt buckle.

While I stood on the back porch, being as quiet as I could, I heard the sound of singing. At least I thought I did. And for some reason the singing put me in mind of Imogene. Her face came to me, and so did a song. *Nobody knows the trouble I've seen. Nobody knows my sorrow...*

Was I imagining it? Then I realized something—the singing wasn't in my mind. It was real singing, and it was coming from the little colored church out near Junior's house. I stopped breathing for a minute, trying to hear. And then, I don't know why, except I just needed the comfort, I headed toward that song.

I sat on the edge of the porch and eased myself to the ground, picked up my crutches, and started toward the singing.

The moon wasn't full, but there was enough light that I could find my way. I knew I couldn't wade through the chopped-off cornstalks in the field. So I went around the edge. Every now and then I'd have to pass a short row of leftover sagging cornstalks. They put me in mind of crippled old soldiers trying their best to stay on guard.

The singing of Imogene's people got louder as I walked. It pulled me away from home until I got to the other end of the field. I was wore out by the time I got there.

Across the dirt road was a graveyard with old headstones poking out of the earth, and beyond that was the tiny white church with a yellow glow coming through the windows. There couldn't have been more than twenty people in that little building. But the way they sung you would not have guessed it. Their voices were big and their song was like a bulldozer fixing to knock me over.

By now they were singing another song. I had never heard it before. But every so often I could catch a word or two. Something about tribulation. And weeping.

But it wasn't the words that got to me. It was the sound of that song—the way Imogene's people sung it—that wrung me out like a dishrag. Their singing put me in mind of a clean bedsheet billowing on the wash line. It floated up real slow, and down again just as slow. And it seemed like it carried me with it.

I hadn't wanted to sit down, on account of the problem of standing again with only a dried-up cornstalk to grab ahold of. But the song wouldn't let me stay on my feet. So I unlocked my leg brace and let myself go—down onto the dampness at the edge of the field. I curled up like a baby and put my face into my hands. I felt the wetness of the grass against my elbows and the grit of the dirt on my knees.

I hung on to the words of the song they were singing. Something about tribulation and weeping.

9

Surprises
October 1945

My daddy was real sorry about flying off the handle like that. He didn't come right out and say it, but he was extra helpful all of a sudden. Momma didn't have to ask him to draw water, or light a fire in the woodstove when it got cool.

He still didn't get a job, though. One day he said he was going out looking for work, but he come back with something else. He walked into the kitchen and reached for Momma. She only give him the teeniest little peck on the cheek. Then she went back to putting food on the table. "Supper's ready," she said.

Daddy grunted a little and turned to Ida and Ellie. "I left something on the truck seat for you. How about going after it before we eat?"

The girls dropped the game they was playing and raced outside to the truck. Daddy sneaked a biscuit from the batch Momma had made for supper and slipped it into his pocket. Then he went outside too.

I watched them through the window. Ellie got there first, but Ida elbowed her out of the way and yanked the truck door open. Before either one of them could catch it, a black puppy scrambled out.

The kitchen window was shut, so I couldn't hear what

they were saying, but I could see every little detail. Daddy made the girls start by letting the puppy sniff their hands, and then he pulled a biscuit out of his pocket and give a piece to each of them. They took turns feeding the dog.

Mostly what I noticed about that dog was, it was the same kind President Roosevelt had. So I knew that even though Daddy had got it for the little girls, that part of it—the fact that it was a Scottie—was for me.

I picked up my crutches and went through the living room and out to the front porch. Momma followed. I sat on a rocking chair and Daddy brought me the dog. I held him close and he licked my face. "How did you find a dog just like the president's?" I asked.

I heard Momma sighing and knew she was worried Daddy had spent money we didn't have. "Well," said Daddy, "of course I couldn't afford a purebred Scottish terrier. This one is a mutt, really. But you can hardly tell it. Just look at that long nose and square jaw."

"But where did you find him?"

"Someone in town was giving puppies away. Ann Fay, you get to name him."

"Wait a minute," said Ida. "Why does she get to pick a name? I want to call him Pete."

"Yeah," said Ellie. "We need another Pete."

The girls were crowding around my chair trying to put pieces of biscuit into the puppy's mouth.

Pete was our dog that followed my brother to the polio hospital. But just like Bobby, he died there. I'll always believe he knew the minute Bobby died. And that he just give up on living himself.

"No," I said. "We got to come up with something more original."

"How about Blackie?" asked Ellie.

"Or Midnight?" asked Ida.

"Nah," I said. "That's boring." Then I noticed that the dog's front paws were white like he was wearing a pair of shoes. "I know," I said. "Let's call him Mr. Shoes."

"Yeah!" said Ida. And Ellie agreed. So that's what we called him.

The girls wanted to teach Mr. Shoes to do tricks, so they started giving him all kinds of commands—*sit, roll over, stand, lay, bark!*

"Hey," said Daddy. "Take it easy. How would you like me ordering you to do all them things at the same time?" Then he took charge of the training. "Sit!" said Daddy. If Mr. Shoes sat back on his haunches, Daddy give him a piece of biscuit and scratched him behind the ears.

At supper Ida brought an extra chair to the table so Mr. Shoes could eat with the rest of us. But of course Momma wouldn't hear of it. "No dogs at the table," she said. "And after supper, no playing with him until your homework is finished."

Later, after I finally give up fighting the girls to play with Mr. Shoes, Daddy and I huddled on the porch and watched the stars come out over Bakers Mountain.

That's when he come up with the second surprise of the day. "Ann Fay," he said, "how would you like a job?"

"A job?"

"I was in Whitener's Store today. Ruth Whitener was asking about you. Said she could use some help in there."

Whitener's was just a little country store where people could stop in and buy a drink on the way home from work. Or pick up some light bread or maybe get a baloney sandwich if they didn't feel like cooking. Before the war Daddy used to sit around the potbelly stove in there and play rook with the other men. But not anymore. Now he'd just buy his cigarettes and leave again.

"But Daddy," I said. "That doesn't make sense. Ruth Whitener has six children of her own. Why would she need me?"

Daddy shrugged. "Maybe she likes you, Ann Fay. She said if you help out she'll pay you in food. Day-old light bread and whatever else she can spare."

I thought about that—how it would help put food on the table while Daddy wasn't working. Maybe I should take the job. But I still couldn't understand why Mrs. Whitener would hire me—unless she was feeling sorry for us.

Maybe someone was talking.

It was probably her daughter Jean. She was the one who carried my books every day. And when Rob Walker knocked me down at school, Jean was the one who give me her handkerchief to wipe the blood off my skinned-up elbow. Maybe she went home and told her momma.

And then again, there was Junior Bledsoe. He liked to talk. He could've told Mrs. Whitener that Daddy wasn't working. Ruth Whitener had a reputation for being big-hearted. People said if someone couldn't pay his bill, she would often let it go. I had a feeling her wanting to hire me had something to do with that soft spot of hers.

"Ruth says if you want the job, all you gotta do is show up on Saturday morning."

It hit me all of a sudden that if I took a Saturday job it would mean giving up going to the movies with Peggy Sue. But then we hadn't been going every week anyway. And it seemed like more often than not, Peggy Sue dragged Junior along with us.

I thought about Daddy and how he hadn't got a job yet.

And about my momma getting impatient with him. She was standing at the front door right that minute, listening. I looked up and seen the light from the living room behind her. And her face looking gray through the screen on the door.

I thought how I could make her eyes light up just a tiny bit by bringing home groceries from Whitener's Store each week. It wouldn't be much. But right now it was better than nothing. I could feel that Momma wanted me to take the job. It looked like I was going to have to be the man of the house all over again.

"All right, then," I said. "I'll give it a try."

10

Otis Hickey
October 1945

When Saturday come, I was as nervous as on the first day of school. Not because of Mrs. Whitener. I thought she'd be patient with me. And of course I liked Jean. But what about the customers? Every time I'd been in that place, there was a group of men sitting around playing cards or talking about soybean crops. Would they be watching every move I made?

Lucky for me, the men weren't at the store when I got there.

The first thing Mrs. Whitener did was give me a stool. "There," she said. "Sit as much as you like. And keep your crutches close by in case you need them."

She helped me with the first three or four customers, taking money and giving them change. After that, I was on my own. "You're a natural storekeeper," she said. "Maybe I'll take the day off and let you run this place."

Before she was done talking, a man come in and bought himself a Coca-Cola and a pack of peanuts. He poured the peanuts in his drink and sat down by the woodstove to enjoy it. Then one at a time the others started coming.

They didn't stay all day, of course. One would sit and chew the fat with a couple of others and then he'd finally stand up and make some excuse to leave. One man said, "I 'spect if I don't get home soon the old lady will be putting extra pepper on my eggs in the morning." But it wasn't long before another one took his place.

Mrs. Whitener went out the back door a few times and over to her house next to the store. "Have to check on my clan. Be back in a minute," she'd say.

It wasn't like things was busy in the store. Mrs. Whitener had a sewing machine in the corner and even sat down and worked on a shirt she was making for one of her boys. It was hard telling why she needed me.

Sometimes the men would sit for a long time without talking. They'd stare at the jars of mayonnaise on the shelf or scrape the toes of their work boots along the cracks in the cement floor. I got to wondering what was going on inside their heads.

Just before eleven o'clock a man named Clarence looked out the window. "Lord help us. Here comes Otis," he said.

He meant Otis Hickey. I'd known about Otis all my life on account of he walked wherever he wanted to go and sometimes my daddy would give him a lift. Otis's right eye had been destroyed in the war, so now he had a glass one. When he turned his eyes from side to side, they didn't move together like most people's eyes do.

But even *before* the war, people called him a strange bird.

Otis lived with his mother in a little gray house that you could hardly see for all the trash sitting in the yard. He collected junk that other people would use or sell—old cars, wood cookstoves, and other things he sold to people. He was the only reason my momma had a Frigidaire instead of an icebox. Why, we even had a refrigerator before Peggy Sue's family did! All on account of Otis getting it from some rich people. When I went with my daddy to get that refrigerator I even thought I seen a bathtub hiding in the weeds.

During the war the government begged for metal to build more ships and bomber planes. But according to Clarence, Otis never turned his in. Clarence said some people felt it was their patriotic duty to go clean up the place. But Otis's mother met them at the door. "No sirree," she said. "Otis makes his living fixing and selling that stuff and you better leave it there for when he comes home."

Otis come into the store. He stood there for a minute while his eyes adjusted to the darkness and then he headed for the counter.

"Good morning, Otis," said Mrs. Whitener. "Do you know Ann Fay Honeycutt? She's my new employee."

He give me a nod and his good eye twitched a little. "We've met," he said.

"Otis will have one of those dills," said Mrs. Whitener. She tapped the gallon jar of giant pickles sitting on the counter. So I took off the lid, fished one out with the tongs that she kept on the counter, and wrapped it in wax paper.

Mrs. Whitener asked Otis how his mother's arthritis was doing.

He took a bite of his pickle, lifted his hat, and scratched his head like he was thinking how to answer her. After a moment he said, "She has her good days and her bad days, she does." He chewed on his pickle for a while, and then he said to anyone who would listen, "I reckon you seen in the paper where them Nazis are being tried for their war crimes. It's about time they get what's coming to them."

Well, that got the men by the stove to talking. Most of them agreed with Otis, whether they'd seen war crimes firsthand or not. I learned that Otis had helped to liberate Poland and seen a concentration camp up close and personal. "You would not believe the size of them prisoners," he said. "They looked like they wasn't nothing but one bone apiece. Like a fence rail with empty eyes."

The men didn't mind Otis talking about the war as long as he was bad-mouthing the Nazis and the meanness they done to people in Poland. But then he made the mistake of telling a story about one of his buddies getting blown apart. And just like that, Clarence told him to shut it up.

He was done with his pickle by then, so he shrugged and crumpled the wax paper in his fist. "Guess I'll be getting a wiggle on," he said. Then he went out the door.

It got quiet for a while, which made me wonder what each of them men was seeing in their minds. After a bit, Clarence picked up the tin can sitting by the woodstove. He spit a stream of black snuff into it. "I declare, Ruth, I don't know why you let that crazy man darken your door," he said.

Mrs. Whitener was sewing on a button by this time. She pulled a long thread through the buttonhole and pointed her needle at Clarence. "As far as I'm concerned, Otis Hickey's two cents is worth just as much as yours."

I had a feeling she was talking about something besides the money Otis spent on a dill pickle. One thing for sure— there wasn't any doubt about who run that store. People come in there with all sorts of opinions. And gossip. But if Ruth Whitener didn't agree with someone's viewpoint, she was quick to say so.

Just before one o'clock a man named Frank Huffman come in, set up a small table, and pulled out some rook cards. Before long, two more men had joined him. But of course they needed a fourth player. "Ruth, are you going to play?" asked Frank. "Or does little Miss Honeycutt want to be my partner?"

Mrs. Whitener laughed. "Good idea! Go ahead, Ann Fay."

Was she serious? Did she want me to play while I was on the job?

"You deserve a break."

She meant it. I shook my head. "I don't want to play." But the truth was, I didn't know much about playing rook. When me and Peggy Sue and Junior got together we always played rummy.

"Deal me a hand," said Mrs. Whitener. She sat up to the table, and next thing I knew she was bidding on how many points she could take.

I picked up a copy of the *Hickory Daily Record* that was under the counter. I read the funny papers first and then I moved on to what was happening in the real world.

I seen an article called HANDICAPPED GET ATTENTION. It was about how President Truman had proclaimed this week "Employ the Physically Handicapped Week." The article said that the war had wounded lots of people who could do a good job in spite of their handicap.

It seemed like an easy thing to say, at least if you were talking about a soldier who come home with a bad arm. But what if something was wrong on the inside? If it was just a weak arm that was wrong with my daddy, he'd find a way to work. But whatever was ailing him wasn't something you could see.

And because I couldn't see it, sometimes I got real impatient. I'd get the biggest urge to tell him to snap out of it! But I would never talk to my daddy like that.

The newspaper article didn't say anything about people being handicapped by polio. But after our epidemic I knew there were plenty of us around too. And I started wondering if maybe that's why Mrs. Whitener had hired me.

Was she feeling sorry for me on account of polio? Or having pity on my whole family because Daddy wasn't working?

I got to thinking maybe I didn't want the job after all. For one thing I didn't care much for being pitied. And for another I was starting to feel sorry for myself. Especially when I remembered that I could be at the movies with Peggy Sue just then.

But of course Junior would probably be there too. I didn't know which bothered me worse—the idea of Junior tagging along or him and Peggy Sue going without me.

11

The Car

November 1945

Because of my job at the store, I didn't get to the movies with Peggy Sue and Junior even once during October. Junior got a second job helping some mechanic fix cars. So that meant Peggy Sue wouldn't be able to take him to the movies either. "I suppose I'll have to get Melinda to go the picture show with me," she said. "Since you and Junior deserted me."

I thought how strange it was that Junior could work two jobs and my daddy couldn't do one. Momma asked Daddy wouldn't he, at least, take advantage of the GI Bill and go back to school. One day she pulled out the papers he'd brought home from the American Legion office and reminded him that veterans could get expenses paid for college or special training.

But my daddy had quit school after ninth grade and he wasn't likely to go back. "What's the matter?" he asked. "I'm not educated enough for you? Just when did you get so highfalutin?"

Momma put the GI papers on the table then and started scrubbing the Frigidaire. Next thing I knew she was taking everything out and wiping it down. Daddy went outside, letting the screen door slam behind him. If one of us young'uns had done that, he would've made us come back and shut it real quiet.

And lately, he probably wouldn't have been too nice about it either.

Of course the whole point of veterans going back to school was job training. But apparently Daddy wasn't worried about any of us starving or Momma not being able to pay the light bill. He seemed to think we could live off the small amount of money the government give to unemployed veterans. Even that wouldn't last forever, but Momma had quit bringing it up.

Every Saturday when Daddy brought me home from my store job, I turned my pay over to Momma. The bread and canned goods always put some of the shine back into her eyes. She'd give me a quick hug and say, "Ann Fay, I don't know what I'd do without you."

I knew she was actually telling Daddy that *he* should be the one working. And that made me feel guilty for the distance my job was putting between them. For some reason it seemed like keeping peace in the family was my responsibility. If it looked like Momma and Daddy were fixing to argue, I would change the subject. If the girls was bothering him, I'd make them go outside. It was getting colder, though, and I started wondering how we'd get through the winter if we was stuck in the house with each other.

One Saturday evening it was unusually warm for November, so me and Daddy was sitting on the porch shelling parched peanuts. We heard a car coming down the road. I didn't recognize it, and I could see Daddy didn't either. But the driver was waving out the window. Then he got closer and I realized that it was Junior Bledsoe—grinning like a lovesick fool.

The twins were running circles in the yard with Mr. Shoes chasing after one and then the other. The minute Junior came to a stop those girls were on the running board of that car, bombarding him with questions and begging for a ride.

"Course I'll take you for a ride." Junior tried to shake the girls off, but they followed him to the porch. "Good evening, Leroy," he said.

"Evening," said Daddy eyeballing the car. "That yours?"

"I bought it off a man in Startown. He got himself a brand-new Chevrolet with a chatterbox in it. This one doesn't have a radio." Junior looked at me. "Wanna go for a ride?"

I looked at Daddy and he nodded. The twins hightailed it to the car, racing to get to the front seat. Daddy lifted me off the porch, and Junior made the girls get in the back so I could sit up front.

We headed out the dirt road with him just a-grinning. "So are you proud of me, Ann Fay?"

"Maybe I am," I said. "But as much as you like to talk, I can't figure how you been saving up for this and never said a word about it."

"Well, see there! You don't know me like you thought you did." Junior took us to the Hinkle sisters' house, pulled into their driveway, and tooted his horn. In a few minutes the two of them come out, Miss Pauline first and then her sister looking just like her—same dark-rimmed glasses and hair pulled up into a bun. Only difference was Miss Dinah was shorter.

"Is it yours?" asked Miss Pauline.

"Yes, ma'am," said Junior. "And it's paid for, too."

"Well, am I ever so proud of you! You have sure grown

into a fine young man. And to think, I was there when you were born."

"Wanna go for a ride?"

Miss Pauline looked at Miss Dinah, and the two of them nodded. Next thing I knew, Junior had hopped out and leaned the back of his seat forward so they could climb in with Ida and Ellie. And Mr. Shoes, of course.

Miss Dinah fell right in love with our dog. But Miss Pauline? She made Ellie sit between her and Miss Dinah so he couldn't lick her elbows. When Mr. Shoes tried to make friends with her, she swatted her hand to keep him in his place.

After we got back, Miss Pauline invited us in for milk and cookies and of course we accepted. But evidently she never expected Miss Dinah to bring Mr. Shoes inside. By the time she realized he was in, it was too late. He slipped between her feet and took off on a tour of their house. "Dear me!" said Miss Pauline. "How did he get inside?"

"Ellie," I said, "get that dog out of here. And put him in the car so we don't lose him."

"Oh, no!" said Miss Dinah. "Poor little Shoesie would be lonely out there all by himself. Let him explore."

I thought Miss Pauline was going to start a squabble with her sister then. "Dinah, what are you thinking of? You know we have never allowed critters in this house." The way she talked, you would've thought Mr. Shoes was a rat.

But Miss Dinah just ignored her. "I'll pour the milk," she said.

Ellie followed Mr. Shoes into one of the bedrooms. But when she came back she said, "He's under the bed and he won't come out."

"Oh, let him go," said Miss Dinah. "If necessary, I'll find

some leftover ham. A bit of meat will bring him running."

Miss Pauline hustled us all into the bathroom to wash our hands, and she made sure her sister scrubbed up at the kitchen sink. Then Miss Dinah set out cookies on individual plates with a glass of milk beside each one.

We were sitting around the kitchen table when Mr. Shoes came back with something in his mouth. Miss Pauline saw it first. "Where did he get that sock?" But then it moved and she squealed. "A rat!" And just like that, she picked up her feet and held them straight out in front of her. Mr. Shoes dropped it. It was only a mouse.

It started to run, but he caught it again and tossed it in the air like a toy. Miss Pauline was really squealing now. "Oh, how dreadful! Stop it, you mean little dog!"

Mr. Shoes put the mouse down and let it run across the shiny tile floor just a few feet and then caught it again. And threw it in the air a few more times.

"Junior Bledsoe, do something!" said Miss Pauline.

Junior called to Mr. Shoes, trying to lead him out the back door. But at that moment Mr. Shoes put the mouse down and it ran under the big iron radiator by the table.

By then Ida and Ellie and Miss Dinah was standing on the chairs. I wasn't scared of mice, but I didn't want one running up my leg. So I lifted my feet too. My right leg, anyway. My left leg was just too hard to pick up with that heavy brace on it.

Miss Dinah grabbed up one of my crutches and give it to Junior, who used it to scare the mouse out from under the radiator. Miss Pauline was screeching and the girls were laughing and squealing and everyone was giving Junior directions.

Mr. Shoes caught the mouse again, and this time Junior

opened the back door. Sure enough, our dog went outside with that mouse's head hanging from one side of his mouth. And his tail and hind legs dangling from the other.

Miss Pauline shuddered and run to shut the door. "I declare!" she said. "I don't know how that critter got in, but I do *not* want it coming back." She started gathering our dishes whether we was finished or not. So we drank the milk in a hurry and ate the cookies on the way out.

We were fixing to climb in Junior's car when Miss Dinah come running after us. She had a box camera in her hand. "Wait!" she called. "I want to take a picture."

So we lined ourselves up beside the car. Junior stood with his foot on the running board, and me and the girls stood beside him. Just when we thought Miss Dinah was done snapping pictures, she said, "Hold it right there. I want to get in the picture." Then she went back in the house and come out with Miss Pauline.

"Stand right here," Miss Dinah ordered her sister. "And don't snap it until I tell you to." She scooped up Mr. Shoes, who was digging under her yellow bell bushes.

Miss Dinah stood beside me with our dog in her arms, and Miss Pauline took the picture. She took three altogether because Miss Dinah wanted one for each of our families. "To remember this day by," she said.

Miss Pauline just shook her head. "I doubt that *I* shall ever forget it," she said.

12

Georgia
November 1945

In November, Mamaw Honeycutt sent us a letter saying her and Papaw wanted us to come to Georgia for Thanksgiving. I heard Momma telling Daddy we couldn't afford it. But that same evening Daddy picked me up and carried me out to the truck.

"Where're we going?" I asked.

"To see your friend Peggy Sue. I need to use their telephone."

There were lights on in the colored church when we went by. I sure wished Daddy would stop and let me listen for a minute, but he was bent on getting to a telephone.

We drove past the Hinkle sisters' house. "Why don't you just stop here?" I asked.

He laughed and rolled down the window just a tad so he could flick the ashes off his cigarette. "I thought Miss Pauline might not want to share her telephone with us after the way our dog behaved at her house."

I knew that wasn't true. So I figured Daddy would rather talk to Mr. Rhinehart than two old maids. Or maybe he wanted me and Peggy Sue to have some time together.

When we got to Peggy Sue's, Daddy carried me on his back and knocked.

Mrs. Rhinehart opened the door. I think it made her feel uncomfortable to see Daddy carrying me like I was a child. Right away she said, "Please. Have a seat, Ann Fay."

Daddy set me in a chair by the door. I looked around and noticed that something was different. Their kitchen had a fresh coat of paint. And new curtains.

Peggy Sue pulled out a chair for Daddy, and then her father came out of the living room and joined us at the table. Him and Daddy started talking. According to Mr. Rhinehart, the hosiery business would soon be picking up. "Nylon stockings will be more in demand than ever," he said. "I have a job for you if you want it."

I crossed my fingers and said a quick prayer. But Daddy shook his head. "I work in wood," he said. He looked at his rough hands. "I just can't see me handling women's nylons."

Mr. Rhinehart nodded like he understood. "But you can fix just about anything, can't you? You'd be a natural to keep our machines running."

I thought I seen Daddy's eyes brighten up just a tad when he said that. Mr. Rhinehart must've seen it too, because he slapped him on the shoulder and said, "Come by on Monday morning and take a look. I'd be proud to have you on my crew."

Daddy shrunk back in his chair a little. "I'll think about that," he said. Then he asked could he use the telephone, and Mr. Rhinehart led him into the front hall. I figured that was the end of that job prospect.

"Want to see my room?" asked Peggy Sue. "I got a new bed this week."

"Sure," I said. Then I remembered I didn't have my crutches along. So I called for Daddy, and he come back and carried me to Peggy Sue's room. If I was home, I would've just crawled. But not at the Rhineharts', I wouldn't. I could feel their embarrassment following me down the hall.

Peggy Sue's room was painted a bright pink, and her new bed had four tall posts and a pink and green canopy and bedspread. Just like a princess. Which is kind of how I always thought of her, anyway. It seemed like Peggy Sue lived a fairy-tale life compared to mine. Her daddy owned a hosiery mill. He didn't have to serve in the war because he had a contract with the government to make socks for the army. From the changes in their house, I guessed it had paid off.

Peggy Sue also had a dressing table with a green-striped skirt to match her new curtains. She showed me how it had little drawers for her hair barrettes and ribbons. On top was a handheld mirror and matching comb-and-brush set. And a tray with a neat little row of fingernail polish, rouge, and lipstick.

To look at Peggy Sue's room you would never know we had just come through a war. It never used to bother me that Peggy Sue was richer than me. I liked it on account of she shared what she had with me. But now, for some reason I felt annoyed by it.

I sat and looked in her mirror. My hair was a mess, so I started combing.

"Here, let *me*," said Peggy Sue. She pulled my hair to one side and started to part it with a comb.

Looking at our two faces there in the mirror, I thought how easy it was to see that me and Peggy Sue was going our separate ways. I looked like a simple country girl with no makeup and no special style. And Peggy Sue was doing her best to look like the stars in her movie magazines.

She fastened my hair with a barrette and added a yellow ribbon from her drawer. "You can keep the ribbon," she said. "Yellow doesn't show up on a blondie. There! What do you think? Maybe I could cut your hair. Make you look like a modern girl."

I had to admit I kind of liked what she did with my hair. Maybe I *should* let her cut it.

"I can't do anything with mine," said Peggy Sue. It wasn't true. Her thick hair was shiny and smooth and looked good even when it was messed up. She combed the front part of her hair into a pouf and fastened it. "What do you think?" she asked.

"Beautiful!" I said.

"Will Junior like it?"

So it didn't matter what I thought. Junior Bledsoe's opinion was all that mattered. I shrugged. "Why not?"

Then I heard Daddy coming down the hall and knew he'd made his phone call. And just like that, the visit was over.

"Oh, dear," said Peggy Sue. "Do you have to leave already? We were just getting started."

"I'm afraid so," said Daddy. "But Ann Fay can come back another day."

"Yes," said Mrs. Rhinehart. "Please do."

But I didn't think Peggy Sue would invite me. It was starting to feel like we'd never get back to the way we were. While I was in the polio hospital she had gone from wading in creeks to drooling over boys.

And me? I'd give anything to run through the woods and play in the creek again. Instead I wore a hideous brace on my leg and my daddy carried me around like I was a little girl. Either that or I had to crawl on the floor like a baby.

For some reason just thinking about it give me the nerve to ask Daddy to stop in front of the colored church so we could listen to those people sing.

Daddy slowed down. "Whatcha want to do that for?"

"I just like the sound of it," I said. "It's different from how we sing. More meaningful or something. And besides, it reminds me of my colored friend."

"Hmm." Daddy stopped his truck and I cranked down my window. He lit up a cigarette and rolled his down too. It was chilly outside, but I didn't mind as long as I got to hear them people sing. But we didn't hear music. Instead it sounded like the preacher was putting forth a powerful sermon.

"Looks like we missed the singing," said Daddy. He started up his truck again.

I grabbed his arm. "Can't you just finish your cigarette while we wait?"

"No telling when the preacher will quit," he said. But he turned the truck off.

I leaned my head against the door frame and looked up at the stars. It was so clear that it seemed like every star in heaven was winking at us.

"I wish you could take me to Greensboro," I said. "To see Imogene Wilfong."

Daddy took a drag on his cigarette and held it out the window. He give it a little flick and the breeze carried the bright sparks out into the darkness. "What's wrong with the friends you got?" he asked. "They're a far sight closer than Greensboro. Didn't you just have a good time with Peggy Sue?"

"Peggy Sue didn't have polio," I said. "Or any other bad thing, for that matter. So she doesn't understand. She's got a fancy bed and a dressing table, and she's wearing makeup. Would you let *me* wear lipstick?" I reckoned I knew the answer to that one.

But Daddy surprised me. "Would it make you more comfortable around Peggy Sue?"

I got the feeling if I said yes, he'd tell me to go ahead and wear makeup. As if that would make everything in my life just peachy keen.

I took my little wooden Comfort from around my neck and held her out to Daddy. It was too dark for him to see her, so I put her in his hand. "Remember when I said the stick reminded me of a friend? I was talking about Imogene. She knows my suffering. And she knows how to make me feel better, too."

Daddy nodded. Then he give his head a little jerk in the direction of the church. "Listen," he said. "They're singing you a song."

And sure enough—the people in the church was going at it. Singing a song I hadn't ever heard before. Something about *Fix me, Jesus, fix me*. It was real slow, with a pleading sound to it that made me want to get on my knees.

But of course I just sat with Daddy and listened. While they was singing, Daddy reached across the seat and put Comfort into my hand. I folded my fingers around her and he wrapped his around mine and squeezed. It seemed like his hand was shaking a little—like he was taking that song real personal. Like he thought they was singing it for him too.

We listened to the end and I sent up a quiet prayer for God to fix me and Daddy both. The people in the church started on another song, but Daddy pulled his hand away and cranked up the truck. We both left the windows down till we got to the house. As if closing them would break something.

The song followed us home—*Fix me... Fix me...*

Later I heard Daddy telling Momma about his talk with Papaw. "I invited them here for Thanksgiving," he said. "But Pap insisted we should go there. He's sending us money for the trip."

I saw Momma turn away and I knew she was embarrassed that Papaw was picking up Daddy's responsibilities. But I also knew we were going to Georgia.

The Wednesday before Thanksgiving we packed our one suitcase and some pasteboard boxes with our clothes onto the back of Daddy's truck. He covered it with a tarp and we all climbed in up front. It was a tight fit, but we were used to it. I sat in the middle next to Daddy. Ida squeezed in between me and Momma. Ellie sat on Momma's lap. Later, the twins would change places.

We didn't have room for Mr. Shoes to ride the whole way to Georgia, so we dropped him off at Junior and Bessie's on the way out. When Junior seen how we was scrunched up in the truck, he said, "Why didn't you ask to borrow my car?"

"Oh, son," said Daddy. "I couldn't do that. This won't be the first time we've squeezed us all in."

"But those girls aren't little anymore," said Junior. "As many times as I've borrowed your truck, you're gonna have to take my car. I won't hear tell of anything else."

Well, the girls begged and Momma looked real hopeful and then Junior and Daddy started untying that tarp and moving all our stuff and my crutches into the trunk of Junior's car. Once the girls realized how much room they had in the back seat, they begged to take Mr. Shoes along.

So next thing I knew, we were going over the river and through the woods with an excited dog bouncing in the back with Ida and Ellie. Momma and I sat up front with me by the window and her next to Daddy. He held her hand and she didn't pull away.

Daddy had actually took that job with Mr. Rhinehart. So after a week and a half of him working it seemed like everything was just swell. Not exactly like a fairy tale, but I felt almost rich knowing Daddy had a job and we was riding to Georgia in a car.

It was late when we finally got to Mamaw and Papaw's house. The girls was sound asleep. Daddy and Papaw carried them upstairs to the bedroom and Mr. Shoes went right up behind them.

Mamaw had made a bed for me on the sofa. "You get the front room, Susie Q," she said. "So you don't have to mess with the stairs." That's her pet name for me—Susie Q. She gave me a glass of milk and an oatmeal cookie. While I ate, I stared at the pretty carnival glass in her corner cupboard. Especially the light brown and rainbow-colored vase that reminded me of my time in the hospital with Imogene. When Imogene and I decided on bottle colors for each other, this was the one I picked for her.

Then I went into the bathroom and brushed my teeth and put on my pajamas. I thought again how nice it must be to have a bathroom right inside the house.

It was lonely on the sofa and I couldn't sleep on account of I was used to hearing my sisters breathe in the same room with me at night. And also because I never slept downstairs at Mamaw and Papaw's.

I wanted to lay in bed and listen to the voices of my grandparents coming through the heat grate from their room below. And when I woke up in the morning I wanted to look down on the yard with the birdbath and the hedge that went around their property.

So finally I decided to go get what I wanted. I wasn't afraid of that big stairway. I'd been up and down it on my behind many times playing Penny Penny with my sisters.

I crawled to the steps and sat on the bottom one and pretended Ida was standing in front of me with her fists held out, saying, *Penny, Penny, who's got the penny?* When I pretended to guess the right one I'd move backwards up one step.

I took my time getting to the top because I liked being on that staircase making believe my sisters were with me and we'd never heard of polio.

I crawled to the bedroom where I'd always slept. There were two beds, but Ida and Ellie were in the same one. So I crawled into the other one. I intended to keep my eyes open and take in the shadowy look of things, but that bed felt so much like home that I don't remember seeing much at all. I slept so sound that when I woke up I couldn't remember dreaming.

Thanksgiving Day was pretty as a picture. Not just the look of it out the upstairs window but also the dinner table. It was covered with all the best cooking, and we ate so good I could almost forget that we'd been through a war and that food was scarce.

On the Friday after Thanksgiving, Papaw's newspaper showed a picture of the people over at the Georgia Warm Springs Foundation. It talked about how President Roosevelt was missed because he often used to eat Thanksgiving dinner with the polio patients.

"I almost went there for therapy," I said. "But then the president died, and now...I just don't know."

Papaw surprised me then. "Well, I have a grand idea," he said. "Why don't we just drive over there and take a look at the place?"

And that's exactly what we done. First thing Saturday morning we all piled in Papaw's car and he took us to Warm Springs. It was a wonderful fall day, almost as warm as summer. We rolled down the car windows. The smell of the pine trees was so strong it reminded me of Hickory's polio hospital.

You would think a body wouldn't get homesick for a hospital, but all of a sudden I was. It came back to me how Imogene would be in her bed beside mine. And the sun coming through the window screen would make lacy pine-needle shadows on her white sheets.

She'd be telling me some silly story or maybe even singing one of those Negro spirituals. Whenever Imogene sang I'd just lay there and listen. Seemed like the songs knew what I was feeling. Or maybe it was Imogene who understood and that's how she picked the songs.

I stared out the car window and thought about Peggy Sue and how we used to understand each other like twin sisters. But that was before my life got cut in two with polio making an ugly line down the middle.

Sometimes it felt like I was on the garden side of Daddy's ditch and Peggy Sue was still in Wisteria Mansion, under those purple blossoms where nothing bad ever happened. We'd look at each other and try to talk across the ditch, but neither one of us could step over it.

The closer we got to Warm Springs, the more I missed Imogene. And President Roosevelt too. I sure wished he was going to be there!

When we arrived, Papaw took us right into the grounds

of the Georgia Warm Springs Foundation. It seemed like it was open to just anyone. He drove real slow by a huge white building with tall columns and lots of windows. A girl in a wheelchair was going toward the building, and when she got to it, I couldn't believe my eyes. The door opened for her and she hadn't even done a thing!

"Well, if that don't beat all," said Daddy.

I thought how I had to struggle to get doors open while I was propped on my crutches. Was every door in this place so easy to get through? What would it be like to live in a place designed especially for crippled people?

While we sat there and stared, the door opened again and a man came through in a wheelchair. Not a big wooden one like all the ones I'd ever seen, but a shiny metal one. He must've thought we looked a little lost because he wheeled his chair over to the car.

"Good afternoon," he said. "How may I help you?"

Papaw told him we just wanted a glimpse of Warm Springs. "We saw a picture in the paper," he said. "And it made us want to visit Franklin Roosevelt's favorite place."

Mr. Shoes poked his head out the window, and the minute the man saw him he got a big grin on his face. He let Mr. Shoes sniff his hand. "You sure do bring up some good memories," he said. "The president had a dog like this, you know."

Then Papaw told him about me having polio. And right then and there, the man invited us to park the car and join him for a tour! None of us ever expected that.

He waited for us to get out and then he introduced himself. "Fred Botts," he said, shaking hands with every single one of us. "I'm the registrar here at the foundation."

Mr. Botts turned his chair toward the building with the

tall pillars. "This building is called Georgia Hall." He looked at Ida and Ellie and asked, "Which one of you wants to open the magic door?"

Of course they both wanted to. So he said, "Whoever steps first in front of the all-seeing eye." He pointed to the door, and Ida and Ellie about knocked each other down to get there first. Just like that, the door opened and Mr. Botts took us inside. The lobby had tall windows that let in lots of light. It was a grand entryway that stretched way out from side to side but wasn't very deep. There was sofas and chairs and potted plants and pictures in fancy frames hanging on the walls.

Mr. Botts led us to a big dining room off to the right. He showed us just where the president would've sat if he'd been there for Thanksgiving dinner. "We always looked forward to our Thanksgiving meal with the president," he said. "This year we left an empty space at the table to honor him."

I asked him what was it like to actually talk to President Roosevelt.

"Meeting Franklin Roosevelt was like meeting your next-door neighbor. That's what he called us. 'Hi ya, neighbor,' he would say when he drove up to people's houses or saw folks in town. He loved to talk about farming and trees and horses and fishing."

After we toured Georgia Hall, Mr. Botts wanted to show us the rest of Warm Springs. So he talked to a man in a bow tie at the desk in the lobby of Georgia Hall. "Ed, could you call for the trailer?"

The man picked up the telephone right away.

"We'll just wait here for a few minutes. Someone will come get us," said Mr. Botts.

And sure enough, before long a bus pulled up out front.

The driver opened some doors in the back and pulled out a ramp. With his help, Mr. Botts rolled his wheelchair right into the back of that bus. And we followed.

We sat on seats that were lined up against the walls facing each other like sofas in a living room. While we rode, Mr. Botts showed how the bus had places to store crutches and even room for people on stretchers to ride along.

We stopped next to a big building with huge glass windows. "This is our new pool that we use for therapy," said Mr. Botts. "We won't go inside, though, because I want to show you the original pools."

The bus took us to some other swimming pools and we got out and walked around. A man was crawling to the pool. "See that gentleman?" asked Mr. Botts. "Before he was president, when he had more time to spend here, that could have been Franklin Roosevelt. At Warm Springs he was a polio like everyone else. If he needed to get somewhere and crawling was the easiest way, then that's what he'd do."

That really surprised me. In every picture I'd seen of the president he was standing or sitting at a table. I just couldn't imagine him on his hands and knees.

Mr. Botts told us to put our hands into the water. "Feel how warm it is? Almost ninety degrees."

I could see why the place was called Warm Springs—on account of the water, of course. But everything about this place seemed warm. There was a breeze, but even though it was late November it wasn't the kind of wind to make you shiver.

On top of that, everybody was real friendly. A couple of patients came up to me and asked when I had polio and if I was coming there to stay. Mr. Botts said, "Oh, we're working on that." He looked at me. "You really should come."

All the way back to Papaw and Mamaw's house I kept hearing him say that line. *You really should come.* Even the tires on Papaw's cars were singing those words. *You really should come. You really should come...*

13

Staying in Warm Springs
November–December 1945

I guess you could say I didn't actually leave Warm Springs.

Something about that place felt so much like home, and driving away was making a big homesickness inside of me. Even after we got back to North Carolina the feeling of belonging in Georgia stayed with me.

Mr. Botts had given me some papers with information about Warm Springs and even a registration form. In case I decided to come back. "Talk it over with your doctor," he'd said. My daddy promised that we would.

Back when I was in the polio hospital, a Warm Springs specialist named Dr. Bennett used to come and check on us. He had told me that with the help of the March of Dimes and people who make donations, anybody can go to Warm Springs.

But my daddy was just home from the war when I got out of the hospital. The thought of being away from him again was more than I could take. So I decided I didn't want to go just then.

Of course that was before we started noticing changes in Daddy. And now that things had got bad with him I was sure I couldn't go. I often heard him hollering in the middle of the night. And then I'd hear Momma's voice—almost like she was soothing a squalling baby.

All this time I had thought that if he just got a job and went to work every day, somehow that was going to fix things between him and Momma. But evidently there was something wrong with him that a job couldn't fix. He still complained about headaches, and we never could predict how he'd act when he got up in the morning or what mood he'd be in when he come home from work.

When Daddy emptied that Bromo-Seltzer bottle, I claimed it for my own. I set it on my nightstand and thought back to my days in the hospital and my friendship with Imogene.

One day, the first week in December, Daddy got up in a specially foul mood. When I said good morning, he growled at me like I'd woke him out of a deep sleep. Then Momma didn't refill his coffee fast enough to suit him and he told Ida to do it.

He knew good and well Momma didn't let the twins take hot things off the stove. So I tried to get it instead. There was only a few steps from the stove to the table, so I thought I could hand a cup of coffee over to Daddy without having a disaster. But I got off balance and dropped the cup.

It broke. Hot coffee splashed on Daddy's pant leg. He jumped up so fast his chair went clattering to the floor. "Ann Fay, who asked for your interference?"

"I'm sorry. I was just trying to help."

Daddy acted like he didn't hear me, but I knew he did. He left without his last cup of coffee. And he forgot his lunchbox, too.

Momma brought the dustpan and started picking up the pieces. I thought she would be annoyed with me. "Do you know what I think?" she asked. "You're trying too hard to fix this family. I think you should go to Warm Springs the first chance you get. There isn't a thing you can do about your daddy anyway. And if you can learn to walk again, we'll all be better off."

I thought about that all the way to school. About how I kept trying to fix things when I needed to be fixed. I thought maybe I should go. But could I really leave my family?

On that very same morning, before I went to my class, I stopped off at the water fountain. But before I could prop myself on my crutch to get a drink, Rob Walker jumped in front of me. He slurped the water real loud and said, "There ought to be a law against people with polio using public water fountains." He made a big show of brushing polio germs off his arm. Then he turned around and marched down the hall.

I tell you what's the truth. I felt like chasing him down and tripping him with my crutch. I wanted to see Rob fall flat on his face. But of course I couldn't run. So I just watched him go until someone behind me said, "Hurry up and get a drink, why don't you!"

That's when I made up my mind. Daddy had told me polio can make you stronger. And I decided to be strong enough to leave home. To get out of that school filled with normal people and away from my house where we couldn't remember what normal felt like.

Somehow or other I *would* go to Warm Springs.

So one night that week when Daddy was in a good mood I told him I wanted to go. I was half afraid he'd get ill-tempered when I mentioned it. But instead he pulled a piece of wood out of his pocket and started whittling. "I wondered how long it would take you to make up your mind."

"You mean it's okay with you?"

Daddy give me a hurt look. "Why wouldn't I want you to walk again?"

The next time we went to the polio clinic he handed the papers to the doctor. "What do you think?" he asked.

Dr. Gaul glanced over the pamphlets, but I'm pretty sure they didn't change how he felt about the matter. He just looked at me and said, "It's not so important what I think. What matters is how Ann Fay feels about it. If she wants to be at Warm Springs, then the staff there will help her make big strides. If she isn't ready yet, there's no point in wasting her time or someone else's money."

Right off I started defending myself. Trying to explain why I didn't want to go when I first came home from the hospital. "Back in June," I said, "my daddy was just home from the war. And I hadn't seen my sisters or my momma in so long that—"

Dr. Gaul put his hand on my shoulder. "I understand all that," he said. "But now that it's December, how do you feel?"

"I want to go."

"Why?"

I thought of everything I'd seen at Warm Springs. The beautiful white buildings with doors that opened up for crippled people. The warm water where Mr. Botts said I could improve my muscles. The sight of people moving all over in wheelchairs and on crutches.

But I didn't say any of that. What I said was, "People can crawl on their hands and knees at Warm Springs and nobody thinks a thing about it." Then I started to cry.

For some reason that was enough for Dr. Gaul. "Warm Springs will do you good," he said. "You've been working hard on your exercises, and your muscles are getting stronger. But there's more that can be done." Then he gave me a warning. "It won't be easy, Ann Fay. When you get to Warm Springs, you'll have to endure many examinations and they'll put you on a rigorous therapy program."

My daddy spoke up. "This girl can work hard as any teenager in North Carolina or Georgia, either one."

Dr. Gaul nodded. "I know that's true. We'll send all your medical records to Warm Springs with your application. But don't expect to be admitted before Christmas. These things take time."

Before Christmas? As much as I wanted to be at Warm Springs, I didn't want to go yet. I'd been in the polio hospital the December before and I didn't want to be away from home for another holiday.

But it felt like Christmas had come early just to hear my doctor say he'd help me get to Warm Springs.

14

Christmas
December 1945

In the middle of December I got a letter from Mr. Fred Botts saying he had a space for me starting in late January.

I'd been holding my breath waiting for this. But when it happened I could hardly breathe for the fear that come over me. I'd lay awake at night feeling like I had to get to Warm Springs. But then I'd think, *No. I can't leave home.*

Or I'd be watching Momma and Daddy doing some ordinary, everyday thing, like her sweeping the floor while he held the dustpan for her. And I'd get this fear that I'd never see that again. That if I didn't stay and hold this family together it might fall to pieces.

Momma was right—I couldn't change anything. But at *least* if I stayed home, I would know what was going on—even if it was bad, like the time he threw a drinking glass at the screen door when Ellie let it slam! Or the way he went to bed before the twins every night and got up looking like he hadn't slept a wink in spite of it. Seeing my daddy come apart like that was hard. But I was afraid that *not* seeing him would be even worse. What if he quit going to his job and Momma didn't write and tell me about it?

When it was definite that I was going to Warm Springs, Momma started sewing two new dresses for me. Daddy took care of all the arrangements. Phone calls, doctor visits, and talking to my teacher.

"I'm sure going to miss you," said Mrs. Barkley. And the next day she handed me a little blue book with blank pages. "It's a diary," she said. "Why don't you record your experiences while you're away?"

When Ruth Whitener found out I was going, she sent Jean back to the house for a canning jar. "This is a community responsibility," she said. "Our customers will want to help." The way she said "our customers" made me feel almost like I was her business partner.

She pulled a fountain pen out of her metal money box and made a small sign on a piece of paper.

Donations for Our Polio Girl
Ann Fay Honeycutt
(so she can learn to walk at Warm Springs, Georgia)

Jean taped the sign on the jar and stayed in the store all morning. "We're going to fill this and then we'll start over again," she said. She wasn't a bit shy. The minute anyone walked through the door, she'd come right out and ask for money. "How about a dollar for Ann Fay going to Georgia?" Or, "Hey, mister. You gotta dime to spare?"

And I do declare, just about every customer come up with something. Mrs. Whitener had a big pot of pinto beans on the stove. She started dishing them up for anybody who put money in the jar. "A bowl of beans for a donation," she'd say. "No amount is too small. And don't forget to tell your neighbors."

Well, that store got so busy Mrs. Whitener run out of beans the first day. "I see I'm going to have to break out my biggest pot," she said. She looked mighty pleased with herself.

The sight of that jar filling with coins and even dollar bills brung tears to my eyes. But the thing that touched my heart the most was Otis Hickey. He come in every morning at eleven o'clock for his dill pickle. But as soon as Jean told him about the collection he said, "Never mind the pickle, then." He put his two cents in the donation jar. It was just a mite, but I figured he didn't have much. So it felt like a whole lot to me.

I had a soft spot for Otis on account of most people wouldn't give him the time of day. Seemed like he was always bringing up the war. And more often than not, one of the other veterans in there would tell him to dry up.

So he never stayed for long. Just long enough to tell us his mother's arthritis was good on some days, bad on others. And maybe he'd try to start up a conversation. If he didn't get any satisfaction he'd just turn around and leave again. It got to where I wanted to run after him. If only I could run! If I could, I would've caught him by the arm and said, "Talk to *me*, Otis Hickey. *I* want to hear about the war. What was it like? What happened over there to change my daddy like it done?"

Maybe that was a lie. Maybe I didn't want to know. Maybe I wasn't as brave as I thought I was. Because I saw Daddy every day of the week and I never did ask him those questions. As a matter of fact I was fixing to run off to Georgia like nothing had happened to him at all.

One Sunday at church I was talking to Peggy Sue about that. "Your daddy's problems are not your fault," she said.

Answers come easy to people who never have problems.

Then Peggy Sue cocked her head and studied me for a minute. "Can I cut your hair before you go?"

"Oh," I said. "Well, I'd have to ask my mother."

So Peggy Sue asked Momma if I could go home with her for the day. "I want to give her a new hairdo," she said. "In case she meets any boys down there in Georgia."

Momma laughed. "Ann Fay's not going there for boys." She looked at me and asked, "Do you want to have your hair cut?"

"I might," I said. "I'm still thinking about it."

Like I said before, Peggy Sue has a knack for getting what she wants. After we ate dinner at her house, she sat me down at her dressing table. She handed me a magazine with movie stars in it and showed me a style one of them was wearing. "What do you think of that look? Your hair will curl more if you cut it shorter." And just like that, she started snipping.

Sure enough, when she was done, it fell into soft waves. She fluffed them with her fingers, and I couldn't believe how she made me look. "Daddy will think his tomboy has disappeared," I said.

"Well, for Pete's sake, it's time to take advantage of your *strong* points. You've got the prettiest black hair and blue eyes. But that's what you've got to call attention to."

Later, when Mr. Rhinehart was driving me home, I started wondering what Peggy Sue had meant by that. What was she saying—that if I got all dolled up maybe boys wouldn't notice my crippled leg?

Momma and the girls loved my new style. "Don't she look like a movie star?" Ida asked Daddy.

Daddy looked at me a long time and I was scared he was going to fuss. But finally he said, "She looks too good for her raising, that's for sure."

I think he liked it, though.

Nobody at school even saw my hair because we had snow about a week before Christmas. So we got out early for Christmas vacation.

It seemed like Warm Springs was the theme of my Christmas. I got a box of stationery with matching envelopes, a pen, and postage stamps for writing home.

And Momma had made me a swimming suit. "You'll need that for the water-therapy sessions," she said. She held it in front of me and said, "Oh, you should see how the blue brings out the color in your eyes."

The twins got a family of tiny wooden dolls Daddy had carved for them and furniture for a dollhouse. But he didn't have the house made yet. "Some things you just have to wait for," he said.

You should've heard the girls. Especially when Ida found a bathtub, a sink, and even a little toilet in there. "Look, Ellie!" she squealed. "Our doll family don't even have to go to the outhouse!"

They hugged Daddy's neck and thanked him and told him it was the best Christmas ever. He just grunted and pulled a cigarette out of his pocket. Then he got up and went outside. He didn't seem one bit pleased about all the happiness he had just give.

After Daddy left, the girls was playing with their new toys and Momma and I sat there guessing if it was going to snow or not. But really, we was waiting on Daddy to come back in with Momma's gift. It's a tradition that the last surprise of the day is always some piece of furniture he made for her.

But Daddy didn't come back in. Finally Momma started gathering the wrapping paper and pressing it out smooth so it could be used another year.

I put my gifts in a pile in my room, waiting until I could pack them up for Warm Springs. Through the window I seen Daddy pacing back and forth between the johnny house and the mimosa tree. And sucking hard on his cigarette.

After a while Momma went to the kitchen. Bessie and Junior were coming over for Christmas dinner and she wanted to be ready.

When they got there Bessie had two pumpkin pies and Junior carried in a pan of green beans. He almost dropped them when he saw me. "*What* did you do to yourself?"

"Huh?"

"Your hair."

"Oh, that! What's the matter? Don't you like it?"

Junior shrugged. "It's different." He set the pot of beans on the stove.

"Of course he likes your hair," said Bessie. She set down the pies and pulled me into a big hug. "Have mercy! Ann Fay, you belong in a magazine."

At dinner we each told what we got for Christmas. When it was Momma's turn, Ida spoke up. "Daddy," she asked, "where's Momma's present?"

Daddy had been picking at his food and looking like he wanted to be someplace else. When Ida said that, he got up and headed for the bedroom.

Oh good, I thought. *He does have something for Momma.* But then he stopped halfway across the room and turned. "I'm giving your momma a—bathroom." He hesitated a second before he said "bathroom." Like he just reached out and grabbed that idea off the ceiling.

"A bathroom?" asked Ida.

"A real live bathroom?" said Ellie. "In the house, with a tub and a toilet and everything?"

"You heard me," said Daddy. "With a real live every-thing. And while I'm at it, I'm putting in a kitchen sink with hot and cold running water."

"Oh, Leroy!" Momma sounded disgusted—like she knew he couldn't afford a bathroom or a kitchen sink either.

"Oh, Leroy, *what?*" Daddy come back to the table and stood over Momma. "Are you telling me you don't want a bathroom?"

"Where would you put a bathroom in this house?"

"That part is easy. I'll—I'll close in the back porch. And Junior will help me, won't you, Junior?"

"Uh, yes sir, I will." Evidently Junior thought Daddy was going to start working right that minute, because he asked, "Can I eat a piece of pie first?"

Daddy laughed then and his smile done me good. "You got time to eat lots of pies before we get started," he said.

Momma just sat there looking stunned. Almost like she wanted to cry, which I didn't blame her. I could see she didn't for one minute believe Daddy. And if you ask me, a bathroom didn't seem too likely.

After dinner Daddy went out for a cigarette, and then he went to his and Momma's bedroom and stayed there. Me and Junior helped clear the food and dishes off the table. Momma poured hot water from the steam kettle into a ba-sin, and Bessie said, "Wouldn't that be something, though? If Leroy got you some running water."

But Momma just shook her head. "You see how much gumption he's got, don't you?" She rolled her eyes in the direction of the bedroom. "I hold my breath every morning, just waiting to see if he'll get out of bed or not."

"Have mercy," said Bessie. "And he was always such a good provider."

After doing dishes, Momma and Bessie went to the living room to visit. Junior pulled out a deck of cards he'd got for Christmas and the two of us played rummy.

It started sleeting in the late afternoon, so Momma made cocoa and Junior got the bright idea that the two of us should sit on the back porch and drink it. We sat on the woodpile next to the back door and listened to the tinkling sound of sleet on the tin roof. I liked being all shivery cold with a cup of hot cocoa to keep me warm.

"Want me to push you on the swing?" Junior asked.

"Oh, sure!" I said. "Why don't I just run on over through the snow and sleet?"

"I could carry you."

"And slide down on your behind from all the ice under there? No thanks, I think I'll stay right here."

"Let's see then," said Junior. "We could crab-walk it."

So that's what we done. He lifted me off the porch and the two of us walked backwards on our hands and feet with our bottoms dragging the ground. Well, actually Junior did. I tried. But mostly I dragged my backside and my heavy left leg along behind me. "I despise this brace," I said. So Junior pulled me most of the way. I got snow and ice in my sleeves. But I didn't care on account of we was having fun.

Junior helped me onto the tire swing. He grabbed the ropes and started twisting until it was wound up tight. "I'm gonna spin you dizzy!" he said. Then just like that, he let go and I went flying around and around with ice from the tree coming down all over me. It landed inside my collar and in my ears too.

"Junior Bledsoe—you're in trouble!"

Junior just laughed. "You look real cute with all that

snow on your head," he said. He dusted me off and then he sat on the ground and leaned against the walnut tree. It was getting dark but the whiteness of the snow lit everything around him. Junior and the trees and the buildings were mostly just dark friendly shapes.

I had a feeling when I got to Georgia I was going to miss the sight of my backyard. And maybe even Junior.

"So, anyway, what made you take a notion to cut your hair?" he asked.

"Blame it on Peggy Sue. It was her idea. Evidently you don't like it."

"I just think it's kind of funny that you decide to get all dolled up right when you're fixing to leave. Must be something mighty special down there in Georgia."

"Must be," I said.

"Why are you so anxious to get away from us?"

"It's not that. I'm just ready to be someplace where I can fit in."

"Well, if *you* don't fit in around here, I don't know who does."

"Oh, really?" I said. "How would *you* like being carried up and down steps and have to crawl wherever you want to go? At Warm Springs if I crab-walked across the room nobody would think a thing of it. But what I really want is to learn to walk. And get rid of this hateful brace."

"I'd help you get anyplace you wanted to go," said Junior. "But I can't blame you for wanting to do it on your own. Just make sure those people down there treat you right. And don't go liking them better than us—understand? After all, nothing could be finer than to be in Carolina."

He started singing the song then. "*Nothing could be finer*

than to be in Carolina in the morning. No one could be sweeter than my sweetie when I meet her in the morning..."

Junior couldn't carry a tune if he put it in the trunk of his car. So I decided I better help him out. *"Where the morning glories twine around the door..."*

He stopped singing and let me finish the song. When it was over, he said, "If the roads weren't so slick, we'd get in my car and go to town. See the Christmas lights."

"Well," I said, "I wouldn't mind it. I'm tired of being penned up in the house. Reckon those lights'll still be up after the roads are clear?"

"Wanna go?"

"Why not? It might be the last chance me and you and Peggy Sue can get out before I leave for Warm Springs."

"Peggy Sue? What's she got to do with this?"

"Well, I just figured she'd go too. She's going to be upset with me if I ride into town with you and don't ask her to go along."

"Whatever for?" Junior sounded surprised. All along I thought he knew Peggy Sue had a barn-sized crush on him. And that he was loving every minute of it. Now I saw he didn't even realize it.

I thought it was unbelievable how someone like Junior, who knew so much about everybody and every little thing, couldn't see something as obvious as that. Some people are plumb stupid when it comes to love!

15

Warm Springs, Georgia
January 1946

One morning toward the end of January, Junior drove us to the train station so I could leave for Warm Springs. The twins was irritable and getting on Daddy's nerves. Momma was teary and Junior hardly said a word.

And it was all my fault everyone was so unhappy.

Daddy lifted me onto the train and Junior carried my suitcase and another box of my things to the porter. Every one of them came on the train to help me get settled and to give me hugs and kisses. Even Junior give me a quick hug. "Don't forget," he said. "Nothing could be finer than to be *here* in North Carolina."

I decided to ignore that comment. "Are you gonna write to me?" I asked.

From the look he give me, you would think I had asked for Junior's car. "I'd do just about anything for you, Ann Fay," he said. "But writing letters is not one of them. If I wanna talk to you, I'll get in my car and drive down there." Then he winked and said, "Of course, I don't mind if *you* write to *me*."

The train whistled then and Junior and my family scrambled off. The five of them looked so lost there on the platform, shrinking away from me as the train headed out of Hickory. Was I making a big mistake to leave them?

Was this how my daddy felt the day he went off to war? I remembered how I couldn't see him looking out the train window at us. Maybe he had the best way of coping. Not looking back was probably smart.

But I kept thinking about the girls getting dropped off at school on the way home from the train station. And Daddy and Junior going to work late, on my account. And Momma at the house the same as every other day. Only this day she'd have one less family member coming home for supper. One less helper to keep after the girls and do little jobs around the house.

Would she be able to stay on top of things?

"It mostly hurts at first," I whispered. I took Daddy's shoelace from around my neck, and the whole way to Georgia I held my wooden Comfort. I studied her little face with its tiny nose and eyes. And her mouth, which was too small for me to see if she was fixing to frown or smile. Mostly what I loved about her was her brace and her crutches. Funny how in real life I hated mine!

Still I rubbed my Comfort between my fingers until I figured she'd be smooth as one of Momma's clothespins by the time I got to where I was going.

Somewhere along the way, the clacking of the train going over the rails picked up the tune of "Nothing Could Be Finer." It played over in my head like a stuck record until it made me plumb ill. The closer we got to Warm Springs, the more I knew I was going in the wrong direction.

It was afternoon when the train pulled into Warm Springs. As the conductor lifted me down from the train, a tall fellow with broad shoulders stepped up. He glanced at the paper in his hand. "Ann Fay Honeycutt?"

"That's me."

"I'm Toby." He stuck out his hand and I shook it the best I could while leaning on my crutches. "I'm a push boy at the Warm Springs Foundation. Have a seat." He pointed to a wheelchair.

I shook my head. "I don't need it. I've got crutches."

"Oh, but you're at Warm Springs now. I've got to take good care of you, and that means you get pushed around until the doctors decide otherwise. There's no point in getting injured before they even examine you."

Even though I called myself a cripple, I hadn't expected to be treated like one at Warm Springs. I reckon Toby saw the surprise on my face on account of he started singing:

"I've got those polio blues, those polio blues.
Wish I could lose those polio blues!
Sent me to Warm Springs to get treatment there,
Took away my crutches and put me in a chair."

Well, that made me laugh. From the sound of that song it seemed like getting demoted to a wheelchair was a normal thing. There was even a song about it. So I sat, and Toby strapped my crutches onto the back of the wheelchair and pushed me to a black car by the railroad platform.

The porter was unloading bags. I pointed mine out, and Toby said he'd go back to get them. But first he helped me into the car.

It only took a few minutes to get to the fancy rock pillars at the entrance of the foundation. Toby drove me right up to the big building with the door that opened by itself. "This is Georgia Hall," he said. "It's where you'll socialize. And meet boys."

Then he winked and I thought, *Is he flirting with me?*

But I decided probably not. For one thing, he was perfectly healthy, so why would he notice a cripple like me? And for another, he looked like he was about twenty years old. Or maybe a little younger. But at least as old as Junior Bledsoe.

"You need to see Mr. Fred Botts," said Toby. "The registrar's office is your first stop. So we won't be getting out at the portico." Hearing him use that rich-sounding word, *portico*, and seeing the beautiful white building with the tall glass windows—all of a sudden I thought about Cinderella arriving at the palace.

And I *felt* like her, too—but the way she was *before* the fairy godmother stepped in. Not that it would matter what I was wearing. Even in a ballgown I wouldn't know how to act going through that fine entrance with perfect strangers staring at me. So I was relieved to go to Mr. Botts's office at the end of the building.

"Welcome, Miss Honeycutt. I see you made it." Mr. Botts reached across his desk to give me a handshake. "Did the railroad people treat you well?"

I was feeling shy, but I made myself look right at him. "Yes, sir. Everyone was good to me."

"It looks as if your paperwork is in order. So now you can settle in and meet your roommate." He chuckled. "At least, I hope so. Olivia flits from one thing to another, so I can't be certain that she's in your room at the moment."

Mr. Botts asked Toby to deliver my suitcase and box to my dormitory. "And please ask the folks at Kress Hall to send an attendant for Ann Fay," he said.

While we waited for the attendant, he asked how my family was doing. I thought about how miserable they looked on the railroad platform that morning. Were they at home right this minute regretting sending me here?

Mr. Botts must've seen how I was struggling to come up with an answer. "It takes awhile for soldiers to adjust to life at home," he said. "We have some Navy men staying here, and I can see that, besides them having polio, war has left its mark."

That really surprised me. "What did my daddy tell you?" I asked. I knew Daddy had talked to Mr. Botts on the phone to make plans for me coming here. But surely they hadn't discussed *his* problems. As far as I could tell, Daddy wouldn't even tell my momma what was weighing him down.

The only other person I could think of who might've talked to Mr. Botts was my doctor. But how would *he* know about Daddy changing after the war?

I guess Mr. Botts saw in my face how confused I was because he went on to explain. "I spoke with your benefactor, the gentleman who is sponsoring your stay at Warm Springs. He says your father is reporting to work and the two of them have an agreement."

An agreement? My benefactor? It must be Peggy Sue's daddy he was talking about. I knew that people had donated money through Mrs. Whitener's collection jar. But Mr. Botts made it sound like Mr. Rhinehart was helping to pay my way. Daddy hadn't told me about that.

That explained why he was sticking with his job even when he couldn't lift a finger at home unless Momma kept after him. He was doing it so I could walk again!

Suddenly lots of thoughts was spinning around in my head. Thoughts about Mr. Rhinehart talking about my daddy's problems. How much did he know? And was Daddy acting strange at work?

"Have I let the cat out of the bag?" asked Mr. Botts. "Mr.

Rhinehart didn't mention that his involvement was confidential."

I shook my head. "It's okay," I said. "But I didn't know he told you about my daddy's problems."

Just then someone tapped on the door, and a woman in a white uniform dress stepped inside. "Good afternoon, Mr. Botts," she said.

While the two of them swapped greetings I noticed every little thing about her. She was slender and had pretty auburn hair and green eyes. Something about her voice and her smile put me in mind of my momma. Mr. Botts introduced us.

"Mrs. Trotter, this is Ann Fay Honeycutt from North Carolina. She'll be staying with you in Kress Hall."

"I'm so glad to meet you, Ann Fay." Mrs. Trotter offered me her hand. Soon I was saying goodbye to Mr. Botts and she was pushing the wheelchair out the door.

We stopped at a counter with a man in a suit and a bow tie standing behind it.

"Ed Frogge, I'd like you to meet Ann Fay Honeycutt," Mrs. Trotter said. She looked at me and added, "Ed is the manager of the front desk. He handles the mail, and as you'll see, he's generally in charge of gossip and rumors around here. But don't you believe a word he tells you!" Mrs. Trotter laughed. It was easy to see that she and Ed enjoyed teasing each other.

Mr. Frogge just shook his head and gave me a big grin. "It's nice – to meet you." He spoke in a breathless way and took short gulps of air between his words. When I heard that, I was pretty sure he'd had polio too—maybe even the same kind my brother had. At the Hickory polio hospital I'd met other patients who'd been in iron lungs. Some of them sounded like Mr. Frogge.

"Young lady," he said. "Don't you – believe that nonsense – about gossip. I just report – the facts." He winked at me then and said, "But if you see a young – man of interest here – just let me know. Maybe I can help."

Mrs. Trotter waved him off. "You watch out, Ann Fay," she said. "Ed will be telling every eligible boy on campus that a pretty young girl has arrived."

We turned to go then, but Mr. Frogge wanted to chat. So while he and Mrs. Trotter talked, I practiced turning myself around in that wheelchair.

There was Georgia Hall stretching way down to the dining room. It was a grand hallway with black and white diamond shapes in the tile floor—just as beautiful as I remembered. Along the walls were wicker couches and chairs with flowered cushions. And there were lots of lamps and potted plants all around.

Just looking at all that beauty made me feel downright shabby—even with my Peggy Sue hairdo and the new dress Momma had made me. I was pretty sure this place had never seen a girl in overalls.

There were people scattered about, reading on the couches or chatting and laughing with each other. Three girls sitting near a fireplace saw me watching and lowered their voices. I turned away.

Mrs. Trotter was finishing her conversation with Mr. Frogge. "We shall see what we shall see," she said, wagging her finger at him. Then she turned to me. "Ready, Ann Fay?" She pushed me out a nearby door, and we followed a red brick walkway under a covered roof.

I couldn't help noticing the big white columns holding up that roof. It seemed like everywhere I looked there were more of them. "This is the colonnade," said Mrs. Trotter.

"And the grassy area ahead is called the quad. I'm sure you'll spend lots of time out here during warm weather."

The quad was like a park, with lots of trees and grass. There were fancy white iron benches here and there. And black lampposts with four white globes hanging so pretty on each one. The weather was warmer than back in North Carolina. So even in January there were people sitting outside and laughing and talking

There were buildings all around the quad—like a frame around a landscape picture. "See Kress Hall?" Mrs. Trotter pointed to a white brick building on the left side of the quad. "That's where you'll be staying."

There were two men in wheelchairs on the porch of Kress Hall. One of them called out to us. "I have something to show you," he said.

So Mrs. Trotter took me to meet them. "This is Ann Fay. Meet Lou." She gestured toward one man and then the other. "And Hubert. These men served our country during the war."

Hubert and Lou were both covered over in smiles. And for some reason, that seemed odd to me, like they were up to something. But of course I didn't know them. So who was I to be suspicious?

"Good to meet you," said Hubert. He wheeled his chair a little closer and reached out his hand. I thought he wanted to shake, so I reached too. But his hand was closed. Just before our hands touched, he opened his, and right there, smack-dab in his palm, was the biggest, ugliest brown bug you ever did see! It was at least two inches long. All of a sudden it lifted its wings and flew right past me.

"Aaaah!" I pulled back fast. It's a good thing I wasn't on crutches or I would probably have lost my balance.

I heard Mrs. Trotter gasp. "Oh, Hubert, you rascal! Is that any way to welcome our new friend?"

She wagged her finger at the two men. They were both laughing like naughty boys. She patted my arm.

"Ann Fay," she said. "It's just a palmetto bug. They thrive in this warm climate. But they're harmless. Really, they are."

Hubert winked at me. He was still laughing. "Welcome to Warm Springs," he said. "And don't worry, I wouldn't have put it in your hand."

I didn't know what to say. He seemed like a nice enough fellow. But my heart was thumping extra beats on account of him.

"Consider yourself initiated into the Warm Springs family," said Lou. "Practical jokes are what makes this place tick."

Mrs. Trotter just shook her head and took my chair again. She pushed me around the building and to a lower door at the back. "Hubert was right," she said. "Someone is always playing tricks on someone else around here. You had better keep on your toes, Ann Fay."

She went on to explain that Hubert and Lou were two Navy men who had polio and had come there for treatment. "The sailors are staying on the main floor of Kress Hall," she said. "So the girls have been moved to the lower level. For now, you have to use this back entrance."

I think she was trying to get my mind off that horrible bug because just as we were getting to the back door Mrs. Trotter told me to snap my fingers. So I did, and just like that, the door opened. We laughed, because of course it would have opened without me doing that.

But I decided I was going to have a good time snapping my fingers at all the doors around that place.

We went into a hallway with shiny tile floors and pale green walls. "Welcome to your new home," Mrs. Trotter said. Then, before she could say another word, a tall girl come out of a nearby room and headed toward us.

"Ann Fay Honeycutt, you're here!" she squealed. "I'm Olivia." She ran straight to us, stopped me in my tracks, and gave me a clumsy hug. Olivia had that kind of upturned mouth that looked like she was always smiling. I noticed right off that her arms was real skinny, so I knew they were the part of her that was affected by polio.

I watched her waltz into the room ahead of my wheelchair.

There were two beds in the room and one of them had a large piece of paper on it that said:

Ann Fay, Welcome to Warm Springs

The letters looked like they'd been colored by a child.

"I know it's sloppy," said Olivia. "I tell my hands to color in the lines, but they don't listen. Mother says they get tired of hearing me talk, so they just ignore me." She laughed. "Sometimes I think she wishes polio affected my tongue instead of my hands."

I wasn't paying much attention to Olivia either, because, just then, I realized there was a bathroom off our room. "Is that just for the two of us?" I asked.

"Sure," said Olivia. She shrugged like she was used to such things. "Do you need to go?"

"Yes," I said.

Thank goodness Mrs. Trotter let me use my crutches and go to the bathroom by myself. At first I just stared at the shiny white commode and sink. And the shower stall that was covered with gray tiles. I couldn't get over this bathroom being just steps away from my bed. And me sharing it with only one other person.

I wished my momma could see me right that second. I thought about Daddy promising to make her a bathroom. For some reason, seeing this room made it seem more hopeless than ever. We could dream about being high society but I had a feeling that staying at Warm Springs was as close as I would ever get.

When I finally came back out, Mrs. Trotter picked up my suitcase and laid it on the bed. "Shall we put your things in the bureau?" she asked. And the next thing I knew we had an assembly line going—with me pulling clothes out of my suitcase and handing them to Olivia, who gave them to Mrs. Trotter, who put them in the drawer.

A couple of times Olivia dropped things. "I'm so sorry! Oh, I wish my hands would behave themselves."

"Really, it's okay," I said. I could see how her hands frustrated her.

The closet was nearly full already with all the clothes that Olivia had in there. I didn't think even Peggy Sue had that many dresses.

I only had two everyday ones, four for school, and two for church.

I decided to leave the everyday dresses in my suitcase. I knew already I wouldn't be wearing *them* around this place.

Mrs. Trotter told me that her son was in the medical building at the other end of the quad. "That's why I work here," she said. "We live in Alabama, but dear Leon has had so many surgeries that Warm Springs has become another home to us."

There was a table beside my bed, so I told Olivia to put my diary and my blue Bromo-Seltzer bottle there. She shook her head. "What if I drop the bottle?" she asked. From the way she stared at it, I could see that saving an empty medicine bottle seemed strange to her.

"It reminds me of something Imogene told me," I explained. "She was my friend at the Hickory polio hospital. According to her, God keeps a separate bottle for each one of us—just for storing our tears inside."

"There's not much to cry about at Warm Springs," said Olivia. "This is a place for laughing. Right, Mrs. Trotter?"

"Yes," said Mrs. Trotter. "And a place for friendships."

I had a feeling they were right. They had both been so kind to me already. So I didn't mention the tears I cried on the train for leaving my family the way I did. As long as the two of them were talking, I could forget about the song Junior put in my head.

"If we hurry we can still make it to the picture show," said Olivia. She was already moving to the door.

"Well," I said, "I only have a little spending money. I should probably save it to buy keepsakes for my family."

"Oh, pooh! It doesn't cost us a thing. The movie company donates the films to Warm Springs."

"Really? I can't imagine it."

Olivia laughed. "Isn't it swell? Let's go."

16

New Friends
January 1946

Mrs. Trotter said I would have to sit in the wheelchair to go to the picture show. It felt like I had took a step backwards all of a sudden. I'd come there to learn how to walk, and instead it seemed like I was more of a cripple than ever.

My disappointment must've showed on my face. "I'm sorry," said Mrs. Trotter. "Perhaps after the doctors examine you they will let you return to using crutches. Until then, this is a safety precaution."

As we were going out the door, we nearly bumped into a large woman coming in.

"Hi, Ma," said Olivia. "Ann Fay is here."

The woman gave Olivia a hug. "Wonderful! I hope you're taking good care of her."

Then she turned to me. "I'm Ma Harding, your house-mother." She was wearing a nurse's uniform and a stiff white nurse's hat. But she was large and soft and her round face was covered in smiles. "You're officially one of my girls now," she said.

I started to shake her hand, but she reached down and pulled me into a hug.

"We were going to the Playhouse," said Olivia. "Please, Ma?"

Ma Harding checked her wristwatch and let go of me. "By all means! Do have a good time and be sure to introduce Ann Fay to your friends."

Olivia led the way through the quad. Mr. Botts was right when he said that she flitted about. She was always ahead of me and Mrs. Trotter, chatting with friends. By the time we caught up with her, she'd be taking off again to go talk with somebody else.

The Playhouse was an old white building with a wide porch and several ramps for wheelchairs. There was vines growing around the porch posts. They didn't have any leaves or flowers, but I knew right off that it was wisteria. I'd recognize that vine in my sleep.

The Playhouse had lots of theater seats going up like stair steps. It also had extra room down front for wheelchairs and stretchers. There were plenty of those. Everyone seemed to be smiling. And all of a sudden I felt exactly like I did when I first visited Warm Springs. Like I hadn't left home at all.

We found seats next to the front row. Mrs. Trotter left us then and said she would be going off duty. "A push boy will take you to the dining room," she said. "And I will see you bright and early tomorrow morning."

Before Mrs. Trotter left she went to a boy on one of the stretchers that was lined up at the front of the theater. The boy had a cast on his whole body. It got me to wondering if that might be the next thing they decided to do with me.

"That's Leon," said Olivia. "Mrs. Trotter's son." Olivia waved at Leon, and he grinned and waved back. It looked like Mrs. Trotter was explaining to him who I was.

I listened to all the jabbering around me. "Where do these people come from?" I asked.

Olivia laughed. "Wherever polio has struck." She started pointing to different people. "He's from Texas. And she's from Michigan. That man over there is from South America even."

Then she pointed to a girl about my age who walked with two canes and wore braces on both legs. "And there's Suzanne. She doesn't live at the foundation and she never even had polio," Olivia said. "But she's got a free pass to the Playhouse and the swimming pool whenever she wants. And she even walks from her school to get here." Olivia jumped up and brought Suzanne over to meet me. "This is Ann Fay, my new roommate," she said.

"Hi." Suzanne sounded a little out of breath. She plopped into the seat where Olivia had been sitting. "I can't believe I actually got here before the show started." She looked around to see who was listening and then lowered her voice. "Olivia, don't tell anybody, but I accepted a ride." Then she looked at me. "You're going to love Warm Springs," she said. "I've been here for over ten years and I wouldn't be anywhere else."

"Over ten years?" I wanted to hear more. "Did you know President Roosevelt?"

Suzanne grinned and her big brown eyes looked pleased as peaches. "You bet I did. I was just a little thing when I met him. My real name is Suzanne. But Mr. Roosevelt asked, 'Do you mind if I call you Suzie?' And guess what we called him? Rosey. Of course that was before he became Mr. President."

I almost couldn't believe it—here was someone who was on a nickname basis with Franklin D. Roosevelt! I wanted to ask her so many questions. But Suzanne was already on to another subject. She pointed to the framed pictures of movie stars and famous musicians on the walls. "They've all been here to visit," she said. "And I even met Bette Davis and Jimmy Dorsey."

A boy rolled up to us in a wheelchair. "Hi, Suzanne," he said. He looked at me and then at Olivia. "Is this your new roommate?"

Olivia laughed. "How did you guess? Ann Fay Honeycutt. From North Carolina."

The boy stuck out his hand. "Gavin," he said. "I'm from Florida." He had green eyes and blond hair that fell over his forehead. And a big smile that was just the least bit crooked.

Seemed like everyone at Warm Springs was smiling.

Then the lights went off and we heard music. Olivia found a seat on the other side of the aisle and Gavin wheeled himself away too. And just like that, the picture was showing. But it wasn't the feature movie. It was a March of Dimes film asking people to donate money. And what do you know? It was the one with Greer Garson called *The Miracle of Hickory*.

"Look!" I said. "That's my hospital. Oh, there's Nurse Amanda!" I tried to spot Imogene. As far as I was concerned, she was one of the reasons for that hospital being such a miracle. I didn't know any other hospitals that put white and black people side by side. But apparently coloreds wasn't something to brag about in a movie.

Then the feature come on and I tried to enjoy it. But I was too worked up to pay close attention. I watched the dark shapes of people on stretchers and wheelchairs and the way the light from the screen danced across them. Some of them were odd shaped because of special equipment they wore or the way polio had distorted their bodies.

At first it was a little shocking to see all that. But to tell you the truth, it was comforting at the same time. It was a relief after being the oddball. I was among my own people now.

Off and on I'd think about what my family was doing right then. Momma was probably making supper, and more than likely the girls was pestering Mr. Shoes. And Daddy? I just hoped he was helping Momma with whatever needed to be done. And not yelling.

When the show was over, the push boys who brought people on stretchers and wheelchairs took them back. And one of them—it was Toby—noticed me sitting there and pushed my chair too. We followed a line of wheelchairs down the ramp that led out of the Playhouse.

Olivia pranced along beside Gavin and jabbered to him while Suzanne stayed with me. She told me how she had to walk to the foundation if she wanted to swim or go to the movies. "Sometimes," she whispered, "like today, I sneak and get a ride. But if I get caught, I lose pool time. That's because walking here is part of my physical therapy."

"But Olivia said you never even had polio."

"That's right. But I was born with club feet. In other words my feet twisted inwards. My doctor asked if I could come here for surgery, and Mr. Roosevelt let me. I've had more surgeries than you can count. After each one I stay in the medical building. But once I'm walking again, I live at home. It's not far from here."

We went through a back entrance into Georgia Hall. Just riding into that big space made me feel small and shabby again. And to make matters worse, Suzanne pointed to a car sitting in front of the building. "There's Mama, waiting to take me home. I'll talk to you tomorrow."

"Oh," I said. "Bye."

She left me there, and all of a sudden I felt lost. I looked around for Olivia and saw her going into the dining room. She was still talking to Gavin. Then Toby took me into the dining room. I declare, if I'd been on crutches I would've stopped dead in my tracks.

I couldn't help but stare. The tables were covered with white cloths and china and silver. It was fancier even than the Hinkle sisters' dining room. All that finery—it scared me. What if I didn't have the manners for a place like this?

Toby pushed my chair up to a table with three people who were about my age. One boy was skinny and had black hair and heavy brown glasses that sat crooked on his nose. "Hi, Ann Fay," he said. He wiggled his nose to get his glasses back in place and his whole face squinched up. He stuck out his hand. "I'm Sam."

I almost forgot to shake his hand on account of I was busy worrying about messing up. Like dropping my fork or saying something stupid. "How do you know my name?" was all I could think of to say.

The other fellow at our table spoke up then. "We knew you were coming. And it's a good thing, too. Sam here needs someone to talk to, dontcha, buddy?" He gave Sam a punch on the arm. "My name's Howie, and this is Loretta."

Sam rolled his eyes. "They're too sweet on each other to carry on a conversation with me."

Loretta blushed a little at that. "I'm pleased to meet you, Ann Fay," she said. I could tell right off she was a southerner. And from the way she talked, I thought she was probably used to eating her supper off china plates.

If it wasn't for all the wheelchairs with crutches hanging on them and poles with slings to support people's arms, a body would've thought she was in a fancy restaurant. There was flowered draperies from the ceiling to the floor, and arched doorways, and fancy lights above the tables. Straight ahead of me was a portrait of President Roosevelt hanging on the wall.

I thought about my family sitting down to eat. Their table was covered with a green-and-white-checked oilcloth. Their dishes didn't all match and they sure didn't have cloth napkins. What was *I* doing here?

A colored waiter in a white coat and black bow tie brought food to our table. A slice of pork, mashed potatoes, cooked cabbage, and black-eyed peas. And a nice soft roll with peach jelly.

All the colored waiters in white coats got me to looking around for colored patients. Since our hospital in Hickory had coloreds, I thought maybe a place like Warm Springs might take them too. What if me and Imogene could get together here? Would she want to come? And would she still want to be my friend?

I didn't know. She hadn't kept up the letter writing like I thought she would.

"Where's the colored people?" I asked Sam.

"What?"

"I don't see any colored people here."

"The waiters are colored. Did polio affect your eyes?" Sam laughed like he had made a big joke.

"I mean colored *patients*."

"Patients?" asked Sam. "We're not patients, and we're not cripples either. We're *polios*. Like President Roosevelt. And for your information, colored polios go to Tuskegee Institute in Alabama. It's like Warm Springs—only for Negroes."

"I should've known," I said.

Before I got polio, coloreds and whites being separated was as normal to me as walking. But being stuck in the hospital beside Imogene and hearing how things looked from her side of town made me see things in a new light.

"What else would you like to know?" asked Sam. "Because I can probably tell you." He squinched his nose again to straighten his glasses. "Some people call me Mr. Encyclopedia."

He seemed proud of this. Him knowing so much about every little thing made me think of Junior Bledsoe. "Well, I just left one Mr. Encyclopedia back home," I said. "Does there have to be one everywhere I go?"

Sam just grinned like I had paid him a big compliment. "Evidently someone thinks you need us." He rolled his eyes up so I would know he was talking about God. And then he went on to tell me the whole history of Warm Springs.

"Franklin Delano Roosevelt came here in 1924 to learn to walk," he said. "This place was a run-down resort with a three-story inn that was a firetrap. So in 1933 they built Georgia Hall."

While he was talking, I changed my mind about Junior Bledsoe being another Mr. Encyclopedia. I thought how Junior seemed more like a farmers' almanac—full of down-home news about crops and weather. And what was the best brand of mayonnaise. And who had the lowest prices on motor oil.

And right about that time, with Mr. Encyclopedia filling my ears with facts and figures, a friendly almanac was starting to feel like a good thing to have around.

17

Examinations
January 1946

The next morning Ma Harding stopped by our room before we were out of bed. "Good morning, my dearies," she said. "Ann Fay, Mrs. Trotter will bring your breakfast to your room today. There's no time to go to the dining room, since you have an appointment with Dr. Pat first thing."

Mrs. Trotter did bring my breakfast. And she helped me get dressed, too. Then she took me to my appointment.

Dr. Pat checked me all over and asked all kinds of questions about what I eat, how often I go to the bathroom, if I sleep without pain, and whether I get headaches. "Polio shocks the body," he said. "We need to know how it's affecting your bodily functions."

It seemed like he checked every muscle I ever owned. I had to get x-rays while I was sitting and then more laying down. Dr. Pat seemed concerned about scoliosis. "Curvature of the spine," he explained. "Since some of your muscles are stronger than others, they can pull your spine out of its proper position."

And I saw Dr. Bennett too. He's the doctor who had come to Hickory during our epidemic. I was looking forward to seeing him on account of he was the one who suggested I come to Warm Springs in the first place. But

I don't think he remembered me. It seemed like his mind was somewhere else when he was going over my charts.

Then it was time for the physiotherapist. Well, not just one but a whole row of them, because Warm Springs is where some physios get their training. The head physio showed about five of them how to check my range of motion—that's how far I can move my legs and arms and every other little part of me.

Thank goodness Dr. Bennett decided I did not have to go around in a wheelchair all the time. Instead they fitted me with new crutches that were made of aluminum and had bands that fit around my upper arms for support. That was more comfortable than having crutches shoved against my armpit.

They took some getting used to, though, so I used my wooden ones to go to dinner. And wouldn't you know? I had to sit with Mr. Sam Encyclopedia again! He explained that we had assigned tables. "So I'm stuck with you," he said. "Just like Howie and Loretta are stuck with me. If they let us choose our own tables, some people wouldn't have anyone to sit with them."

Of course, I thought. *Who would choose to eat with a whole set of encyclopedias?*

I wanted to talk to Loretta for a change. The first chance I got, I started a conversation with her. "Are you from Georgia?" I asked.

She shook her head. "Louisiana."

Loretta's right arm was in a sling attached to a pole on her wheelchair. And there was a hinged device that helped her move it. An attendant stopped by the table and cut her meat.

"Are you right-handed?" I asked.

She nodded. "And my left hand wasn't even affected by polio. I was learning to use it, but the doctor thought I should strengthen my right hand too. After my first day here, when I sent my meat flying into another girl's face, I decided he was right." Loretta laughed, and the sound of it put me in mind of water running over the rocks in our creek.

"Are you serious?" Suddenly I felt less worried about dropping a fork in this classy dining room.

"Oh, yes!" said Loretta. "When I first came here I was trying to look as normal as possible. So I didn't want to ask for help."

"No one is normal at Warm Springs," said Howie. "That's the whole point of it. You were just showing off for *me*, weren't you?"

Loretta blushed. Listening to the two of them made me feel safer in this big place. At least here I wouldn't have to worry about bullies like Rob Walker pushing me down, or people calling me a cripple. And so far I'd hardly had a minute to fret about my daddy.

"Are you listening?" asked Sam.

While my mind was wandering, he'd changed the subject from Loretta's meat story to President Roosevelt's death. "It happened here at Warm Springs on April twelfth," he said. Like he thought I'd been born just that morning.

"I remember," I said. "That day is as clear to me now as that water you're drinking. I was laying in my hospital bed in North Carolina when the announcement come on the radio."

"Came," said Sam.

"What?"

"It's *came*—when the announcement *came* on the radio."

By the time I figured out Sam was correcting my grammar, he was back on the subject of Roosevelt dying. "He was down at his Little White House getting his portrait painted. And all of a sudden he said, 'I have a terrific headache.' Then he slumped down in his chair. That was at one fifteen in the afternoon and by three thirty-five he was gone."

From the details Sam was giving, you would've thought he was the clock itself, watching from the Little White House wall.

"Were you here?" I asked.

Sam shook his head. "I was back home in Tennessee. I didn't even have polio yet."

"I was here," said Howie. "In the medical building, because I'd just had surgery. But I wanted to say goodbye like everyone else. So they brought me on a stretcher to Georgia Hall and lined me up with everyone else."

"You should've seen how they crowded everyone around the portico," said Sam.

"I thought you were in Tennessee," I said.

"Oh, I saw the pictures in *Life* magazine. With everyone crying and that colored man playing 'Going Home' on his accordion while the tears ran down his cheeks. Even Suzanne was in the picture, but she was mostly behind one of the columns."

"Really?" I asked.

"Really," said Sam. "Is there anything else you want to know? I've read practically everything that's ever been written about FDR."

Well, there was lots I wanted to know about Franklin Roosevelt, but I would ask Suzanne, not Sam the Encyclopedia Man, that was for sure. It just amazed me how that boy could take a perfectly good conversation and turn it into a speech!

After lunch Mrs. Trotter took me to my room. "Time for rest," she said. She explained that resting was an important daily ritual. "Try to sleep if you can."

And Ma Harding came down the hall too. Before she got to our room, I heard her calling out advice. "Rest! Rest! And more rest!" she said. When she got to our door she blew us kisses and said it again. "Rest! Rest! And more rest! And that means you too, Olivia."

But Olivia was full of talk. As soon as Ma's footsteps disappeared down the hallway, she started. "Gavin wants to know, are you going to play bridge with us tonight? Or rook, if you prefer."

"Maybe I'll watch," I said. Now I wished I'd played rook with those farmers and Mrs. Whitener at the store.

"Ah, come on. Watching is no fun. If you need a teacher, Gavin would love to do the honors." She lowered her voice. "If you ask me, I think he's sweet on you."

I didn't for thirty seconds think that was true. "Does everybody around here have to have a sweetheart or something?"

"Why not?" asked Olivia. "This is Warm Springs. Romance is in the air." She laughed. "Or maybe it's in the water. Do you have a boyfriend at home?"

"Of course not," I said. "The boys in my class are younger than me. And anyway, as far as they're concerned, I'm nothing but a pair of crutches and an ugly old brace."

"See there?" said Olivia. "At Warm Springs, we don't have that problem. We're all in braces and crutches and wheelchairs. And guess what—we can have dates and our parents will never know!"

While Olivia chattered, I wrote in my diary—about the bathroom we had for just the two of us, the Playhouse and free movies, and Sam the annoying encyclopedia. And all the other people I'd met so far. After I filled the page, I slid my diary under my pillow and drifted off to sleep.

My daddy was waiting in my dreams, standing at the Warm Springs train station with tears spilling out of his blue eyes. "We need you at home, Ann Fay," he said. He grabbed my hand and kissed it, and when he did, his tears froze on my arm.

The train whistle blew a mournful wailing sound and the train started out of the station. The wheels began clacking and the sound of that song chimed in again. *Nothing could be finer than to be in Carolina...*

I *wanted* to go with Daddy. But what about the Warm Springs Foundation? It had a glow around it like an enchanted forest. The sunlight came in long, straight beams through the trees. A soft breeze rippled the pine needles so the whole forest shimmered. I wasn't ready to leave that place.

But I felt Daddy tugging on my hand. "I've come to get you, Ann Fay," he said.

He started running to catch the train, and next thing I knew, I was riding on his back and he was running away with me.

The train was clacking real loud. If it hadn't woke me up just then, I reckon I would've gone back to North Carolina.

18

Fun and Games
January 1946

I felt all groggy and grumpy when I woke up from my nap. Olivia wasn't in the room, and the bathroom door was open so I could see she wasn't in there either. All of a sudden I got a sick feeling in my tummy. What was I doing in this strange place with no family around? What was I thinking when I told my doctor I wanted to come here?

I knew the answer to that. I was thinking about walking again. About getting back to normal. And being with people who wouldn't care if I *wasn't* normal. That's why I was here. But my dream about Daddy made me feel like I was in the wrong place.

I went to the window and looked out. A car drove by slow on the road behind the building. Otherwise I didn't see a soul moving about. I looked at the clock on Olivia's nightstand and saw that our rest time wasn't over. But where was Olivia?

I decided to write to my family. By now, Momma was probably wondering what I was up to.

Dear Momma, Daddy, Ida, and Ellie,
I want you to know I got here just fine. The train trip was good except for wishing I wasn't leaving you all.

Everybody has been real good to me here. I'm making friends fast! My roommate is Olivia and she introduces me to just everyone. I eat at a fancy table with Howie, Loretta, and Sam. They're all about my age or a little older.

I met a girl named Suzanne who never even had polio. But she came here for surgery when she was little and keeps having more and more surgeries to fix her club feet. She knew President Roosevelt and Sam says her picture was in Life magazine when they took his body away from here last year. I don't know if it's true. But Sam seems to know everything, so it probably is.

I saw the doctors this morning, and they sent me to the brace shop for new crutches. Now I am learning to use Canadian crutches, which are lightweight. Once I get used to them they will be lots more comfortable. This afternoon I took a nap. We have two hours of rest time every day!

How are you doing? Please write and tell me every little thing.

Ida and Ellie, give hugs to Mr. Shoes for me. And when you see Peggy Sue, tell her to write me.

Daddy, if you stop in at the store, please tell Mrs. Whitener and Otis that I am doing just great down here!

Love,
Ann Fay

Of course I wasn't feeling as wonderful as my letter made it sound, but I didn't want anyone worrying about me. And besides, I hoped my homesickness would go away real soon.

After a while Olivia came back in the room. "Rest time is over," she said.

"Where'd you go?" I asked. "Didn't you sleep?"

"Are you kidding?" Olivia sat on her bed and pulled her hairbrush through her hair. "I can't lay still in the middle of the day." She lowered her voice. "I was just visiting with some friends down the hall. But don't tell Ma Harding. If I get caught again, she's liable to send me home!"

That didn't sound funny to me, but Olivia laughed.

Then she got up from the bed. "I'm off to OT," she told me. "That's occupational therapy. They have me crocheting another handbag. I'll give this one to you." She headed toward the door but then stopped. "And oh, by the way, Suzanne is here. She wants you to meet her in the library. It's that way—in the school building."

And just like that, Olivia was back out the door. I had a feeling I'd never be able to keep up with that girl!

I needed something to pull me out of my blue mood. Maybe going to meet Suzanne would help.

The school building was close to Kress Hall, so it didn't take me long to find her. She was sitting at a table looking through a large album, and there was another one next to it. "Want to see my scrapbooks?" She patted the chair beside her, and I sat down.

The album was filled with Suzanne's favorite movie stars—June Allyson, Doris Day, Susan Hayward, and lots more. She had pictures she'd clipped from magazines and ticket stubs from the theater over in Manchester. "That's about five miles from here," she said.

I was mostly interested in her pictures of Franklin Roosevelt. She had plenty that were taken in Warm Springs. They all came from the newspaper and it wasn't like they showed him and her together or anything really special. But still, it seemed special that she was there at the same time he was.

"Were you really in *Life* magazine?" I asked. "Sam said you were."

"Well then, I guess I was," she said. Suzanne squinched up her nose like she was Sam adjusting his glasses. "Because, of course, Sam knows everything."

We both laughed.

"My momma has the magazine. She would never let me cut it apart to put in an album. Hey! I've got an idea. Maybe you can come to my house one day. If you do, I'll show it to you."

I looked through both of her scrapbooks and even helped her glue photographs in the one that wasn't full. We wrote little notes about each picture. Then she told me to keep that album in my room. "That way we can work on it some more," she said.

I felt like Suzanne really wanted me to be her friend. In that way, she reminded me of Imogene. And she wasn't even stuck with me in a hospital ward the way Imogene was.

We walked over to Kress Hall, and I tucked the scrapbook in the drawer on my nightstand. Suzanne asked to see pictures of my family.

So I pulled out my diary and showed her the photographs tucked in the back. One was of Momma and Daddy taken before he went off to the war. And another one was my whole family before my brother died. Only you couldn't see Bobby good because he had his hand over his eyes.

I had school pictures of Ida and Ellie and Peggy Sue. And I had the picture of us with Junior and Miss Dinah at the Hinkle sisters' house.

"Who's that?" asked Suzanne. "Is he your boyfriend?"

"Are you crazy? That's my neighbor. He's too old for me. And if he wasn't, he still wouldn't be my boyfriend."

"Is that his car?"

"Yes, and I think he'd owned it for about two hours when that picture was taken. That's my neighbor Miss Dinah holding our dog."

I told Suzanne the story about Mr. Shoes and the mouse and Miss Pauline. Actually I told her lots of things. All about my neighbors and Whitener's Store, and Peggy Sue, and how I got polio and met Imogene at the hospital. And Bobby, of course, and the blue bottle sitting on my nightstand.

Suzanne told me that once when she was staying in the medical building, she tried to sneak one of her friends out to see a movie at the Playhouse. She was in a wheelchair, but that didn't stop her from pulling her friend's stretcher down the hall!

"But then," she said, "I got my wheelchair hung up in the elevator door. Before I could get unstuck, along came the head nurse. And believe me, she wasn't too happy about my shenanigans!"

Of course, I had to tell Suzanne about the time me and Imogene sneaked out of our hospital wards in the rain to see each other. "We got caught too," I said. "But it was worth it because Nurse Amanda stuck us in the warm water tubs to get the chill off. So we got to spend more time together."

Swapping stories made me see how much the two of us had in common. Nothing against Olivia or anything, but in some ways I wished Suzanne could be my roommate. But of course she had to go home most days before supper.

That evening Olivia talked me into going to Georgia Hall to play rook.

"I'm just planning to watch," I warned her. But when we got there an older girl named Martha invited us to play with her and Gavin. I shook my head. "I'll watch."

"Sure!" said Olivia.

"We need one more person," said Gavin. He winked at me. "I think that means you." And right off he started dealing cards into four piles.

Thankfully, Mr. Encyclopedia came then and wheeled his chair up to the fourth pile. But Gavin shooed him off.

"Ann Fay is playing," he said. "You can't just butt in here."

So Sam backed his chair away and I seen how some of the shine went out of his brown eyes. It put me in mind of Otis and how those veterans at the store didn't want him around if he was going to talk about certain ugly parts of the war.

Thinking about Otis made me feel sorry for Sam. "You can teach me how to play," I said. That was all Sam needed to get sparked up. He pulled his wheelchair as close to my seat as he could get. And right away he started giving me instructions.

It wasn't that hard. I just had to learn which cards had the most points and play them at the right time. And Sam wasn't shy about telling me.

Olivia was sitting across from me and winking every time Gavin opened his mouth. Like she thought every word was intended just for me. I was sure it was all in her head. For one thing, Gavin didn't know the first thing about me. And besides, I wasn't half as pretty as Loretta or Olivia. Or Martha either, even if she was older than us.

I kept watching the other people in the room, sitting at tables playing games or putting jigsaw puzzles together. It seemed so natural to be here with all these people enjoying each other. If you closed your eyes and listened, you would hear two people playing checkers and arguing over whose move it was. Or a table full of people laughing so hard you'd want to find out what you were missing.

For a second there I felt sorry for everybody who wasn't at Warm Springs, Georgia. I wanted my family to be here. Especially my daddy. There was just something about this place—a softness in the air and a welcome at every door that made you feel like a body could overcome anything.

Then I heard Olivia's voice. "Ann Fay, are you sleeping? Sam is stealing this game away from you. Don't you even care?"

Well, I *didn't* care. I was happy to let Sam play my trump cards and get the credit for winning. Watching the rest of them play was all I'd come to do in the first place.

For all the fun Sam was having, at exactly twenty minutes after nine he pointed to the clock on the wall and said, "You watch, Ann Fay! The manager of Georgia Hall will come run us out in ten minutes."

And sure enough, at nine thirty someone come and started shooing us off. "Thirty minutes until lights out," the man called.

I wasn't ready to go back to my room. And everyone else seemed to feel the same way. Except for Sam. He seemed to think that clock on the wall was God talking. The second that long hand hit the six he started rolling away from the card table. Squinching his glasses into place as he went.

"You're on your own, Ann Fay," he called back to me.

After that, a girl at another table picked up her crutches and struggled to her feet. People put their games into boxes. And big wooden wheelchairs backed away from the tables. The next thing I knew, there was a whole train of them rolling out the doors.

The people at my table were determined to finish our

game. I played my last card, hoping my partner would back me up with the rook, but wouldn't you know—Gavin played it instead. "Gotcha!" he said.

I felt a little kick under the table and Olivia made eyes at me. As if Gavin saying "Gotcha" in a game of rook actually meant something else. Then she faked a yawn and elbowed Martha. "How's about you and me get out of the way?" she said.

And just like that, she stood and motioned for Martha to follow. Then it was just me and Gavin sitting at that table. If I didn't hurry, I'd end up being alone with him.

I started gathering the cards. I don't know if Gavin was watching every move I made, but it sure felt like it. And it flustered me so bad that I dropped a whole bunch of cards. They scattered on the floor. "Oh, brother!"

Gavin just laughed and said, "Now you did it!"

He was stuck in that chair and couldn't help me pick those cards up. So I hung on to the table and lowered myself to the floor. I knew I looked ridiculous with my legs sprawled out and my skirt hiked up to my knees. If Gavin had thought about liking me, he was about to get over it.

I started picking up the cards and Gavin reached out to take them from me. I heard a man ask, "Hey, Gavin, need any help over there?"

"No thanks," said Gavin. "I'm just putting these cards away. I'll be right there."

I could tell that the man thought Gavin was alone in the room. He couldn't see me on the floor because of the tables and chairs in the way.

"Okay. I'll be going then. Better hurry. The night watch will be around soon to shut things down." And just like that, the man was gone.

Gavin could've told him I was there. But he didn't. I looked at him and he was laughing at me. "Thanks a lot!" I said. "Now who's going to help me off this floor?"

"Think of it this way," said Gavin. "In about nine hours, breakfast will be served in the next room. You can sleep right here. It'll save crutching to your room and back." He wheeled his chair away from the table like he was going to leave me there. "See you in the morning, Ann Fay."

But he was watching me—maybe to see if I'd get mad. And to be honest, I almost did. But then I noticed something. Gavin had real cute dimples. How come I hadn't seen *them* before?

I was in the middle of trying to think up some clever answer when he came back and reached his hand out to me. It was solid and cool. Mine felt sweaty! But between hanging on to him and his chair, I managed to pick myself off the floor. I reached for my crutches and started across the room.

"*You* can sleep here if you want to," I said. "*I'm* crutching back to Kress Hall."

"You are so welcome for my help," Gavin called after me. "Anything else I can do? Give you a tour of the foundation, maybe?"

And just like that, the Little White House popped into my head. I turned. "Really? What about the president's house? Can you take me there?"

Gavin was close behind me, but he stopped his wheelchair in its tracks. "Um, uh, I'm afraid you got me on that one. Even if we talked a push boy into taking us, we'd get caught for trespassing. They've got guards over there."

"Why? It's not like we want to hurt anything."

"I suppose someone might, though. They can't take the chance." Then Gavin placed his hand on his chest and said, real dramatic-like, "But take heart, dear friend! I read in the *Warm Springs Mirror* that the state is preserving it as a memorial. It's just a matter of time until they open it to the public."

"For real?"

Gavin laughed at me. "You should see your face," he said. "Do you really care that much about going there?"

I could feel myself blushing. I must have looked like a silly child at a candy counter. Like a ragged young'un from the foot of Bakers Mountain, a place so small Gavin didn't know it existed. I wanted to escape Georgia Hall—quick, before the night watchman showed up. And before I gave Gavin something else to laugh at.

I looked for the nearest door. "Well," I said—and I know I sounded mad—"wasn't history made right there? Isn't that enough reason to want to go?" I turned my crutches around and stepped in front of the door. I snapped my fingers.

Thank goodness it opened. And just like that, I was outside and Gavin was in.

19

Changing
January–February 1946

On my second full day in Georgia I went to the famous Warm Springs pool for the first time.

There was an attendant named Betty in the dressing room who helped me get my suit on. It felt strange having people wait on me hand and foot. Especially dressing me. I was used to pulling clothes out of the drawer for my sisters and helping *them* get dressed. But it seemed like there was lots of being waited on at Warm Springs. In one way it made me feel like a child again, to be helped with every little thing, but in another way I felt like Cinderella.

"Just relax and let us take care of you," said Betty. When I had my swimsuit on, she helped me into a wheelchair and a push boy took me to the pool. It was in a tall building with high windows all around. There was tiles the color of North Carolina clay on the floor and halfway up the walls. The morning sun coming in through the windows made long slants of light on the red tiles. And it rippled on the water.

In all my fifteen years I had never been in a real pool. The only swimming I'd ever done was in the rivers of Catawba County, North Carolina. I always thought swimming in pools was for rich people.

The physiotherapists were busy, so I had to wait my turn. But that was fine with me because I just wanted to sit there and take it all in. I watched how the physios talked so quiet to the polios and how gentle they worked at massaging their muscles.

After a while Mr. Fred Botts went past the window. Later in the day there would be plenty of people in the quad. But it was quiet there this early in the morning.

From the pool I could see the walking court, a platform with steps going up on three sides. It was empty now, but the day before, I'd watched one of the Navy men practicing the stairs. A push boy and a physio helped him go up with no crutches or canes. The physio was in front, going up backwards so she was facing him. She talked him through each step and the push boy stayed right behind him hanging on to his belt. Sweat was dripping off that man's chin. And it was still January!

Thinking about it now made goose bumps come up on my arms. Sam had already told me I'd have to walk those steps before I could go home. I turned back to the pool and got the biggest urge to be inside the warm water. I wanted to be covered over by it—to let it fix me.

Sitting there with the sunlight streaming over my legs, it was easy for me to believe that this place could fix whatever was wrong. Someone called my name then. It was a physiotherapist. I started to get out of the wheelchair, but the push boy stopped me. "That's my job," he said, reaching down to take me from the chair. You could tell he had done this a million times because he knew just how to lift me.

He carried me like a baby down into the water, and I felt the wetness hit my backside and then my feet. It wasn't as warm as I thought it would be, but it wasn't cold either. He laid me on a table that was in the pool. It was sloped up at the top so my head could be out of the water.

The physio took my hand then. "Hello, Ann Fay." When she smiled, the shine in her eyes was just as warm and magic as the water itself. "My name is Janice. I'll be your physiotherapist."

Janice talked to me for a few minutes about where I was from and how I liked it at Warm Springs, and then she got right down to business.

The first thing she did was start moving my legs to loosen them up. She was so gentle it reminded me of what the attendant had said: "Just relax and let us take care of you." And I have to tell you it felt so good after all the bearing up I'd done with my family, and going back to school, and even working for Ruth Whitener. I couldn't hold on anymore. The tears started slipping out of the corners of my eyes.

Janice was turning my leg in a circular motion, but she stopped. "Did that hurt?"

I shook my head. I kept my eyes shut, but they still leaked and the tears ran off my face and into the Warm Springs pool. It seemed to me like that clean sparkly pool was a good place to let go of my sorrows.

Janice explained everything she was doing to me. She bent my legs in different positions. She rotated them. She rested my feet on her shoulders and massaged my leg muscles with her fingers. I don't think she missed a single muscle from my belly to my toes. And she worked on my left arm because it had been affected by polio too. "You still have some weakness in your shoulder," she said.

I think I must have cried the whole time. Not out loud or anything, just to myself. It was like Janice was working loose all the sadness and worry in me. I hoped it would go down the drain without clogging the pool filters. And I hoped the polios around the pool weren't watching me.

Finally, Janice said we were done for the day. "If you'd like, you can splash around in the pool for a few minutes," she said. She helped me off the table. And right away I could feel how much easier it was to move in the mineral waters of Warm Springs. Almost like magic! "Stay close to the edge," Janice told me.

So I did. I hung on to a bar with one hand and held my nose shut with the other one, and I went down into the water. The way it felt covering over me—oh, I just can't describe it. I felt free. Like I was going down a cripple but I'd come back up and start walking around again.

It wasn't going to be that easy, of course. I knew it wasn't. But it helped me to think about it like that. To dream about change and getting better and turning sad things in my life into happy ones. I thought about my daddy, and how if I could get better, surely he could too.

I reckon that was the moment when I really, truly settled in to Warm Springs. That first time in the pool was when I quit thinking I should be at home and started realizing that *this* was where I belonged.

I still thought about my family. But I quit trying to be in two places at one time. I figured that only God in heaven could fix my daddy. So I should let Him do it.

On Sunday I went to the Warm Springs chapel right across from Georgia Hall. Like all the other buildings at the foundation, it was filled with light. At first I just stared at the pew where Franklin Roosevelt used to sit. And wished that he was there. But then the service started and I was so interested that I forgot all about the president.

There was lots of kneeling and reading prayers and

things we never done at my little church in North Carolina. But I told myself it was the same God who my family was worshipping right that very minute in our little country church.

I liked knowing what my family was doing back home each day. Church on Sunday and maybe visiting with the neighbors in the evening. Then on Monday it would be the regular routine—breakfast, Daddy's job, and school for the girls. And Momma at home scrubbing the house or doing laundry.

I got into a routine of my own at Warm Springs. Breakfast. Water therapy. Dry therapy. "Rest! Rest! And more rest!" And of course meals in the dining room and games in Georgia Hall.

And school even, right there on the campus. Some teachers went into the medical building, to the patients' beds, to work with them. But I had to go to class. With Olivia and Gavin and all the others who were ambulatory. Because of our handicaps we were closer than my class back home was. Except for Mrs. Barkley and Peggy Sue not being there, I liked this school a lot better.

When I wasn't in school or therapy, I was usually with Suzanne. We worked on her scrapbook. And we joked about how we'd have to divide it between us when it was time for me to leave. One day Suzanne brought a camera and Ma Harding took pictures of us together. When she got them developed we put one in the scrapbook. And I sent one to my family.

Dear Momma, Daddy, Ida, and Ellie,
   I am having a good time in Warm Springs. What about you? Is everything fine at home? Please tell me what's going on

up there. Ida and Ellie, after all the times I helped you study your spelling words, the least you can do is write me a letter!

Daddy and Momma, remember Mr. Botts? He said to give you his regards.

I have lots of friends here and all the staff is so good to me. I'm sending you a picture of me with Suzanne in front of the practice stairs. Just think! Pretty soon I will be walking up and down those steps.

I love the pool the best. It's hard to explain how the water feels. But it's so easy to move around in. It makes you believe you can overcome anything. Just watch and see if I don't come home in no time at all!

Love from your daughter,

Ann Fay

As busy as Momma was, she found time to write to me.

Dear Ann Fay,

I sure do miss you around here. But we are fine and the twins are learning to help out.

It seems like the minute you left they gave up playing with paper dolls and dollhouse toys. Now they are putting on plays with the front porch as their stage. For some reason every story they make up includes Junior and his car.

Virginia Setzer gave birth to her new baby the day after you left. She had a girl. Donna Benfield's baby is two weeks overdue already.

I hope you are doing well and aren't feeling homesick. Are you working on your therapy? I can't wait to see how you improve. We pray for you every night at the supper table.

Love,

Momma, Daddy, Ida, and Ellie

I folded Momma's letter and thought about what she said and what she didn't say. She didn't come out and say that the twins was growing up without me there to take care of them. But it almost sounded that way.

She didn't say a word about Daddy. That could mean just about anything. Was he doing so good that she didn't have to mention it? Or so bad that she couldn't bring it up?

And what she said about those new babies—well, it just wouldn't let go of me. Both their daddies had served in the war. They both came home early on account of injuries. The Benfield man had even lost a leg.

I couldn't help but wonder what else those soldiers had lost. Did they forget how they were before the war? Could they hold down a job? Or take care of their families?

I figured in some ways those new babies were lucky. Even if the war did ruin their daddies, *they* would never know the difference. It wasn't like they ever knew them any other way.

I was pretty sure that having a treasure and losing it is much harder than never knowing what you missed.

I missed the way my daddy used to love the sound of his young'uns playing. Now it seemed like he hated noise of any kind. I missed the way he used to play *with* us. Now he didn't do much of anything except smoke cigarettes and whittle. I missed Daddy being the man of the house, and loving my momma, and taking care of all of us like we was his most prized possessions.

Now I wasn't sure if he prized any of us anymore.

But then I thought about him working for Mr. Rhinehart every day. And how he was doing it so I could be at Warm Springs. I took Daddy's shoestring from around my neck and kissed my little wooden Comfort.

And I knew that Daddy had never really stopped loving any one of us. He was just having a hard time showing us what was inside of him.

20

Valentines
February 1946

There was a commissary at Warm Springs where you could buy drinks and candy and other snacks. It seemed like Olivia and Gavin and Suzanne were buying treats about every other day.

But not me. When I left home the Hinkle sisters had give me spending money. But as much as I loved Cracker Jacks or Coca-Cola with peanuts in it, I tried to stay away from the commissary. I wanted to save my money for souvenirs to take home to my family.

Then, not long after I got to Georgia, the U.S. Mint come out with brand-new dimes with FDR's face. It seemed like everybody was making sure they had some.

So I got in line for dimes too. I sent one to each of the girls and to Momma and Daddy for Valentine's Day. Of course my family could get their own new dimes in Hickory, North Carolina, but just the fact of these coming from Warm Springs made them seem more valuable.

Ida and Ellie both sent me valentines made with red paper and ribbons and lace and even buttons. I could see Momma had let them dig into her sewing things! Momma and Peggy Sue made me cards too. And Peggy Sue filled me in on things at school.

Dear Ann Fay,

How is life in Georgia? Are there any swell guys down there? As for me, I have given up on Junior Bledsoe. He doesn't even know I exist. Good grief! How could he not know? I've been around for his whole entire life (almost).

Anyway, remember Hudson Whisnant? He wants me to be his girl. So I am. Of course, my parents will not let me go anywhere with him until I'm sixteen, but at least I see him at school every day. Whatever will I do when school is out for the summer?

Melinda likes Barry Lail. Personally, I don't know what she sees in him. He thinks he's the cat's meow and all the girls do too. You know he has a new girl practically every week.

As you can see, you are missing out on lots of excitement. Hurry on back!

Your friend,

Peggy Sue

I had wrote to Peggy Sue telling her about Warm Springs, but I guess it hadn't sounded too exciting to her. I wasn't surprised she gave up on Junior, since I never did understand what she liked about him in the first place. Like she said, we had known him for as long as we could remember. As far as I was concerned, he was more like a brother to both of us.

He did send me a valentine, though. That really shocked me on account of how he said he wasn't going to write. And he didn't, actually. He just sent a store-bought card with his name signed to it.

The card said, *So I'm a lemon. How about a little squeeze?*

When I showed it to Olivia she said, "Don't let Gavin see that. He'll be jealous."

"Junior Bledsoe ain't nobody to be jealous over," I said. "And Gavin wouldn't care a hoot in the first place."

"I'm telling you, he's all swoony over you, Ann Fay," said Olivia.

Well, I didn't believe it. Gavin was nice to me, but he was nice to everybody. And he was very popular with everyone. "Did he tell you he likes me?"

"Not in so many words," said Olivia. "Gavin is a very private person."

Well, good, I thought. *I'm a private person too.* I liked Olivia, but if I was sweet on a boy I wouldn't tell her. She would probably split wide open if she was expected to keep a secret. I had started hiding my diary under my mattress in case she got to feeling nosy.

But all that talk of Olivia's made me start watching him when I thought he wasn't looking. In the dining room he sat about two tables away from me and almost straight behind Sam. I could listen to Sam and still keep my eye on Gavin.

Just like Sam, Gavin was usually talking. But the difference was, the people at his table would be laughing and hanging on to every word. He could tell a story so good that even Olivia would stop talking. If I got too bored with Sam I would imagine I was sitting at their table.

Every so often Gavin would glance my way and catch me watching him. Of course I'd always look away. But for a second there, just before I did, it was almost like our eyes would have a quiet conversation. It made me wonder just the least little bit if Olivia was right. And if

Gavin did like me special—how would I feel about that?

Like Olivia said, romance was in the air at Warm Springs. For the first time in my life I started thinking about it for myself.

21

Magic Hill
March 1946

One evening in March, when the weather was turning warmer, Suzanne decided to have a party at her house. A bunch of us from Warm Springs piled into a couple of cars.

A few able-bodied men loaded wheelchairs and crutches into the back of a truck and off we went. Even Ed Frogge went along!

As much as I loved being at the foundation, it felt great to go someplace else. Of course Sam started in on a history lesson as soon as we were off the grounds. "This town didn't used to be called Warm Springs," he said. "It was Bullochville before Roosevelt came here."

While Sam went on about the improvements FDR brought to Georgia, I thought how amazing it was that a place so tiny could become so famous and so important. All because of one man. And polio. And healing water bubbling up out of the ground.

Suzanne lived in a white house with a big yard full of trees. She took me to her room. I just couldn't get over it. For one thing, it was painted strawberry red. And for another, she had a shiny wood bed with pineapples carved into the four posts. And lots of scrapbooks in the room. "See," she said, "I'm a scrapbook fiend."

She showed me the *Life* magazine with her picture in it. Sam was right—she was mostly behind a big white column, but it showed just enough of her face that you could tell who it was. Out in front of her was the colored man playing the accordion for Franklin Roosevelt with tears running down his cheeks.

"It was a day you could never forget," said Suzanne. And just looking at that picture I could feel the sadness of that day all over again.

Soon we went out to the screened-in porch with everyone else and drank lemonade and ate cookies made by Suzanne's mother. We sat in a circle and played games and told stories about people getting into mischief at Warm Springs—about people shooting peas into the light fixtures with their forks. And having wheelchair races.

Suzanne asked her mother to bring sugar for Ed Frogge because he likes his lemonade extra sweet. But secretly she told her momma to put salt in the sugar bowl. So when Ed took a big swallow, you should've heard him growl. Then he started wheezing and coughing, and I thought for a second he was going to choke to death. But that was just Ed's way of getting Suzanne back. He was fine, really. Every last one of us laughed till the tears was running out of our eyes.

When we finally settled down, someone told a ghost story, and that was the beginning of a whole bunch of spooky tales. It was fun scaring ourselves.

Gavin said there is a place in Florida called Spook Hill where cars actually roll uphill. He told an Indian legend about some chief killing an alligator that was raiding his village. "So now," said Gavin, "the ghost of the alligator haunts the place. Trust me, it's real spooky sitting in a car that rolls uphill."

"Maybe you don't know this," said Sam, "but Georgia has Magic Hill, right over in Manchester. Of course it's not real."

"It's real all right!" said Olivia. "One of the attendants told me about that place. Betty said she was at Magic Hill one night with her soldier boyfriend and they parked for a while. When they were ready to leave, their car wouldn't start."

Sam rolled his eyes and took over the story. "So they went to find help. And when they got back, their car was sitting about a hundred yards uphill! But it didn't happen to Betty," he said. "I read it in the newspaper. A local woman claimed it happened to her."

Well, you should've heard the racket on Suzanne's porch then. There was a big discussion about all the different people who claimed this strange thing had happened to them.

Someone said Magic Hill was just a legend.

"Actually," said Sam, "it's an optical illusion. I've read about those things. There's more of them in other places around the world."

Olivia said, "Why don't we just get in the car and go to Magic Hill?"

Well, we all loved that idea. So we said our goodbyes and thank-yous to Suzanne's family. Her mother said Suzanne could ride along for the fun. The drivers helped us into our cars, and off we went.

Somehow I ended up sitting beside Gavin. It's hard to say if my goose bumps came from going to Magic Hill or from the company I was keeping.

Manchester was just a hop and a skip from Warm Springs. Soon we saw a sign ahead:

SWITCH OFF MOTOR
RELEASE BRAKES

So the fellow who was driving said, "Here goes. Are you ready?"

He turned off the engine. And it got real quiet then, as if every single one of us had quit breathing. Except Ed Frogge in the front seat. You could hear him wheezing, of course. And that just added to the spookiness. Everyone in the back seat grabbed each other's hands and waited.

Maybe that car did roll uphill. Maybe not. It was hard for me to know what was real and what wasn't. My mind was on Gavin holding my hand. And thinking he had give it a little squeeze.

But then again, maybe not.

I'm pretty sure the car didn't move an inch. But Ed and Olivia both declared it rolled a good ten feet. And the polios in the other car started hooting and hollering so loud I figured maybe they did get a spooky ride.

When it was all said and done, it didn't matter one way or the other what happened. People believed what they wanted to about ghosts and Magic Hill. I decided I didn't trust any of it.

Except the part about having a good time in a car with my friends and one of them being a boy. Who just happened to be holding my hand.

That was magic enough for me.

22

Singing
March 1946

If the world was made of water I could've walked without crutches a lot sooner. Even with all the exercising Janice made me do, I couldn't wait to go in the pool each day. Getting around in that mineral water was so easy that I was sure I could walk the second I got out.

But moving my muscles on dry land was a whole other story.

For weeks I worked with my physio. I learned to focus on each little muscle—and if some just wouldn't do their job, I had to substitute others instead. It took a lot of concentration, and during the dry exercises I would get wet from sweating so bad.

The exercise I dreaded most was when she made me lay on my stomach with my arms stretched above my head, raising them off the table as slow and as high as I could. I maybe got as high as four inches. Eventually. But I sweated buckets to do it.

Still, I could feel my left arm getting stronger.

My legs got a workout too, of course. Especially my left one—lifting itself with that heavy brace. I begged Janice to let me get rid of it. But she insisted I needed it for support.

Eventually I got my turn on the walking court. Janice

was in front and Toby, the push boy, was behind me when I first walked between the parallel bars. "Don't worry," said Toby. "I won't let you fall."

But from the way I hung on to the bars, I reckon he thought I didn't believe him. "You don't have to squeeze them, Ann Fay," he said. "You're liable to melt the paint."

So I let up just a little.

When I took that first step, my friends were on the sidelines cheering like I'd hit a home run on the softball field back home. At Warm Springs every new movement was something to root for. We all encouraged each other to keep on trying. It was hard to stay in the dumps around that place.

After I was there about six weeks, Gavin's parents came to visit. And wouldn't you know? Mamaw and Papaw showed up on the very same day.

They watched us exercising on the walking court and joined in the cheering for anybody who was doing their exercises. By then I was learning to go up and down the steps with only the handrails. But just for fun, using my Canadian crutches, I showed how I could go up those stairs backwards.

Papaw was impressed. "Now if that ain't the bee's knees!" He slapped Gavin's daddy on the back. "Can your boy do that?" His voice sounded extra loud.

I saw Gavin's father pull away just the teeniest bit. "My boy had surgery on his back," he said.

"Well, of course," said Papaw. "Maybe next week, then."

I rolled my eyes at Gavin to let him know how embarrassed I was. Suddenly everything about Mamaw and Papaw seemed all wrong. I noticed that Mamaw's hat smelled like mothballs. And Papaw had a spot of ketchup on his tie.

He might as well have wore overalls! Or a sign that said Country Bumpkin.

Don't get me wrong—I think the world of them. But when my grandparents left, I was mostly relieved. They didn't fit in so well at Warm Springs.

Gavin's family was a different story. Later, while we were waiting to go in the dining room, I learned that his father owned a department store. No wonder his mother wore such nice clothes! I heard her telling Mrs. Trotter that she was holding a garden club meeting at her house the next week.

"I just can't imagine your mother picking green beans," I said.

Gavin laughed. "Me either! She mostly grows orchids."

"Oh." Talk about being a country bumpkin! All of a sudden I felt like I didn't belong anywhere. Not back home where people didn't understand how it felt to have polio. And not in Warm Springs trying to mix with high society.

Since they came from Florida, Gavin's parents planned to stay in a guest cottage on the grounds. After supper they played games with us in Georgia Hall. Then his mother went to the baby grand piano and played hit songs like "Let Me Call You Sweetheart" and "Don't Sit Under the Apple Tree (With Anyone Else but Me)."

Someone handed out song sheets so we could sing along. Some people kept right on playing games, but you could see them nodding their heads to the music. Suzanne and I leaned on the piano and sang.

I looked around at all the smiling faces. I saw people in wheelchairs who'd been flat on their backs when I first came to Warm Springs. And others who'd graduated from wheelchairs to crutches. Just like me, they was learning to think of themselves as something besides cripples.

Roosevelt had really started something when he came to Georgia. I felt proud to be part of it. Just the thought of it made me sing louder. But then, out of nowhere, I got this feeling like I shouldn't be enjoying myself when my family was going through Lord-knows-what back home. So right there, while I was singing "Happy Days Are Here Again," a sadness washed over me.

I thought about the singing at the little colored church near my home, and suddenly I wanted to hear *those* songs. So I asked Gavin's mother if she could play "His Eye Is on the Sparrow."

She started right in, and I sang along. At the end she scooted over a little and patted the piano bench. "Sit here, Ann Fay," she said. "I want to hear you sing some more." Then she played "Nobody Knows the Trouble I've Seen."

Well, we hadn't sung more than a few lines when I heard this great big voice singing behind me. But it felt like it was all around me. I tell you, it was so beautiful it put the cold chills on my arms. I just wanted to stop singing and listen. I turned and saw that it was Mr. Botts! I did stop then and just stared. But he motioned for me to keep singing. I tried to match my voice to his, but I know I sounded puny beside him.

When we got done, everyone clapped and Mr. Botts said, "Ann Fay, they like it. Sing some more."

"Mr. Botts," I said, "it's you they're clapping for. Where did you learn to sing like that?"

A sadness crossed over his face then. "Polio interrupted a lot of things," he said. He didn't explain any more. He just took his fancy metal wheelchair with his crutches strapped to the back and rolled out the door of Georgia Hall.

I guessed he didn't want to talk about what polio had

interrupted. But he had sure made me curious.

Sam wheeled his chair into the spot that Mr. Botts had left empty. "I guess you know," he said, "that before he got polio, Mr. Botts was training with William Hinshaw. And Mr. Hinshaw sang for the Metropolitan Opera in New York."

Of course, I didn't know any of that. I'd never even heard of William Hinshaw. But I just said, "Now, ain't that something!"

"Ain't?" said Sam. "Ann Fay, you've got to start using the King's English. Anybody who can sing the way you do shouldn't go around talking as if you're not educated."

It wasn't the first time Sam had fussed at me about the way I talked. He was right, of course! If I stopped and thought about it, I knew *ain't* wasn't a real word. And I knew when to use words like *saw* and *seen* and *come* and *came*. It was just easy to slip into talking the way people back home done—I mean, *did*.

But I was learning to talk more like people at Warm Springs too. For instance, nobody at Warm Springs called themselves crippled. We were polios. To hear people talk, you would think it was something to be proud of. After all, hadn't the president of the United States been one?

Somewhere along the way I had stopped thinking of polio as a weakness and started realizing it could make me strong.

Of course, Daddy had told me that very same thing on the first day of school when I didn't want to go. He was talking about Roosevelt. "Maybe polio made him stronger than he already was," he said.

I knew I didn't come from high society. And my daddy never went past ninth grade. But sometimes I thought he was the smartest man in the world.

23

Hubert

March 1946

There was a brace shop at Warm Springs. Mr. Maddox, the brace maker, made all sorts of things there. Contraptions, as my daddy would say—devices to help people pick things up, hold a spoon, or use a typewriter. And of course they made braces for our legs and arms and also corsets and shoe buildups for people who needed them. I couldn't even begin to list all the things they'd make for you

I had already been there for my Canadian crutches and to get the clicking sound in my braces fixed. And now I was supposed to get fitted with Canadian canes. I was excited because that meant I was really improving.

Since the brace shop was down below the medical building, I was tired when I got there. So I didn't mind waiting for the man in a wheelchair just ahead of me. It was Hubert, the Navy man who scared me with that palmetto bug the day I came to Warm Springs. Mrs. Trotter was with him.

When I come in the door he was telling Mr. Maddox about a stunt he'd pulled the night before. Evidently his practical jokes always had something to do with palmetto bugs. "Compared to the critters we saw in the South Pacific, these bugs are tiny," he said. "Don't tell anyone, but I keep a few as pets."

The way he said "these bugs" made me think he had one with him. I thought maybe I should turn around and leave.

But then he said how, just that morning, he'd sneaked one into an older girl's handbag. "She reached in for lipstick and guess what she got?" Hubert mimicked the girl's scream. "When that bug skittered across her hand, she threw her pocketbook so hard she nearly broke a lamp in Georgia Hall."

Hubert was having such a good time with that story I thought he was going to bust open laughing. And Mr. Maddox too. But Mrs. Trotter had a look of pure horror on her face.

There was a wall just inside the door with a display of braces, special shoes, and other gadgets on it. When Hubert told that story, I jerked back a little and bumped the display. I knocked a heavy metal brace off its hook. It went clattering to the floor.

And I tell you what's the truth—a body would've thought we went straight from a comedy play to a war zone!

Every one of us about jumped out of our britches when it fell. But Hubert? It must've scared him half to death. "Enemy fire!" he hollered. "They're blowing us to smithereens!" He yelled a bunch of other things too, but I didn't understand most of it. He ducked his head, trying to throw himself on the ground.

Only he couldn't. He was paralyzed from polio.

Mr. Maddox just stared at him and then at me. Mrs. Trotter reached out and put her hand on Hubert's shoulder. "It's okay. There's no enemy fire," she said. "You're safe here. You're in Warm Springs, Georgia. You're safe. You're in Georgia now. In Georgia."

Hubert kept on hollering. Mrs. Trotter rubbed his shoulders and said it again, real gentle. "You're in Warm Springs.

Everything's going to be all right." She pulled his head up against her and cradled it there. Hubert was shaking like it was a cold day in January. His teeth were chattering, too.

He did quiet down, though. His hollering turned to moaning and then to crying. Mrs. Trotter held him while he bawled like a baby boy.

I don't know what happened after that because Mr. Maddox suggested I come another time instead. And when he did, I remembered back to second grade when I was talking to Peggy Sue during arithmetic class. The teacher was so annoyed she sent me out to stand in the hall. All these years later I could still feel the mortification of it.

I didn't have what it took to get back up to Kress Hall. I just wanted to crawl under the bushes next to the nearest building. So I let myself to the ground and leaned against the end wall.

The earth felt cool and solid beneath me. My tummy felt wobbly. Why had I knocked that stupid brace to the floor?

I could still hear Hubert sobbing through the open doorway of the brace shop. And I heard Mrs. Trotter's low voice. I couldn't hear what she was saying, but I could guess. "You're in Warm Springs," she was telling him. "You're safe here."

But I knew Hubert didn't *feel* safe. And now, all of a sudden, I didn't either.

Did the war have to come all the way to Warm Springs? Why couldn't there be one peaceful place in the world?

While I was sitting there with my legs sticking out beyond the bushes where just anyone could see, I heard Suzanne's voice.

"Ann Fay? Is that you?" It took her a minute to get there and I tried to wipe the tears away before she did. But she seen right off that I was crying. "What?" she asked. "What's wrong? Did someone hurt you?" Suzanne let herself down to the ground in front of me. Her hair was damp so I knew she'd just come from the pool. Her large eyes looked real worried. "What happened?"

I shook my head. "Nothing."

I thought about Imogene then and what a comfort she was to me in the polio hospital. And how she made me talk when I didn't want to. And how Suzanne had befriended me too. So I started talking.

"I mean, I don't know. I scared that Navy man—Hubert—in the brace shop. I knocked something down and made a bunch of noise, and next thing I knew, it was like he was back in the war. And now he's in there crying like a baby and it's all my fault!" I didn't want to cry in front of Suzanne. But I did. I couldn't stop.

"Maybe he's just having a bad day," she said. "It could've been *anybody* that upset him." She patted my arm.

"But it's not just Hubert," I said. "It's my daddy too. You never know when he's going to go off the deep end." My nose was dripping and I didn't have a handkerchief. I wiped at the snot with the back of my hand.

Suzanne pulled a handkerchief out of her pocket. It was used, but I didn't care.

"When is that stupid war going to go away? Why can't it leave me in peace?"

I leaned my head against the medical building. It felt solid and warm. I looked up at the Georgia sky. It was loaded with puffy clouds stacked one on top of the other, like Momma's clean sheets piled in the laundry basket.

All of a sudden I wanted in the worst way to be at home, breathing in the smell of clothes coming off the line. Eating Momma's fluffy biscuits. Laughing with her and Daddy over something the twins was doing. If I could just be there, *surely* we would be laughing.

"Let's go," I said.

We got ourselves off the ground and started toward Kress Hall. "My mother will be coming for me any minute," said Suzanne. "Are you going to be all right?

I gave her back the handkerchief. "I'll just go to my room and write to my family."

That's what I did, too.

Dear Momma and Daddy,

Is everything okay at home? I really need to know. Sometimes things seem almost perfect around here and then something happens that lets you know everyone else has problems too.

I'll soon be fitted with Canadian canes. They have a band that fits around the forearm but the bottom is like crutches. They're lightweight because they're made of aluminum like the Canadian crutches I've been using.

So, you see, I'm making progress. Soon I will have the stairs mastered and then I'll be coming home. Maybe I should surprise you and just show up one day! Wouldn't that be fun? But of course, the doctor will be sending you a letter first, filling you in on my progress.

Daddy, I bet you've planted the peas by now. I know how you like to get an early start. I wish I was there to help.

All my love,
Ann Fay

I put the letter in an envelope and stuck a stamp on it. I felt closer to my family already. Even though nothing had changed and I sure didn't come out and tell them what happened with Hubert, somehow just writing to them put my mind more at ease.

24

Mr. Botts
March 1946

After that horrible day in the brace shop, I tried not to see Hubert.

I knew exactly where he sat in the dining room, but I never looked his way. And if I saw him coming toward me on a sidewalk, I'd cut across the grass. He probably never knew I was the one who made him go berserk. So it wasn't like he would be embarrassed if he saw me.

But I was trying to protect myself. Just catching a glimpse of him would put a certain dread over me. I'd lose track of whatever game or conversation I was in the middle of.

Mrs. Trotter seemed just as concerned about me as she was for Hubert. She came to my room soon after it happened. "Don't you worry about it, dear," she said. "It wasn't your fault. And there are psychiatrists who can help with war neurosis."

War neurosis? Did it really have a name? That got me wondering if we could get help for Daddy. I started imagining impossible things. Like me getting him to a psychiatrist when I got home.

Dr. Bennett was hinting that I'd be leaving soon.

But first I had to get fitted with Canadian canes. I didn't want to go back to the brace shop, but of course I had to.

On the way I told myself, *It mostly hurts at first... It mostly hurts at first...*

Mr. Maddox was very kind. "Don't worry about that incident," he said. "We often drop things in here. It could have happened to anyone." He fitted me with the canes and helped me practice walking with them.

Once I got used to them, I felt almost like a normal person. They weren't nearly as noticeable or as awkward as crutches. I could get around campus much faster than I did at first. And I had a feeling that eventually I'd be walking without them because he also gave me a wooden cane with a crook at the top. "To use in your room and for short distances," he explained.

One day I just needed a rest between school and my time on the walking court, so I sat down on a wrought-iron bench. While I was catching my breath I thought again how the white buildings around the quad looked like a frame around a pretty picture.

Most of the time I liked being inside that frame. But on this day, the sweet smell of wisteria was putting me in a blue mood. Purple flower clusters had popped out all over the vines on the colonnade. Smelling them was kind of like seeing Hubert. It put jitters in my tummy and a buzzing in my head.

While I was sitting there, Mr. Botts came in his wheelchair and sat beside me. "Mind if I join you?"

"Sure." I was honored that he would sit with me.

"It's too lovely to be inside," he said. "I just want to sit here and enjoy the smell of the pines."

"And the wisteria?"

"Mmm," said Mr. Botts. "It smells good, but it certainly keeps the gardeners busy trimming."

"I know all about that," I said. "My daddy hates wisteria."

"I hope your father is doing well."

It was sweet of Mr. Botts to ask. But I didn't know what to tell him. "I hope so, too," I said.

Mr. Botts didn't ask any more questions. He was quiet, though, so I thought maybe he was waiting for me to talk.

"But the thing is, I just don't know. My mother hardly even mentions him in her letters. It makes me think she's leaving out something important."

"Maybe she doesn't want to burden you with grown-up problems."

"Maybe," I said. "But it's too late for that. I've *had* them from the minute my daddy went off to war."

Mr. Botts nodded. "I guess the war made us all grow up," he said. "But polio complicated things even more. Once you're rehabilitated, that will be one less thing for you to worry about. I'm sure your mother wants you to concentrate on that right now."

"Yes, sir," I said. "I'm working at it. But sometimes it's hard to forget about home."

Mr. Botts was real quiet then, and he looked like he was thinking about someplace far off. Maybe he was missing his home. I knew he'd been at the foundation almost from the beginning. So I asked him how he got there.

"Oh," he said, "I'm from Pennsylvania. I heard about Warm Springs from a newspaper. I came on the train, same as you. Except I started out riding in the baggage car with some chickens."

Well, that just astonished me. "Chickens?" I asked. "The baggage car? But why?"

He laughed. "I was just a lame-stepper, after all. At least that's how I thought of myself. So that's how people treated me. But also, because of polio, I couldn't sit up for the whole trip. So I asked my brother to make a crate for me to lie in. The baggage car was the only place for it."

I looked at Mr. Botts. He seemed so sure of himself, and he could sing better than anyone I ever heard. Was he saying that he used to think he was low as the chickens?

"How did you get this way?" I think my question surprised him because he looked at me quick and squinted his eyes nearly shut. "I mean, how did you get to feeling so strong and confident? Did you feel better the minute you got to Warm Springs?"

Mr. Botts laughed. "Actually," he said, "when I arrived I was so worn out they fed me and put me to bed. But my brother was with me, and the next day he took me to the pools. That's where I met FDR for the first time."

"What was that like?"

"Oh, it was just grand. I was lying in the pool on some inner tubes—as pale as an envelope and just as skinny. Everyone worried that I'd be sucked down the drain. The fancy guests at the resort—that's what it was before polios heard about Roosevelt and showed up here—looked exceedingly nervous about catching my disease. So I was feeling quite conscious of my bony white self. Suddenly I heard this booming voice say, 'Good morning!'

"It was Roosevelt himself. The next thing I knew, he was giving me instructions to move about in the water and concentrate on my muscles. To go lie in the sun and get myself some color. We called him Dr. Roosevelt."

I could hardly believe that Mr. Botts had been so sick when he arrived. "Did you feel bad at first?" I asked. "Did you feel out of place, I mean?"

"In some ways I did. The tourists resented us because

168

they were here first. Many of them were afraid of polio even though we no longer had it. And it was uncomfortable being stared at. But I was more afraid of giving up the ghost, as people thought I was about to do."

Mr. Botts tapped the arm of his wheelchair like he was keeping time to a slow song playing in his head. His soft tapping and the sounds of birds and the shushing of the pines were all I heard for a few minutes.

Finally he spoke again. "Everyone in life has a handicap, Ann Fay. But the struggle to overcome it is worthwhile."

I thought about that. About how far Mr. Botts had come. And how far I still had to go. By this time I knew I could overcome my polio handicap. But I didn't have any idea how I could fix my falling-apart family. Still, I would do whatever I could—if someone would just tell me what that was.

Mr. Botts went back to his story. "So my health improved. Mr. Roosevelt bought the resort and decided tourists and polios didn't mix well. So he sent the tourists away and turned it into a place where polios could really live again."

"Did you ever go home?" I asked. I wondered if he tried going back to the opera.

"Home?" Mr. Botts took in a slow, deep breath. "The smell of these pines is home," he said. "I expect to die right here taking one last whiff of pine needles on my way out."

I took a deep breath too and knew how he felt. But I also smelled the sweetness of wisteria blossoms. And something in me felt sad and pulled apart.

25

Gavin
March 1946

"Someone's sweet on – you, Ann Fay." Ed Frogge handed me an envelope with only my name on the outside.

I didn't recognize the handwriting. I looked at Ed. His bow tie was just a little bit crooked and his smile was kind of off balance too. There was mischief in his eyes. "What is it?" I asked him.

"Go ahead. See for yourself."

I looked in the envelope. There was another, fancier one inside. It had four stamps on it and each one had a drawing of Franklin Roosevelt with the Little White House in the background. And the envelope had his picture too.

I know my mouth fell open with the surprise of it. "Where did this come from?"

The mischief in Ed's eyes was really acting up now. "State secret," he said.

I looked all over the envelope, thinking I might find a name. But there wasn't any.

So now I had two envelopes and no letter. "What am I supposed to do with it?"

Ed laughed. "If I were you – I'd put it in a safety – deposit box. See that?" He pointed to some words stamped on the envelope:

FIRST DAY OF ISSUE
AUG 24
1945

"And notice the Warm Springs – postmark with the date. Roosevelt himself would – hang on to that. He was a stamp collector – you know."

Really? Why hadn't Sam the Encyclopedia Man told me that? Who was giving me the stamps? And why?

Ed could see I was confused. "I was told it was a – late valentine," he explained.

"Valentine? From who?"

Ed grinned and straightened his bow tie. "As Mrs. Trot ter – would say, 'We shall see – what we shall see...'"

I tucked the envelopes in my pocket and didn't show them to anyone. Not at first, that is. But I knew if anyone could find out who gave me those stamps, it was Suzanne. That girl got around campus like a box of chocolates.

So the next time she came I hunted her down in the library. "I need a detective," I said.

I showed Suzanne the stamps. But first I swore her to secrecy. The minute she realized what I wanted, her big brown eyes started swing-dancing. But she squinted at me, put on her deep detective voice, and held out her hand. "I'll need the evidence."

I hugged them to me. I couldn't believe she thought I would hand them over. "I can't let you take these."

"Then maybe you don't want to know where they came from." Suzanne knew how to take charge of a situation.

"Know who you remind me of?" I asked. "My friend Peggy Sue. If she wants something, she finds a way to get it."

Suzanne held out the Nancy Drew book she was reading.

"Put them in here," she ordered. "I'll guard them with my life. And I'll bring them back to you in two days."

And sure enough! On Sunday, Suzanne showed up just as I was going into the dining room for supper. She took the stamps out of the book. "Put these in your pocket before Gavin comes by," she said.

"Gavin?"

"He's your Romeo."

"Are you sure?" I looked around to see who was watching. "How do you know?" I whispered.

"I showed him the stamps."

"You did not!" This time I forgot to whisper.

"I did. I told him you didn't care anything about them, so you gave them to me. The look on his face was all I the proof I needed."

"You tricked him?"

"Isn't that what detectives do?"

"I feel terrible."

"Well, don't. The boy likes you and now he knows you like him too."

"Suzanne!" I screeched her name so loud it's a wonder every person in the building didn't stop to listen.

She laughed so hard I thought she'd wet herself. I laughed too. But I didn't think it was *that* funny. Finally she said, "I'm just kidding. But he was sure relieved to know you didn't give them away. And he was tickled you were so curious."

"Just think," I said. "All this time, I thought Olivia was making things up about Gavin and me."

"She probably was," said Suzanne. "After all, if Gavin wanted to keep a secret he wouldn't tell her. But Olivia has a nose for romance, so she figured it out."

At dinner I didn't look once in Gavin's direction. Instead I acted really interested in Sam's conversation about the assassination of President William McKinley—way back in 1901. Of course Sam knew every little detail about where the president was at the time and how long the assassin waited in line to shake his hand. Once his story cranked up, Sam actually kept my attention.

But of course I couldn't avoid Gavin forever. He stopped me on the way out of the dining room. "How about a game of table tennis?" he asked. Gavin had table tennis at home, so he was a good player, one of the best wheelchair players at Warm Springs. And I was terrible. I stuttered around a little, trying to get out of it. But he grabbed my arm and said, "You owe me a big favor."

I was afraid to look at him, but I did anyway. His dimples were deep and adorable. "I—I do?"

"Didn't you hire Nancy Drew to come after me?"

"I didn't *hire* anyone. And I had nothing to do with Suzanne tricking you."

"Well, either way, I already reserved the next game for you and me."

I figured there was nothing to do but make a fool of myself. While we waited for the other players to finish, Gavin told me about his stamp collection. "That envelope I gave you is called a First Day Cover. It makes stamps more valuable."

"Well, I don't know what to say! Don't you want the stamps for yourself?"

"I'm a collector," he said. "I can get more. Those stamps aren't like seeing the Little White House in person, but I figured they were the next best thing. My father's trying to pull some strings, though. If it works out, we'll get a tour."

"Your father could do that?" I just couldn't imagine it.

"Probably not. But he's trying. He donates money to Warm Springs, so maybe. With any luck, we can at least see the outside. But it's heavily guarded, you know. You *will* go with us, won't you, Ann Fay?"

Had Gavin been talking to his parents about me? I wasn't about to ask. I just said, "I wouldn't miss that for anything in the world."

I didn't turn down the table tennis game, either. I sat in a wheelchair to play so I wouldn't throw myself off balance while trying to return the ball. I didn't give Gavin many good hits. But I gave him plenty to laugh about. And I gave our friends plenty of exercise going after my stray balls.

I decided it wasn't so bad, really—making a fool of myself with somebody who actually liked me.

I was already dreaming about more fun and games with Gavin. Then I looked up and saw someone I never expected to see in Warm Springs, Georgia. It took a few seconds for it to dawn on me exactly who I was seeing. Was I imagining things? Or was Junior Bledsoe actually standing there watching me?

26

Disbelief

March 1946

"Junior Bledsoe!" I said. "What in the wide world are *you* doing here?"

Junior looked a little confused. The first words out of his mouth were, "Ann Fay, I thought you was learning to walk. What are you doing in *that* thing?"

He wanted to know what I was doing. I wanted to know what *he* was doing. We just stared at each other and waited for who knows what to come along and make sense of this whole thing.

Then I heard Gavin's voice. "Thanks for the game, Ann Fay." And off he rolled.

"Who was that?" asked Junior.

"Oh, just somebody," I said. "He lives here too. Like all these people." I tried to sound as offhand about it as I could. So Junior wouldn't think that me playing table tennis with a boy meant something.

But he seemed more concerned about me being in a wheelchair than who I was with. "Are you getting better or not?" he asked.

I realized he was worried. "Stop fretting," I said. "This isn't *my* chair. I just borrowed it. Wanna see me walk?" Then I showed him how I could walk a short way without canes. At the end I grabbed on to Junior and he steadied me.

"Ann Fay! That's good. Really good! You're actually walking."

"Yeah," I said. "I reckon I am." I sat back down in the wheelchair to catch my breath. "So why did you come, Junior? Is everything okay at home?"

"Can we sit someplace?"

"Well, sure." I wheeled my chair toward the fountain between Georgia Hall and the colonnade. There was an iron bench under a tree and we went there. I didn't want to be in the wheelchair anymore, so I moved to the bench beside Junior.

He looked around. "This place is dandy. Do you really live here?"

I pointed to Kress Hall. "That's my dormitory there. I have a roommate and we have our own bathroom. Just for the two of us. What do you think of that?"

"I think you probably won't say it's finer in North Carolina. That's what I think. I hope you're not getting too big for your britches."

"Is that what you came here to talk about? How's everything back home?"

"Peggy Sue is the same as always. And my momma too."

"And my family?"

"The girls are growing like kudzu."

Junior had come to Georgia for a reason, but now he was circling the block a few times before he got around to telling me what it was. I grabbed his shirtsleeve. "And Momma? Daddy?"

Junior shuffled his feet a little. And then he pulled his

pocketknife out, opened it up, and started cleaning his fingernails. "Your daddy's still working."

I breathed a sigh of relief.

He didn't say anything more, just folded his knife and put it away. He sat there staring at his brown shoes. He reached down and wiped some dirt off the tips. And for some reason I knew it was too early to feel relieved.

"Junior, you didn't drive all the way down here to tell me my daddy is working."

"Well, Ann Fay, something just don't seem right."

"What do you mean? Like what?"

Junior looked around the quad. "Don't you want to show me around this place?" He pointed toward the pool. "What's that fancy building down there?"

I twisted his sleeve. "Just tell me what you come here for."

"Well, okay then." Suddenly the words came out of Junior in a big rush. "Your momma and daddy wasn't at church last Sunday and we didn't hear nothing out of them all week. So this morning before church I went by your house to check on them. I'm sure your momma wouldn't have shown her face if I hadn't seen her in the yard before she could get back inside."

"Why on earth wouldn't my momma want to see you, Junior?"

"I don't think she wanted *me* to see *her*."

"But why?"

"On account of—on account of—Ann Fay, she had a black eye. It looked like it's been there for a while, which is probably why they didn't make it to church on Sunday."

"A black eye? What happened?"

Junior looked at me then. "What do you *think*

happened?" he said. Like he knew the answer but was giving me a quiz to see if I could come up with it. The only reason I could think of for anyone to have a black eye was if someone else hit him. Or her.

And then all of a sudden I realized what Junior was saying. Or not saying.

"Junior Bledsoe, what are you trying to say?" I balled up my fist and socked him in the arm. "Don't you even *think* it!"

Junior pulled away from me, but I socked him again.

"My daddy is not that kind of person! He would never hit my momma! Do you hear me, Junior Bledsoe?"

I pounded on his arm until he turned and grabbed my fist and held it away from him. That just made me madder.

I tried to twist out of his grip, but he wouldn't let me go. I could feel myself starting to cry. "My daddy is a good man. He would not hit anybody, Junior, and you know it. My momma fell or something. My daddy is a good man!" Right then I hated Junior Bledsoe.

"Well, Ann Fay," he said, "the way I see it, you're a good person too, but you're beating on me. It don't change who you are. It's just how you feel that's making you hit me."

That sure stopped me cold. I didn't hit Junior again or try to get loose from him. I just sat there with the smell of pine trees and wisteria in the air and knew that the beauty of Warm Springs was slipping away. It was a fairy tale after all.

On the outside of this campus, up the road from this enchanted forest, was a real world of dirt and tears. And now it was pushing in on me.

Junior held me while I cried. "Your momma has been talking to mine. This isn't the first time it's happened, Ann Fay."

My mind just couldn't take it in. I kept seeing my daddy coming into the kitchen and taking Momma into his arms—right when she was in the middle of baking pies. Or they'd be on the front porch and she'd be fixing to sit in her favorite rocking chair, but he'd pull her onto his lap instead.

I almost started arguing with Junior all over again. But then, for some reason, the sighing of the pine trees reminded me of my momma. So I didn't. I just grabbed on to my little wooden Comfort and listened.

"I didn't want to tell you. But I knew you'd never forgive me if I let it go on."

Junior was right, of course—he had to tell me. But what could I do about it? Especially from down here in Warm Springs. Then it hit me. Junior hadn't come to *tell* me. He had come to *get* me.

I could've hit him again. But I didn't. "No!" I said. "I can't leave here. You can't make me go, Junior."

He didn't argue with me. He just squeezed my hand and waited. I sat there on that cold bench and all of a sudden I started shivering. The Georgia sun had disappeared off to the west someplace. And the breeze felt chilly.

I wanted in the worst way to slide into the warm water down at the pool. To think about some tiny muscles that I didn't know I had before I got to Warm Springs. To count while I exercised. To focus on getting strong so I could face the real world again.

I wasn't strong enough yet. I had only learned to take a few baby steps. And now I was supposed to jump up and run home? I just didn't think I could do it. I sat there for a long time and stared at the water shooting up from the fountain.

After a while people started coming out of Georgia Hall—rolling past us with their wheelchairs, calling out to each other about who was going to play bridge that night, laughing over one thing or another. Across the yard I heard Olivia calling to Gavin, "I'll let you know when I find out." I figured they were talking about me, wondering who Junior was and why was I crying.

That's when I realized I couldn't send Junior home and go back to playing rook and table tennis with my friends. Warm Springs was a shiny bubble that had already been popped.

"I have to talk to Mr. Botts," I said. I reached for the wheelchair and got myself into it. Junior started pushing me and I let him. The only thing I did was point the way to Mr. Botts's office. But it was Sunday, so of course he wasn't in. I had to find someone who could get a message to him.

It wasn't long until he was right there in front of me. His wheelchair was so close our toes were almost touching. I didn't even think about introducing him to Junior.

"I have to leave," I said.

Mr. Botts leaned forward and looked into my face. "What's going on?"

But I couldn't tell him the truth. It was too hard for me to believe it, and I wasn't going to go telling stories about something I hadn't seen with my own two eyes.

"My momma needs me," was all I could say.

"You should get some sleep before making any decisions," said Mr. Botts. "Things will look different in the morning."

"I wouldn't be able to sleep," I said. "If we leave now, we can be there by morning."

"You want to leave *right now?*"

Of course I didn't. Sometimes I thought I never wanted to leave. I felt safe at Warm Springs. Like being at a second home. But then again, how could such a big fine place be my home?

But I didn't tell Mr. Botts what I was thinking. I just said, "I have to go pack."

Mr. Botts shook his head. "I'm sorry, Ann Fay, I can't let you go tonight." He turned to Junior. "My name is Fred Botts," he said.

Junior shook his hand, but he didn't even tell Mr. Botts his name.

"And you are—?"

"Junior Bledsoe. I'm Ann Fay's neighbor."

Mr. Botts looked at me like he wanted some proof. "Junior's the one who watched after us during the war," I said. "If you can't trust him, you can't trust nobody."

Mr. Botts nodded slowly, but I could see he wasn't taking my word for it, and not Junior's either. "Did Ann Fay's parents send a letter requesting her release?"

"No, sir," said Junior. "The situation at home just doesn't allow for it."

I tried to help him explain. "My momma wouldn't want to disturb my treatment here." I stopped there and took a breath. I didn't want to say the next part, but I had to because I could see how things must look suspicious with Junior just showing up and me wanting to run off with him. "My daddy is hurting her. So *he's* not going to write the letter." I started crying then.

"I'm so sorry," said Mr. Botts. But I couldn't tell if he

actually believed me. "I know you're upset, but we can't fix one thing by breaking another. We've got to go through proper procedures to release you." He looked at Junior. "You're saying Ann Fay's parents don't know that you've come for her?"

Junior's nose started twitching. This was getting to be more complicated than either one of us had imagined.

Mr. Botts tapped the arm of his wheelchair as he spoke. "We can see Dr. Bennett about this in the morning. Perhaps he will sign a release. But first I will need to speak with one of Ann Fay's parents on the telephone."

I just can't tell you the agitation that was building inside of me while I listened to Mr. Botts talking about procedures. As if doing things in the proper order was the only thing that mattered!

Junior spoke up. "Sir, Ann Fay's family doesn't have a telephone. There would be no way to reach her mother."

Mr. Botts squinted. I could see this news did not make him feel any better about letting Junior Bledsoe drive off with me in his car. "There must be a neighbor with a telephone," Mr. Botts finally said. "*Your* family, perhaps. Could I speak with your parents?"

"Junior's daddy is dead," I said. "And his momma doesn't have a phone. We always use the Hinkle sisters' phone, but they don't know anything about my family's problems. Please believe me, Mr. Bot—"

"Yes, they do," Junior said, interrupting.

"What?" I said.

"The Hinkle sisters know. Your momma talks to my momma, and she talks to Miss Dinah and Miss Pauline." Junior's voice went soft, like he realized how bad it sounded. Like the whole neighborhood was gossiping about my family.

I just couldn't believe what I was hearing, and I didn't

think I could stand the humiliation of it. "Oh!" I practically shouted. "So *I'm* the last one in the wide world to find out? Is that what you're saying? Well, thanks a lot for leaving me in the dark, Junior Bledsoe! Like I don't have nothing to do with it. How *could* you?"

"There, there," said Mr. Botts. "Try to remain calm. I can call the Hinkle sisters in the morning. You understand, however, that I will need more information about them, such as their relationship to the family. And I would feel much better about this if we could get your doctor to verify your story."

Doctor? Did he mean Dr. Gaul from the polio clinic? Or Dr. Johnson, our family doctor? I couldn't stand the thought of either one of them getting in on my family's shame.

"Sir," said Junior, "we can call the Hinkle sisters right now if you want. They can confirm my story. But the doctors don't know nothing about this. Mrs. Honeycutt is much too proud to go telling—"

Mr. Botts cut him off. "Young man, I can see how sincere you are. And I want to help. But while Ann Fay is at the foundation, we are her legal guardians. So I suggest we sleep on this. I'll make arrangements for you to stay in a guest cottage tonight and we'll take care of it in the morning."

Mr. Botts began to turn his wheelchair. "Ann Fay, you may begin packing if you like. Mrs. Trotter is off duty right now but I'm sure she'll be happy to help. I will ask her to meet you in your room. Junior, would you come with me, please?"

And the next thing I knew, Junior was following Mr. Botts into his office. I heard Junior saying, "Sir, I'm very concerned about Ann Fay. And her whole family."

Then I heard Mr. Botts asking him to shut the door. And just like that, I was left out in the cold.

27

Desperation
March 1946

I started to knock on Mr. Bott's door. "Ann Fay," someone said. I turned and saw Martha, the older girl who sometimes played rook with me and my friends. She was with Lou, one of the Navy men staying in Kress Hall. "What's the matter, Ann Fay? Can I help you?"

I couldn't talk to her about it. I just couldn't. Not with Lou sitting there listening. "Where's Suzanne?" I said.

"I'll find her," Martha said. "Shall I tell her to come here?"

I didn't know the answer to that. Part of me wanted to break Mr. Botts's door down. And another part wanted to start packing. "Tell her I'll be in my room."

Kress Hall was close by, and Suzanne got there soon after I did. Olivia was with her. "Martha sent us," Olivia said. "Who's that fellow you were talking to? And what's going on?"

I just looked at my two friends. The sight of them made me want to lock the door and stay at Warm Springs. How could I explain about my complicated, falling-apart life? "My neighbor is taking me home."

"Home?" asked Olivia. "To North Carolina?"

"I've got to pack." I pulled open my underwear drawer.

"Wait!" said Olivia. She shoved the drawer shut with her body and stood in front of it. "Tell us what's going on."

"Are they making you leave?" asked Suzanne. "Did I get you in trouble?"

Sweet, naughty Suzanne—if anyone could get me in trouble, it would be her. I shook my head. "It's my momma," I said. And then I started crying. "My daddy—he's hurting her."

I couldn't believe I said that out loud. I'd shown my little wooden Comfort to Olivia and Suzanne. And told them how my daddy made Wisteria Mansion for me. And how he served our country in the war.

Of course, ever since I told her about that incident in the brace shop with Hubert, Suzanne knew that the war had changed my daddy, too. But who would've guessed he could hurt a living soul?

All of a sudden neither one of them had a word to say. They were probably shocked and disappointed to find out what I came from. Maybe they thought I was lying when I told them the good things about my daddy.

"He never used to do that," I explained. "He never *did*."

Olivia put her awkward arms around me and then Suzanne grabbed on to me too. We stood in the middle of the room and they rocked me like I was their baby. And I think we all cried.

Mrs. Trotter came in and put her arms around us all. And then finally, when I couldn't take any more hugging, I pulled back and opened that bureau drawer again. Mrs. Trotter got my suitcase and pasteboard box out of the closet and put them on the bed. I handed Olivia my clothes one piece at a time, she handed them to Mrs. Trotter, and Mrs. Trotter put them in my suitcase.

Suzanne gathered my personal belongings and put them in the box—my hairbrush, my diary, and other odds and ends. Including the scrapbook we'd started together. "I want you to have it," she said. Before I could argue about the scrapbook, she handed me the blue bottle I'd brought from home. "Truth and faithfulness." Her voice sounded shaky. "That's you."

Apparently truth and faithfulness meant I had to leave Warm Springs with no warning. But first I had to lay awake worrying about Mr. Botts calling my doctor.

If it was any other night, I'd be in Georgia Hall having a good time. And that was what I should be doing on my last night at Warm Springs. But I couldn't play when I had all these problems on my mind. So I told Olivia would she please tell Gavin and Martha and Sam I'd see them in the morning. "I just don't feel like talking to people," I said.

Olivia made a sad face—like she was going to miss me. But I saw her inching toward the door. I had a feeling she was anxious to tell Gavin all about Junior and me. I wished I hadn't opened my big mouth about Daddy.

She hugged me one more time and said, "I'll talk to you later tonight, okay?" And then she was gone.

Mrs. Trotter checked the nightstand and bureau drawers one last time and then she left too. But first she gave me a sweet hug and promised to check on me first thing in the morning. I knew she would, too. She was like a mother to us all.

She was hardly out the door before Ma Harding came by. "What's this I hear about you leaving us?" she asked.

I didn't feel like telling the whole story again. Ma pulled me up against her. "My little darling," she said. "Mr. Botts told me everything. I'm so sorry."

I didn't want to start crying again either, but I was fixing to do just that if she didn't stop hugging me. Why did everyone at Warm Springs have to be so sweet?

"I'm going to Atlanta first thing in the morning," she said. "So I won't even be here to say goodbye. But I have something for you. It's just a little remembrance of your stay in Georgia."

She handed me a small package wrapped in tissue paper. And when I opened it there was a peach inside. Not a real one, though. It was made of ceramic and was about the size of a softball. It had a slot in it for coins and a plug in the bottom.

"Oh, it's a bank! I love it."

"To save your money," said Ma Harding. "So you can come back to visit. I'll be watching for you."

I didn't tell her I didn't have much money for saving, but I think she knew that already. She gave me a big hug and told me to write once in a while. I told her I really wanted to come back.

Then it was just me and Suzanne there in my room. I showed her the bank. "It's so—peachy keen! How will I get it home without breaking it?"

Suzanne helped me open my suitcase and squeeze the gift into the very center, where my clothes would protect it. "I'll stay with you till my mother comes," she said. "I don't feel like playing games tonight either."

Suzanne was a true friend. How could I ever leave her? But then again, how could I stay? Even for one more night?

"I've got to stop Mr. Botts from calling my doctor," I said. "What if the doctor decides to investigate? My family would be humiliated. And for no reason. Momma and

Daddy will never let me come home just because of their problems. Oh, Suzanne, my momma will die of shame! If I wait till tomorrow morning it will ruin everything."

Suzanne just nodded, but I saw that her brain was working on my problem. "Well," she said, "you *are* all packed up."

I wasn't sure what she was getting at. And not knowing wasn't helping the pain in my stomach. But then it hit me. I was ready to go. All I had to do was get in the car with Junior and leave. Without anyone knowing, of course. But where was Junior?

"I don't even know where Junior is," I said. "Mr. Botts was going to put him in a guest cottage."

"I know where the guest cottages are," said Suzanne. "I can tell him to meet you behind Kress Hall after everyone settles down. How about eleven o'clock? And I'll warn him about the night watchman."

"But what about my things? I can't carry them."

"Oh, that's right," she said. "Maybe I can find someone to help."

"No! They'll get in trouble. I have to do this myself." I looked around the room, trying to think of a solution. "The window," I said. "We'll put them through the window."

So that's what we did. First we looked outside to make sure no one was watching. Thank goodness it was getting dark. Together we lifted the pasteboard box. Just before we let it fall, I saw the blue bottle peeking out the top.

"Wait!" I said. I wasn't taking any chances on breaking my bottle. I pulled it out and we let the box fall to the ground. Then we both busted out laughing.

For a few seconds the excitement of getting away with something made me forget my troubles. But then I looked at my suitcase. And evidently Suzanne and I were having the exact same thought in the exact same minute.

"What about Olivia?" she asked. "If we put it out the window, she might notice that it's gone when she comes back."

Oh, why did it have to be so complicated? Part of me just wanted to give up. To send Junior home without me. I didn't want to leave Warm Springs anyway.

But there was that blue bottle. I *had* to help my family. Maybe if I could find a way to leave Warm Springs without getting caught, then I could come up with some answers for back home too.

"I'll carry the suitcase when I go," I said. "I'll put the Canadian canes outside and just use my wooden one. It's not far to the door. I can do it. But be sure to tell Junior if I'm not there at eleven to wait fifteen minutes, someplace where the night watchman won't be suspicious. Then he can come back. I have to be sure Olivia's asleep before I sneak out."

"Well, don't talk to her. Go to bed now. And if you're not asleep when she comes in, act like you are." Suzanne picked up her canes. "I've got to find your friend Junior and then get over to Georgia Hall for some games so no one suspects anything." All of a sudden a worry crossed her face. "What if Junior says no and you're outside waiting on him all night?"

"Trust me," I said. "Junior Bledsoe doesn't know how to say no. Not if someone needs help."

"Well, if you're sure."

"I'm sure. Now go!" When I said that, it hit me that I might never see Suzanne again. "Thank you, Suzanne," I said. "What would I ever do without you?" I wanted to grab her and hang on.

We both started crying. But we didn't hug or hold on to each other. We just stood there with tears running down our faces. Then she left me. I watched her go down the hall. The outside door opened right before she got to it. She went through and started to walk away, but then she turned. I thought for a second she was going to come back in. But then the door closed between us.

I went back into my room. And almost tripped over the lump in my throat.

I took my canes to the window and looked out. I didn't see anyone, so I dropped them one at time into the dirt at the edge of the building. Then I shut the window. I put the nightgown and change of clothes into my suitcase, then set it and my blue bottle by the door. I sure hoped Olivia wouldn't notice anything missing.

After I went to the bathroom, I crawled into bed with my clothes on and pulled the covers tight around my shoulders so Olivia wouldn't see I was wearing my sweater.

At first I just laid there and cried. Then I started praying that Suzanne would find Junior and that she wouldn't get in trouble. And that Mr. Botts, sweet kind Mr. Botts, would forgive me for going against him.

I never slept. I was too keyed up and too worried. About Momma and Daddy and how things were at home right that minute. About how mad they would be when they found out what I did. And what if I got caught?

When Olivia came in, I made my breathing sound slow and even. "Ann Fay," she whispered. She waited a few seconds and then tried again. "Are you awake?"

I ignored her and prayed she would turn off the lamp and get into bed. She did. First she went to the bathroom. Then she got undressed and crawled under the covers. After that I waited for her breathing to change. It was a long time before I had the nerve to even move one leg.

The lights were off in the hall, so I knew it was after ten thirty. It was time to make my move. I could wait outside in the shadows for as long as I needed to.

I turned in my bed and watched Olivia in the darkness. I couldn't see much except her dark hair against the white pillow. She lay still as a rug. I sat up ever so slowly and kept my eyes on her the whole entire time.

Olivia would think this was a great adventure. She'd wish she could go along. I felt bad enough for involving Suzanne, but at least she didn't live on campus. And she'd been at Warm Springs so long that her only punishment would probably be losing some afternoons at the picture show.

I made one last trip to the bathroom. I hated leaving that little room with shiny ceramic tiles and white porcelain fixtures. Having it so close and handy when I needed it had made me feel rich. Like Cinderella at the ball.

Leaving it was like Cinderella losing her glass slipper. But I couldn't stay in the bathroom forever.

I sneaked to the door of our room and opened it just a crack. I'd never noticed before that it creaked.

Olivia turned over. Why now, right when I was going out the door? I waited until I was sure she was sleeping and then I opened it a little more. I waited again. I tucked my blue bottle into my dress pocket and slid my suitcase into the hall. Then I picked up my wooden cane and squeezed myself through the opening.

I decided I could open that outside door so quiet that no one would ever know. But of course when I stepped in front of it, the door opened all by itself. And I could not control how much noise it made.

It scared me so bad I almost dropped the suitcase. But I hung on to it and to the wall. Then I went through the door. I slid into the shadows close to the building and waited to see if anyone was around. Nothing happened. Ma Harding did not come out looking for me.

I held on to the brick wall and followed it around the end of the building. I waited in the shadows until I saw headlights coming on the dirt road that ran behind Kress Hall. Junior! He got the message. I almost stepped out to wave when I realized something—it wasn't Junior's car! I ducked back into the shadows as fast as I could, but that threw me off balance, so I fell to the ground. I huddled there and waited for the car to go by.

It passed and I breathed. I waited. I heard someone cough. Was the night watchman standing over me?

28

Leaving Warm Springs
March 1946

I slowly turned my head and realized I was under an open window. Probably someone was coughing in their sleep.

Where was Junior? Had he worked up his nerve to say no to the plan? Or maybe Mr. Botts had locked him up someplace. That was a ridiculous idea and I knew it. For some reason it made me giggle. I was real nervous so the giggling turned to crying but I knew I couldn't cry out loud or I might get caught. So I covered my mouth and huddled there on the ground, forcing back the sobs and telling myself to hang on just a little longer.

Then I heard a car and saw its lights coming on the road. I kept myself on the ground until I heard the low sound of the bobwhite call. Then I knew for sure it was Junior. I was too scared to whistle back, but I pulled myself up and stepped out of the darkness. Junior saw me and got out of the car.

"There's my suitcase," I whispered. "My canes and a pasteboard box are back there—under the second window."

I was really scared now because Junior had to leave his car sitting in the road while he went after them. He ducked and ran. He helped me get in the back seat and then he put my canes on the floorboard. He set my suitcase and box in the front seat. "Stay low," he said. Then he went around the car and slid behind the wheel. He shut the door as quiet as he could. "Keep your head down, Ann Fay."

"Did you see the night watchman?"

"No. And that has me worried. I'd feel better if I knew he wasn't around the next corner."

I sat up.

"Get down!"

"How are you going to get out of here?"

"Don't worry," he said. "I took a walk around this place earlier. I know where this road goes. We'll be on the highway in a minute."

And we were, too. But it took me a long time to let go of Warm Springs. As bad as I wanted to sneak away, that's how bad I wanted to get back. And as much as I'd wanted Junior to sneak me out, that's how much I hated the sight of him. My feelings were so tangled up I didn't know what I felt. Fear and relief and thankfulness and anger swapped places inside of me. I rolled the window down a few inches.

"Ann Fay, are you hot?" asked Junior.

"No," I said. "I just want to smell Georgia, that's all. And whatever you do, don't start singing, *Nothing could be finer.*"

Junior kept quiet.

The truth was, the smell of pines put me in mind of Mr. Botts, and thinking about him made me ache inside. He was going to be so disappointed in me. What had I just done? I was pretty sure they'd never let me come back again. Even for a visit.

But it wasn't like I had a choice about this. The thought of Mr. Botts telling the whole ugly story to my doctor was more shameful than me leaving Warm Springs without permission.

I thought about Gavin. He came from a real good family and was popular with everyone, but for some reason he liked little ol' me! If Junior Bledsoe hadn't come along with bad news, I could've had me a sweetheart. For the first time in my life I was interested in a boy. And then, just like that, it was over!

I hung on to my blue bottle with one hand and my wooden Comfort with the other. And I cried a puddle into the back seat of Junior's car.

Somewhere along the way my crying turned to dreaming. It was a jumbled dream about me losing some little shiny thing—I don't even know what it was. I would see it, but when I reached out it would be gone. I must've tried a dozen times to pick it up, and every time it disappeared. And I dreamed Junior was driving my daddy's truck and I was in the back under a pile of hay. Ida and Ellie were there too, and a police car was chasing after us.

I was glad when I finally woke up. I didn't tell Junior about my dream, but I did look to see if there was any red lights flashing behind us. What if Mr. Botts sent the police to chase us down?

Then I saw that we were in South Carolina and I breathed a little easier. I could tell because we passed a sign that said GAFFNEY 30 MILES.

"Gaffney's just ahead," said Junior. "Wanna stop?"

"Well, I wouldn't mind stretching my legs," I said. "And going to the bathroom. But nothing's open at this time of night."

"No, but..." Whatever he was fixing to say, he must've changed his mind.

"But what?"

Even from where I was sitting, I could see Junior's nose

was twitching. So I knew he was nervous. But why would he be nervous?

"I bet," he said, sounding a little croaky, "if we went to see a JP, he'd let us use his bathroom."

"A JP?"

"You know—a justice of the peace."

"Junior, I know what a JP is, but I'm sure not going to wake one up in the middle of the night just to use his bathroom."

"Of course not. But that's not the main reason people go to see a JP, now is it?"

Well, I just couldn't believe what I was hearing. The reason *anybody* from North Carolina went to see a justice of the peace in Gaffney was to get married. That's because North Carolina has stricter marriage laws.

Junior Bledsoe knew good and well my daddy wasn't about to let me get married. And what in the world was he talking to me about marriage for?

"Junior," I said, "are you out of your ever-loving mind? You don't want to marry me, and I *sure* don't want to marry you!"

I thought he would agree with me. I thought he'd say, *Ah, Ann Fay, you know I'm just teasing.* But he didn't. Instead his voice got kind of smallish and he said, "How do you know what I want, Ann Fay? When was the last time you asked me what I want?"

I didn't know what that was supposed to mean. "Well, okay then," I said. "What *do* you want, Junior Bledsoe?"

"I'm old enough to get married. And I could make you a real good husband. It seems like you could use a good man in your family right now."

I tell you what's the truth. If I hadn't been mad at Junior

already, I for sure would've been angry by this time. For one thing, I didn't like him bad-mouthing my daddy like that. And for another, the idea of me and him getting married was the most ridiculous thing I ever heard of. And I told him so, too.

That's when he said, "Ah, you know I was just teasing you, Ann Fay." But something about the way he said it—the way he swallowed real hard first and how his voice came out real croaky this time—made me wonder. *Was* he teasing me? Or was Junior Bledsoe trying to tell me something?

He didn't say a word to me after that. It was about two hours to home, but it felt longer than the rest of the trip and my train ride to Georgia put together. Every now and then I snuck a peek at Junior. His jaw was clamped tight and a muscle in his cheek was twitching.

I started feeling real bad. Why did I always have to go spouting off exactly what I was thinking? Especially with Junior. When I was at Warm Springs, I could be annoyed with Sam the Encyclopedia, but I would never come out and tell him what I thought, the way I did with Junior. It was like Warm Springs brought out a whole other side to me. A better side.

And right now, heading back home, I did not like what I felt coming out of me.

But I thought I had a right to be mad at Junior. Even though I was the one who decided to leave, it felt like he had come down there and jerked me up and dragged me off. And before I was even over the shock of it, he had to drop some crazy idea on me.

I thought how I'd known Junior for as long as I could remember. He was practically family, so I guessed I loved him. But good grief—did that mean I had to *like* him too?

Part of me wanted to tell him I was sorry. But another part wanted to jump out of the car. So I settled for something in the middle. I huddled in the back seat of the car and felt sorry for him and me both.

There was a faint glow in the sky ahead. I knew it would be almost light when we got home, and Daddy would be getting ready for work. Soon I would have to face him.

And it felt bad—worse than I ever imagined!

29

Home
March 1946

I had a real sick feeling when Junior turned onto our road. Part of it was the way you feel from getting up too early in the morning. But another part was a hurting in my tummy and a clamping feeling in my chest. How was I going to explain why I left Warm Springs?

The sight of familiar places should have made me feel better the Hinkle sisters' house on the corner, the mailbox by Junior's lane, and the misty blue of Bakers Mountain straight ahead. And of course, the little colored church on the right. But I didn't feel better. I laid my head against the window and closed my eyes until I knew Junior had turned in by our mailbox. Then I opened them and there was my house.

It had never been painted. Compared to all the white buildings at Warm Springs, it looked like a shed. Everything about our place looked like it had shrunk while I was gone. The mailbox. The house. Even the driveway looked shorter than I remembered.

What would Gavin think if he saw where I lived? *His* house probably had gingerbread trim and fancy shutters. Or maybe it was even made of brick.

I sneaked a peek at Junior and saw his nose was

twitching again. I figured the least I could do was let him out of facing my family. So I said, "You can just drop me off and go on."

But Junior wasn't about to take me up on that idea. "Don't be ridiculous, Ann Fay. Who's going to carry your suitcase in?"

"Well, you can just set it on the porch. And my box too. I know you have to go on to work."

I guess Junior thought that would be cowardly. "No," he said. "I'm the one who brought you home. And I'm the one who's going to face the music."

The light in the kitchen was on. Daddy was probably drinking coffee. And I figured Momma was making pimento cheese sandwiches to go in his lunchbox.

They must've seen us drive in because Daddy came to the front door. By then I was getting out of the car and Junior was taking my suitcase and box out of the front seat.

"Ann Fay? Are you paying us a visit?" asked Daddy. And before I got started toward the porch, I felt his arms around me.

So right then, before I could lose my nerve, I said, "Daddy, I'm home to stay."

Daddy pulled away just a little then and looked at me. He lowered me to the ground and said, "Can you walk now? Why didn't you tell us?" I could see the happiness in his face, like he thought me and Junior had worked up a big surprise for him. He started to let me go so I could show him.

Just like that, Junior was there to steady me. As if he thought my daddy was about to let me down.

I knew I could stand on my own two feet. I could walk all the way to the porch, even. But there were these two men both wanting to be the one to hold me up. And to be honest, I didn't know which one of them was doing the best job of it.

I asked Daddy would he help me get to the porch.

"Well, of course," he said. And he started to pick me up.

"No, just let me hang on your arm." I showed him how I could walk. Junior was on the other side of me, just in case. I could've walked up the steps as long as I hung on to the two of them. But when we got to the porch I let Daddy carry me up and set me in his rocking chair.

Junior brought all my canes and slid them onto the porch and said, "Mr. Honeycutt, sir." It was the first time I ever heard him call my daddy anything besides Leroy. "I'm sure the people at Warm Springs will take Ann Fay back any time."

Daddy looked at me then, and behind him I saw Momma coming out the screen door. I saw shades of purple and green around her left eye and I felt that sick feeling in my stomach again.

Seeing her like that gave me the courage to say what had to be said. "I was the one that decided to come home," I said. "On account of Momma needing me."

I saw the surprise in her face and then her hand going to cover her mouth. She lowered her eyes so I wouldn't see her shame, but there was no way I could miss it.

I turned back to Daddy and saw the anger flare up in his eyes. He took a step toward the edge of the porch. Looking down at Junior, he said, real slow and mean-sounding, "Well, who do you think you are, Mr. Bledsoe?"

I, for sure, had never heard Daddy call Junior Mr. Bledsoe. All of a sudden it was like two strangers were talking to each other.

Daddy kept going in that voice. "What do you think you're doing, meddling in my family's business?"

Junior straightened up his shoulders. "Sir, I know you're upset, but I'm just trying to be a good neighbor."

"Upset!" My daddy was like a roaring lion. "You want to see me upset?"

He leaped off the porch then, and I screamed, "Daddy, you leave Junior alone, you hear me?" I hadn't been home two minutes and my daddy had already become my enemy.

I thought he was going to tear into Junior Bledsoe. Maybe it was my screaming that stopped him. Or maybe it was the way Junior squared his shoulders and held up the flat of his hand. "Sir," he said. And that's all he said. Just "Sir," like he wanted to show Daddy every bit of respect he could. But that didn't mean he was going to back off.

Daddy stopped just short of Junior and pointed to his car. "Get. Off. My. Property," he said. "Or I'll show you what I can do when I'm upset."

For just one second I saw Junior glance at my momma, and I knew what that look meant. It meant he'd already seen the damage my daddy could do. But that wasn't going to stop him from doing the right thing.

"Good morning, Myrtle," Junior said. And just like that, he got in his car and drove off. That's when I knew what he meant about this family needing a good man. Junior Bledsoe had just turned nineteen, but he was old enough to know how a man was supposed to behave.

My momma come out on the porch then, and she leaned over and gave me a big hug while I sat in that chair. When she did, I started to cry. I don't know if I was crying for me or her or my daddy. Probably it was just for the shame of it all.

While we was still hugging I heard Ida and Ellie coming through the door. And Mr. Shoes too, and after that everything was back to the way it always was. The girls asked more questions than I could answer. Momma was back in the house in no time, calling for the twins to come and get their breakfast and make themselves some sandwiches to take to school.

But when they didn't answer right away, Daddy pitched in. "You heard what your momma said." The girls moved fast then. It was easy to see how they feared him.

Maybe Daddy was afraid too. Because when Momma said it was time for him to leave for work, he moved just as fast as the girls did. She met him at the door with his lunch box, and he kissed her quick on the cheek. And then he pulled away from her and I saw something I hadn't noticed before.

My momma was going to have a baby!

Well, God in heaven must've thought I didn't have enough surprises already. Maybe He thought I needed one more thing to make my head spin and my heart to argue with itself. I mean, how was I supposed to feel about that?

Good, because maybe it would be a boy to take the place of Bobby? Or worried that he was being born into this mess of a family?

After Daddy left, Momma went back into the kitchen to get the girls ready for school. I sat on the porch for a while, hanging on to Mr. Shoes and letting him lick my face while I stared at my suitcase and my pasteboard box of personal items. Junior had put the blue bottle on top of it. I must've left it in the car.

While I was sitting there getting used to the idea of a baby brother or sister, I heard Ida calling me. "Okay, Mr.

Shoes," I said, "it looks like we're on duty." I picked up the blue bottle and carried it into the house.

Something about it—the smell of Momma's biscuits mixed with the odor of wood burning in the cookstove—grabbed at me and pulled me in. I couldn't help but notice how shabby everything looked, though. My momma kept a clean house, but she couldn't do much about the worn linoleum or the fact that the walls could use a good coat of paint.

In the kitchen Ida and Ellie were eating breakfast and begging Momma to let them stay home from school. "We haven't seen Ann Fay for months," said Ida.

"Yeah," said Ellie. "I won't even be able to think about schoolwork for missing her."

"Ann Fay will be here when you get home," said Momma. "Right now she needs to catch up on her sleep and *you* have to go to school. No ifs, ands, or buts."

Ida stuck out her lower lip and frowned into her cereal. Ellie said, "Can she at least fix my hair?"

Momma was starting to shake her head, but I interrupted before she could even argue. "You don't think I forgot *how*, do you?" I said to Ellie.

Momma turned away then and carried her kettle of hot water from the stove to the dishpan. When she poured out some water, the top half of her disappeared for a moment behind a cloud of steam. She seemed glad to turn the girls over to me.

I figured right then that I could get them to do whatever I asked. So I said, "Eat up. The first one done with breakfast gets French braids. The second one gets them tomorrow."

Well, you should've seen them eating after that. Ellie finished first.

"Get the comb," I said. "And rubber bands. Ida, get dressed while I plait Ellie's hair."

Both of the girls did exactly what I told them. The whole time they were asking questions about Warm Springs.

"Have you been saving these questions up?" I asked. "I'd hate to see how many you'd have if I had stayed any longer."

"Why *did* you come home?" asked Ellie.

"It just seemed like the right time," I said.

After the girls were gone, Momma set a bowl of cereal in front of me. Then she started cleaning up the kitchen. "Won't you sit with me?" I asked. But she kept her back to me while she wiped down the stove.

I didn't want to ask Momma hard questions about how things were with my daddy. It would feel like trespassing on private property. But I had left Warm Springs for this. So I got right to the point. "Junior said Daddy gave you that black eye."

Momma stopped wiping the handle on the oven door. At first she didn't speak. She just straightened up and pushed her shoulders back and didn't look at me. And when she did talk, she seemed to be on Daddy's side of things. "Junior ought to mind his own business," she said.

"I think the way Junior sees it, my family *is* his business. He's worried about you, that's all." I thought how all of a sudden I seemed to be on Junior's side of things.

"Well," said Momma. She turned and started toward the kitchen table. "You should be down in Warm Springs right now working on your therapy. I don't know how I can handle the guilt of having you home." She pulled out a chair at the end of the table and sat down. "I don't see how you can do much about the situation here."

"I don't either. But I could never forgive myself if I was down there having a good time and you were back here getting beat up."

Momma's face twisted then. She gave out a scared-sounding cry, and then she stuffed her fist to her mouth like she wanted to cram the noise back inside. She put her head in her arms and started crying for real.

Well, I just didn't know what to do—but I scooted over to the next chair and reached out and felt her shaking. I wanted to cry too, but I figured it was time for me to be strong. So I put my arm around my momma and rubbed my hand across her shoulders and said, "It's going to get better. Honest it is. Somehow we're going to fix it."

After a while she lifted her head and pulled her apron up and wiped her eyes. "Oh, they ruined my Leroy," she said. "They might as well have killed him. I don't even know him anymore."

And then it was like someone had opened up a bag of dried beans and the whole pile of them came pouring out and clattered all over the kitchen. She just started talking. It wasn't like Momma to pile one sentence on top of another like that.

"He doesn't sleep anymore, so he's always tired. And when he does sleep he has terrifying dreams. I have to wake him up so he won't scare the children, and anyway I can't let him lay there and suffer the way he does. He begs me not to leave him. So I promise I won't, but I don't know if I can stay."

Well, Momma almost knocked me off my chair when she said that. Would she actually think about leaving my daddy?

"I ask him what he sees in those dreams. But he won't

tell me. 'It's better to forget,' he says. 'I have to get over it.' But Ann Fay, he's not getting over it. Sometimes I think he is. But then out of the blue a noise startles him or he goes into a rage about some tiny little thing, and then..." Momma's voice trailed off, and I saw the pain cross her face and her head jerk a little as if she was being smacked right then.

And something about that made me understand why she would think about leaving. I mean, is it right for a woman to be beat by the man she loves? I thought how my daddy always said he and Momma were staying together for better or worse. But how much worse?

My heart was arguing with itself again. And I didn't have any idea which side to take. So finally I said, "Momma, we'll find a way. I don't know how, but I know we will."

30

Telling
March 1946

Before the day was half over, there was a car in our driveway and a highway patrolman standing on our porch. I had the biggest urge to run, but you can't outrun the law. So I decided to try out-talking him.

I spoke to him through the screen door. "Can I help you?"

He tipped his officer's cap. "Good day," he said. He pulled out his badge and told me his name, which I forgot as quick as I heard it. "I'm looking for Mr. or Mrs. Leroy Honeycutt."

I took a deep breath. "My daddy's not here right now, and my momma can't come to the door. Can I help you?"

And then I heard my momma saying it. "May I help you?"

Why couldn't she just stay in the back room and let me handle this? Now the patrolman could plainly see her black eye.

He didn't say a word about her eye. He just told her he was following up on a report that Ann Fay Honeycutt had left the Georgia Warm Springs Foundation without authorization. He wanted to know if she had returned home safe and sound.

Momma put her arm around my shoulder then. "This is Ann Fay. She's just fine, thank you."

The officer looked at me. "Young lady, what made you do such a thing?"

"My momma needed me," I said. How I was going to explain that? "See?" I pointed to her tummy. "She's going to have a baby. And my twin sisters are a handful."

He nodded. But he wasn't looking at her tummy. He was looking at her bruised eye. "And you couldn't have waited for a proper discharge?"

"No," I said. "Junior came after me on a Sunday. He had to work today."

He looked at his paper. "That would be Junior Bledsoe? Can you tell me where he works?"

Now I'd done it! Why did I have to mention Junior?

Momma spoke up. "Sir, it's all right. Please don't give him any trouble. He was just being a good neighbor. We're all happy to have our daughter home."

The officer nodded. He stood there for a moment and finally he said, "May I come in?"

Momma stepped back, so I did too. She offered him a seat, but he didn't take it. He looked around the living room and I saw how his eyes went searching on past the door, into the kitchen. I could tell he was sizing us up. Trying to see if anything looked suspicious. But just like always, my momma had the house as neat and clean as his starched uniform.

"Ma'am, may I ask if you're all right? I see you've got a bruise there."

Momma laughed nervously. "Yes," she said. "I had an accident in the middle of the night."

The officer nodded. "Shall I report that you're content

with your daughter's sudden departure from the Georgia Warm Springs Foundation?"

"Please do," said Momma. She opened the screen door and went on through to the porch.

There wasn't a thing for that officer to do but follow. He gave her a nod and put his cap back on. "You would call on help if you needed it, right?"

"Of course," said Momma. "Of course we would. We've got good neighbors. Thank you for looking in on us."

As the patrolman drove away, she said to me, "We don't need to mention this to your daddy. You understand?"

"I understand," I said.

When Daddy came home from work that night he took his lunchbox into the kitchen and set it on the table. Then he washed up and sat down to eat with the rest of us. Ida and Ellie jabbered about this and that and asked me questions about Warm Springs.

I picked up my glass. It was a jelly jar and there was a chip on the edge. I took a drink of water and acted like I didn't hear their questions. But of course they didn't give up so easy. So I gave in.

"We ate dinner on white tablecloths," I said. "And we used china. And there were real waiters in white coats and black bow ties. I never did get over feeling like I was eating at a fine restaurant."

"I never ate at a fine restaurant," said Ellie.

"Well, don't feel bad," I said. "Neither have I. So I don't really know if it's like eating at Warm Springs. But I think so."

Thinking about Warm Springs ruined my appetite. Right about then, Sam and Loretta and Howie were sitting down to eat without me. Sam was probably telling every detail about how me and Junior sneaked out of there. Just like he was the clock on Olivia's dresser watching it happen.

I never thought I'd say this—but I sure would like to have heard his version!

To change the subject, I asked Daddy had he planted his peas yet. But he just shook his head and said, "Maybe now that *you're* here, I'll get that done. Seems like we just can't get along around here without you."

His voice was flat when he said it, so I couldn't tell what he meant. Was he glad I was there? Or was he being sarcastic because I'd come to check on him?

After supper, I started helping Momma with the dishes, but Daddy took my towel. "Go to bed, Ann Fay," he said. "You look beat."

I *was* tired on account of I hadn't slept much during the day. I had tried, but honest, my mind wouldn't settle down for thinking about that patrolman. And Junior and my family. And Warm Springs and Suzanne and Gavin.

So when I saw how Daddy was going to help Momma with the dishes, I went straight to bed. And I tell you what's the truth—if my daddy or anyone, including me, had a bad dream that night, I missed it altogether. I slept clear through till morning.

I figured there wasn't anything to do but get up and go to school. And that meant going right back to where I started at the beginning of the year. In eighth grade, facing Rob Walker, and sitting out recess.

For some reason it didn't scare me, though. I had been somewhere special. To a historic place that no one else at my school had ever seen. And that made me real proud.

When I got on the bus I went halfway to the back and sat down with the rest of the students. I could see the bus driver was surprised. And people said "Hey" to me. And "Welcome back."

When the bus stopped at Whitener's Store, Jean got on with her brothers and sisters. She caught sight of me just before she sat down. Her eyebrows went up and she smiled like I was a happy surprise. And when we got to school she waited for me outside the bus door. "Nifty!" she said. "No more crutches. Does my mother know you're back?"

I shook my head. "I just got home yesterday."

"What was it like? Did you have a good time? Did you learn to walk?"

Before I could even answer her, one of her friends got off another bus and called her name.

"I'll talk to you later," I said. And then I headed toward the school.

Wouldn't you know, Rob Walker got to the steps just when I did. He was running. I could see he hadn't changed a bit.

But *I* had. At Warm Springs, I learned I wasn't a cripple. I was a polio. And I didn't have to be afraid of anyone.

So when I saw him, I spoke first. "Look who's back," I said. "Can you hold that door?" In my mind I snapped my fingers.

Rob gave me a surprised look, but he actually held the door for me.

"Thanks!" I said. "Where I came from they had magic doors. You would think I was the queen of England the way those doors opened when they saw me coming."

"I know that's a lie," said Rob. And he went on down the hall.

People were talking about me. I heard my name going up and down the hallway. It's a wonder I even made it to my class for all the people stopping to watch me use those canes. I knew my walk was a little lopsided, but I just looked them in the eye and decided not to care what they thought of me.

Peggy Sue grabbed me in a big hug, and then she said, "Are you going to show me how you can walk or not?"

"What makes you think I can walk?"

"I know you, Ann Fay. If you went down there to walk, then I figure you did it. And anyway, you wrote me about that. Remember?"

So I handed her my Canadian canes and I walked the rest of the way to my class. I had to rest a few times and I hung on to the wall some. But it made me think I could almost leave those canes at home—if I took a notion.

When I got to my classroom the smile on Mrs. Barkley's face made me think she was glad to see me. And she gave me a hug too. Later when the class went out to recess she made arrangements for someone else to supervise them. And she asked me to stay in. Then she sat in a desk across the aisle. "Well, Ann Fay, I guess your homecoming was unexpected."

I just didn't know what to tell her. So I sat there and stared at the cracks between the floorboards. And rubbed my foot in a figure-eight pattern in a bright spot on the floor.

"I'm sure they didn't expel you from Warm Springs. You're such a model citizen."

I gave a nervous laugh when she said that. What would she think if I told her I ran away? And that an officer of the law had come looking for me?

"So why did you come back?"

"Warm Springs was wonderful," I said. "Everybody there

was like me—I mean, not exactly like me, but they had problems getting around too. Or maybe it was just one arm they couldn't use. And some people were even twisted out of shape. Maybe they would look funny to normal people, but to me it was the most comforting place in the world. I was real mad when my neighbor came to get me."

Then I stopped. How was I going to tell Mrs. Barkley about my daddy?

Mrs. Barkley got up and moved the desk she was sitting in. She pushed it right up against mine. Then she put her hand on my arm. "I want to help if I can," she said.

And I knew it was true. But I just didn't see how anyone could help. Still, I had told Momma I was going to find a way to change things. And I knew if there was anyone I trusted besides Junior Bledsoe—who would probably never speak to me again—it was Mrs. Barkley.

So I said, "Something is happening to Daddy. At first when he came home from the war it seemed like he was fine. But he's not fine. He has nightmares. He doesn't sleep and then he gets angry. Momma says it's like they killed the man she used to love. It's like his body is home but he's back in Europe, still fighting that war."

"Oh," said Mrs. Barkley.

I didn't know what "Oh" meant. Maybe it meant she didn't know what to say. Or maybe it made her think of something she could do about it. But suddenly I wasn't sure I wanted her to do anything.

"Please don't tell anybody," I said. "Please don't."

"Ann Fay, are you in danger?"

I didn't know what to say about that. Because, to tell you the truth, I didn't think my daddy would ever hurt me, but I didn't exactly feel safe with him either.

Still, I shook my head. "No," I said. "I'm not in any danger."

I didn't tell her about my momma's black eye. I had probably said too much already.

31

Planting Peas
March 1946

That night when Daddy came home from work he had a small paper sack in his hand. After he kissed my momma he took it out the back door. I watched through the screen, and the next thing I knew he was pulling his tiller out of the shed.

"Momma," I said, "he's fixing to till the garden." Then I went out on the back porch and sat with my feet over the edge. I remembered how two years ago I was in this exact same spot—just about the same time of year. Daddy was away at the war. So Junior had come to till our garden. Peggy Sue was here with me.

I couldn't believe how things had changed since then. I had run with Peggy Sue down into the woods while Junior had done the tilling. I'd actually *run* there and back. Now, I was just glad that I could walk without help from the edge of the porch to the tiller.

I watched Daddy pull the rope on the tiller. At first it didn't start, but he pulled again and it cranked right up. I thought I would see a smile cross his face, but I didn't. He jumped back and looked scared for a second like that tiller had just exploded in his face. But then he grabbed the handle and steadied himself and just hung on for a minute or two and breathed real deep.

The simple noise of that tiller—a sound he'd always loved—was scaring him somehow. I saw how hard he was working at convincing himself to do this job. He walked away for a minute and stared into the woods. I saw how he curled his hands into a fist and opened them again. He flexed them a few times and shook his shoulders and arms like he was trying to knock something loose.

Finally he came back to the tiller and grabbed ahold of it. It shook him all over while he walked it to the garden.

The whole time he acted like he didn't even know I was on the porch. Maybe he hadn't noticed. For as long as I could remember I'd helped him get his garden ready. Now I felt shut out.

He'd left the paper sack lying on the ground, so I went to it. I could feel the bumpy shapes of dried peas through the paper. I hugged it to my chest and wished I could take over the tilling for my daddy.

I watched him in the garden—how he leaned into the tiller and how the soil turned up red and soft between the tines. Already Mr. Shoes was chasing behind Daddy, sniffing after moles that had tunneled through the garden space.

I wanted in the worst way to put my toes into that soft, crumbly red dirt. To follow behind Daddy, making a row with the edge of a hoe and then dropping the peas in. I thought I could do it again if I sat in the dirt. I set the sack of peas on the ground and went in the house to get my overalls.

When I came back out, it was getting dark. The tiller wasn't running anymore, and Daddy was sitting in the dirt with his fists pressed up to the sides of his head. He had only tilled about two and a half rows. I picked up the sack of seeds and stuffed it into the pocket of my overalls, and then I walked with my canes down to the garden.

I went and sat in the dirt beside Daddy. I leaned up against him and felt him trembling. "You did enough for over two rows," I said. "If you get the hoe and make the rows, I'll drop the peas in. I can scoot through the garden on my behind."

Daddy didn't say a word. He just got up and walked to the tiller and gave it a hard kick. Then he went to the shed and got a hoe and started making rows. I dropped the seeds in and he covered them with dirt, and by the time we were done it was too dark for me to know how crooked our rows would be.

I could see the shape of the tiller sitting there. I saw Daddy give it one last kick before he picked me up and carried me to the porch. He filled a basin with water from the bucket so I could wash my hands and feet. "I'm going to build you that bathroom before you know it," he said.

That night when I was laying in bed I knew what I had to do. I wasn't looking forward to it because I figured Junior never wanted to see me again. And Daddy didn't want Junior on his property. But we had to get the rest of that garden tilled, and Junior Bledsoe was the one who could do it.

The next day after school I asked the bus driver to drop me off at the end of the Bledsoes' lane. I made Ida and Ellie go on home and tell Momma I'd be there soon. Then I walked with my canes to Junior's house and knocked on the door. I knew he wasn't home from work yet, but I figured I could wait till he got there.

Bessie came to the door and it wasn't two seconds before she pulled me into her big, soft hug. "Have mercy," she said. "I have sure missed you." She pointed me to a chair and said, "I was fixing to bring you a chocolate cake. But since you're here, I'm going to cut it."

She went into the kitchen and clattered around for a few minutes, and when she came back she had a tray with a glass of milk and a slice of cake on a small china plate.

"What a pretty plate," I said. "It puts me in mind of Warm Springs."

"Junior said you fit right in down there."

"Well," I said, "in some ways I did. But I just couldn't believe it was really me in that ritzy place."

I started telling Bessie all about Warm Springs and how, if it wasn't for my momma and daddy, I would love to be there right that second.

"I'm sorry," she said. "It's not all Junior's fault. We both thought it would be best if you knew."

"I don't blame you," I said. "Or Junior either." I didn't mention how mad I was at him for ruining my Warm Springs fairy tale.

The next thing I knew, Junior was coming through the door. When he saw me he stopped dead in his tracks.

"The school bus dropped me off," I said. "I'm hoping you'll take me home." It was hard saying this on account of how I hurt him so bad on the way home from Georgia. But I couldn't let that stop me from doing what had to be done.

"My daddy can't run the tiller," I said.

"Is it broke?"

"The sound of it scares him. He did two and a half rows and just quit. You should've seen how he was shaking."

Junior hung his hat on a hook inside the living room door. And his car key beside the hat. Bessie went in the kitchen to get him some cake and milk.

He balanced the dish with the cake on his knee. He ate it without talking to me. He knew good and well I wanted him to come and till that garden for my daddy. But I could see he was going to make me beg. So I did.

"I'm asking you to till the garden for him, Junior. He wants to do right by his family. But loud noises bother him. And you know how loud that tiller is."

"Your daddy run me off his property and I don't suppose he's going to let me come back two days later, now is he?"

"He won't be home for another hour and a half. You've got time before he gets there."

I knew Junior wanted to turn me down, but of course he couldn't. And his momma was right there to make sure he didn't. "Don't argue. Just go," she said. "Leroy needs you and you'll kick yourself later if you don't help out."

Junior looked like he wanted to kick something right that minute. He ate one last big bite of cake and drank the rest of the milk. Then he stood and his mother took his dishes from him and carried them into the kitchen.

"Let's go," he said.

He went out the door and waited for me to come through before he shut it. He didn't help me off the porch like he normally would. But I didn't need his help. He opened the car door for me but went around to the other side and let me get in and close the door by myself.

Neither one of us said a word on the way to my house. He went straight to the garden and cranked up the tiller and was tilling the rows almost before I got into the house.

Momma was in the living room. She gave me a quick hug. "When Junior's done you tell him to come in for a piece of chocolate cake I made today."

"He just ate chocolate cake," I said. "And right now I don't think he would take it if I offered it. Or even come inside."

I went into the bedroom and changed into my overalls

and went through the kitchen door to the back porch.

It was a warm spring day and I could see little baby leaves fixing to pop out on the trees. I thought how strange it was that the world could be so beautiful and still hurt so bad at the same time. I sat in the grass at the side of the house and watched Junior.

The tiller made *his* arms shake too, but he held it steady and kept his eye on the ground. I could see how he was keeping just the right amount of pressure on the handles so it wouldn't bog down in the dirt. His hair was rumpled and his shirttail was hanging loose. But he seemed so solid and unbreakable.

Not like my daddy, who seemed wobbly when he was behind the tiller. And even when he wasn't.

Once when Junior got to the other end of the garden he looked up to where I sat. He went on with his job. When he was done he took the tiller right past me and put it in the shed.

"Thanks," I said when he came back out.

Junior grunted.

"I sure do appreciate it," I said. "Let me know if I can help you with anything."

As soon as that came out of my mouth, I wished it hadn't. What could I do for Junior? He'd never asked me for a single thing. At least not until we drove past Gaffney, South Carolina.

I knew he didn't mean I should marry him right there on the spot. But he took a chance by letting me know how he felt. And the one thing he wanted from me—a little sign that I felt the same way—he didn't get.

I knew one thing for sure. Junior Bledsoe deserved a good woman. And even if Mrs. Barkley did think I was a model citizen, I knew I wasn't very good at all.

32

Getting Help
March 1946

I was afraid Daddy would be furious about Junior tilling his garden. And that he'd take it out on my momma for allowing it to happen. If he did something to hurt her, it would be my fault.

I wanted to be the one to explain, so I sat on the porch and waited for him to come home from work. While I waited, I thought how if I was in Warm Springs I would be going into the dining room soon.

Before long, Mr. Botts would have someone else filling my place. Would Sam the Encyclopedia Man feed that person the same stories he gave me? Was Gavin mad that I ran off without saying goodbye? And Mr. Botts—would he ever forgive me?

Then Daddy came driving in and I forgot about Warm Springs.

Before he even got out of the truck, Daddy noticed the garden was tilled. He sat and stared at it for a long time. Mr. Shoes went running to greet him, yapping and jumping up against the door, but Daddy didn't open it. He just sat there and stared and Mr. Shoes yipped some more.

Finally Daddy opened the door and Mr. Shoes jumped up into the floorboard of the truck and onto his lap. He greeted Daddy like he always did—licking his face and snuffling in his pockets. But you would've thought he was a rat the way Daddy grabbed him and flung him out the door.

Mr. Shoes landed in the yard with a thump that hurt me to hear. He sat looking stunned for a second and then he ran whimpering up the steps. I snapped my fingers, and just like that, he was on my lap.

"Give *me* kisses," I said. I hugged him close. "Don't take it personal, Mr. Shoes," I whispered. "Daddy's having a bad day, is all." But I couldn't see how that was a good explanation. And I figured Mr. Shoes was too smart to buy it.

When Daddy came up on the porch he stopped right by my chair. "I'm sure your momma's glad to have you home, Ann Fay. I reckon from now on you can just solve *all* her problems, can't you?"

And this time I knew for sure he was being sarcastic.

I burrowed my face in Mr. Shoes' fur. What was I supposed to say? That I hadn't done it for my momma? That I was just trying to help him out? But how would that make him feel?

I hung on to Mr. Shoes and waited for Daddy to go in the house. But he didn't. I could feel him right beside me, breathing heavy. He opened the screen door a few times and let it fall back shut again.

I opened my eyes and saw his fist just a few inches away, clenching and opening and clenching again. I held real still and waited. Then finally he went inside.

Daddy was wrong. I didn't know how to solve our problems. Especially not his.

But the next day at school Mrs. Barkley handed me a book. It was a biography of Eleanor Roosevelt. "Take a look at page thirty-eight," she said.

So I started reading it the first chance I got. The part Mrs. Barkley wanted me to read was about when Eleanor was first married to Franklin. He was the Secretary of the Navy then, so she made visits to the Navy hospital. There were lots of shell-shocked soldiers from World War I. Mrs. Roosevelt described them as "poor demented creatures, ... gazing from behind bars or walking up and down on enclosed porches."

It sounded like those soldiers who'd fought for our country were being treated like prisoners! The book said Mrs. Roosevelt was so concerned that she went straight to work getting Congress to spend money on improving the hospital. And she raised other funds so they could have recreation. And occupational therapy.

I knew what occupational therapy was, and I could understand how making pot holders and crocheting pocketbooks could strengthen Olivia's hands. But I didn't see how it could help my daddy. Still, the book made me think maybe there was help out there somewhere.

During recess I went outside and sat on the bench and watched the rest of the class doing broad jumps and pole vaulting. I asked Mrs. Barkley did she think my daddy had shell shock.

"I think war neurosis may be a common condition," she said. "The Veterans Administration might have a program to help soldiers adjust to life at home. It would be worth looking into."

I didn't see how I could ask Junior Bledsoe for one more thing. But how else would I get to the Veterans Administration to ask about GI benefits?

"And if they can't help," said Mrs. Barkley, "maybe the state hospital in Morganton can."

"The state hospital!" I reached for my wooden Comfort. "That's an insane asylum. My daddy is not crazy!"

Mrs. Barkley put her hand on my arm. "Don't think of it like that," she said. "Surely that hospital has psychiatrists on staff who could help your father. I just want you to think about the possibilities."

"But I read what that book said—about soldiers behind bars. My daddy is not a criminal. And he's not dangerous either."

Maybe I was lying about that—I didn't know. But I couldn't imagine my daddy behind bars. And who was supposed to put him there anyway? I decided right off I wasn't going to look into that mental hospital. At least not until I'd checked with the Veterans Administration.

But there was still the problem of Junior.

On the way home from school, it hit me that there was another way I could get some information. So this time I asked the bus driver to drop me off at the Hinkle sisters'.

Miss Pauline was right there at the back door to let me in. "My, my," she said. "Isn't this a surprise! Dinah, we have a guest." She led me into her kitchen and pulled out a chair. "Sit here. I'll get you something to eat." She opened her refrigerator and brought out a bottle of Cheerwine.

Miss Dinah hugged me so hard it knocked her glasses half off. "Oh, it's good to see you," she said. "I heard you were back. How was Georgia?"

Why did I have to answer the same old question to every new person I saw? Didn't it ever cross their minds I might rather *be* in Warm Springs? Instead of sitting there talking about it?

Miss Pauline put a plate of cookies in front of me. I took one and nibbled at it. "Georgia was just fine," I said.

"I wonder if I could use your telephone. I need to call the Veterans Administration."

"Of course," said Dinah. "I'll look up the number while you finish your treat."

She went into the living room.

I ate the cookie and left most of the Cheerwine in the bottle. "I'll share it with the twins later," I said. Miss Pauline and I went into the living room.

Miss Dinah had her finger on the phone directory and the receiver off the hook. "Do you want me to dial it for you?"

"Um," I said, "maybe not just yet."

What would I say, especially with those two sisters hearing every word? I didn't want to drag them into my family's business. But Junior had told me they already knew some of it. So I decided to take my chances.

"I need to talk to them about getting help for my daddy. Lately he's been...well, he's been..." I just couldn't make myself say that my daddy had turned violent.

Miss Dinah leaned forward and whispered, "It's okay, Ann Fay. Actually Bessie told us about the incidents." Then she sat back and said, louder, "We'd do anything for your mother, wouldn't we, Pauline?"

Miss Pauline nodded. "Perhaps *I* should call," she said. "They'll be more likely to speak to an adult."

She took the phone. She explained all about Daddy not being himself since the war and my momma being in a family way. "Urgent help is needed," she said.

After she hung up, she said that my mother would have to go and fill out papers. "Tell your momma we'll gladly drive her there."

"I think we should pay her a visit," said Miss Dinah.

"Oh, no," I said. "Please don't. She will be so ashamed."

"Nonsense," said Miss Pauline. "If the war taught us anything, it's that women must sometimes take charge of a situation. And we have to stick together."

"Well, maybe."

"No maybe about it," said Miss Dinah. "I'm going to give you a ride home this minute. And get myself a little time with that precious dog of yours. I'll talk to your mother and insist that she let us help."

And that's exactly what Miss Dinah did.

33

Good Days and Bad
April 1946

Miss Dinah and Miss Pauline tried their best to help us out. They took Momma to the Veterans Administration Office, more than once. But to make a long story short, there were so many soldiers needing help after the war that if we waited until they got around to helping my daddy I knew it might not ever happen.

I thought a lot about Imogene and whether her daddy was one of those people needing help after the war. When we were in the hospital she told me her daddy did not get to help in the fighting. They kept the blacks and whites separated in the army just like everywhere else. Except maybe up north.

I figured that was good for Imogene. Maybe her daddy was the same one she had always been used to instead of an angry stranger.

I never saw Daddy hit my momma. But I heard him yelling in their room lots of times at night when he should've been sleeping. And one day when he had trouble opening a jar of pickled beets, he got so mad he threw it against the Frigidaire. Then he stomped out the door and tore up the road in his truck.

As he drove away I thought about Hubert at Warm

Springs. And psychiatrists. And how I promised Momma we'd fix Daddy somehow. "Maybe we should try the state hospital," I said.

I expected Momma to argue. But she just stared at the long, pink drips streaking down the side of the refrigerator. Tears oozed out her eyes and dribbled off her face. "Maybe," she said.

But to be honest, I don't think either one of us could make ourselves do it. We did look into it, but unless he put himself in there, we'd have to get two doctors to sign affidavits saying he was insane.

We needed a better plan.

For one week I almost thought things were going to be all right with Daddy. Now that the garden was tilled, he would go out there and work the soil with his shovel or hoe and plant lettuce and carrots. He even spent two whole evenings chopping away at the wisteria vines that were moving toward the garden again.

I stood at the bedroom window and watched. He looked as mad at those vines as I was when I cut them back during the war. I was just glad he was taking his madness out on the wisteria instead of on us.

Things were better for me at school, too. I still took my canes, but I always moved around the room without them. And every day I could walk a little farther without stopping to rest.

On the school bus I never sat in the front seat. Instead I mixed in with everyone else. Sometimes Jean or Beckie sat with me. One day after I'd been home for a couple of weeks Jean said, "Ann Fay, my mother wants to know why you haven't come by to see her."

I shrugged. "I don't know," I said. "Too much going on,

I guess." I didn't tell her what I meant by that. I probably didn't need to. If you wanted to hear some good gossip, that store would be the place to go. More than likely the people coming and going in there knew more about my daddy than I did.

"Well, she wants you to come by on Saturday." Jean laughed. "But watch out! She's liable to put you to work."

I looked at Jean to see if she was making this up. "Tell me the truth," I said. "Does your momma feel sorry for me or what?"

"Maybe so. Or maybe she just likes you. And anyway, if you're helping in the store it saves one of us young'uns some work."

So on Saturday I asked Daddy to take me to Whitener's Store.

"Look at you," said Ruth Whitener when I came through the door. "Walking in here with only a cane." She pulled out a stool and told me to sit. But first she gave me a big hug. "Everyone's been asking where our little polio girl is."

Her saying that made me feel warm inside. Like I belonged to something bigger than my family and closer than Warm Springs. And after all, her customers had collected a pile of money to get me to Georgia.

Next thing I knew, I had my job back. I can't tell you how good it felt. I had met a lot of people by working at the store. And now when they saw me again it seemed like their faces would light up. The women gave me hugs or patted my hand and asked about my momma. Some of the men even talked me into playing rook with them. They joked with me and teased me about the boys I met in Georgia.

But I didn't mention a single word about Gavin. I hadn't

heard from him. When I first got home, I sent a letter to Suzanne and another one to Olivia explaining that my momma was having a baby and my daddy wasn't doing so good. But I didn't give them any details.

When the people at the store asked about Daddy, I didn't give them much satisfaction either. "Oh, he's busy," I said. "Working all day and planting the garden at night."

It made me wonder what they'd be saying if I wasn't sitting there to hear it.

Of course Otis came into the store right at eleven o'clock. And I do declare, I think even his glass eye twinkled when he saw me. I just had to ask how his momma was doing.

Otis grinned real slow and lifted his hat like always and scratched his head. "She has her good days and her bad days, she does."

I fished a pickle out of the jar for him and he asked about my family.

"I reckon we're like your momma," I said. "Some days are better than others."

I wondered what Otis actually meant when he gave that answer. What were the bad days like, anyway? Was his momma in a foul mood? Or was her arthritis acting up?

It made me stop and think how all those people coming into the store, one or two at a time, were carrying things inside that the rest of us didn't have any idea of. And maybe they liked coming in there because they could count on Ruth Whitener to listen to them grumble. Or they could swap gossip and forget their own worries.

In some ways it was like Whitener's Store took the place of Warm Springs for me. Even if I had different troubles from the people who came in there, they were my friends. It felt like some of the men who came in there offering me chewing gum and asking me silly riddles loved me almost like a daughter.

Or maybe I just wanted to believe that because I couldn't count on anything from my daddy anymore.

One night, the week after I started back at the store, I found out just how bad off my daddy really was. We were fixing to eat supper. Ida and Ellie had both washed their hands and were sitting at the table. I was getting butter and jelly out of the Frigidaire and Momma was at the stove putting food from pots into serving bowls.

"Ida," said Momma, "go tell your daddy that supper is ready."

Daddy was sitting on the front porch, so Ida ran and told him. Then she came right back inside and hid behind the kitchen door. When he came into the kitchen she jumped out at him and hollered, "Boo!"

Well, you should have seen my daddy jump. At first Ida squealed with laughing because she had scared him so good. But it wasn't a good kind of scared—the kind where you're startled but then you realize you're okay.

I could see Daddy thought he was in danger—like Hubert on that day in the brace shop. Like he thought a real enemy was after him. For a minute his whole face went ugly scared, and then he went after Ida like she was the enemy. He let out an awful scream, grabbed her up, and slammed her against the wall.

Ida went dead silent but tears were running off her cheeks. Her teeth were chattering, and her eyes—oh, the fear in them just made my legs go weak. I wanted to grab her away from him, but I didn't. I just stood there staring and hanging on to the open refrigerator door.

But Momma, if she was the least bit afraid of Daddy,

I couldn't tell it. She was taking a pot of stew beef off the stove when it happened. She set the pot back down and stepped ever so quietly to where Daddy was standing. "Leroy," she said. And her voice was low and soothing. "It's your little girl." As if Daddy didn't know who Ida was. As if he was the one who needed comforting. She put one hand on Daddy's shoulder and she slipped the other arm around Ida's waist. "Let her go," she said.

Daddy was shaking every bit as much as Ida was. His face was twisted up and he was making strange sounds. But it looked like he had relaxed his hold and was letting her slide down the wall.

Momma pulled Ida to her, but she kept one hand on Daddy's shoulder.

Daddy shook his head hard—like a dog drying off when it comes out of the creek. Then he went into the living room and out the front door, and left us there.

Ida started crying out loud then. And Ellie too. We was all crying. Momma had Ida's face pressed up against her big belly and was running her fingers through her hair. "He didn't mean it for you, honey. He didn't mean it for you."

She was looking through the window at Daddy's truck driving away. I could see her worrying if Daddy was going to hurt himself on the road. I was worried too, but still I was glad he was gone.

I never did put the butter on the table. But it didn't matter on account of none of us ate supper that night. Later I saw Ellie nibbling on a biscuit, but I don't think she even realized it or she would've put jelly on it.

It was Thursday and I wished in the worst way it was Wednesday. I needed to hear those people singing out at the colored church. I didn't care what song it was. As long as it was about tribulation and making it through.

I took Comfort from around my neck before I went to bed that night. And held on to her while I waited for Daddy to come home. He came in the back door after I'd gone to sleep. I woke up because Mr. Shoes was in the kitchen yapping.

At least someone in the family was glad to see my daddy.

34

Change
April 1946

The next morning I expected to see Daddy at the kitchen table staring into his coffee and smoking a cigarette. But he wasn't there. Momma wasn't elbow-deep in flour either. There was a box of cornflakes out, and the table was set with bowls and spoons.

Evidently Daddy wasn't getting biscuits and gravy for breakfast.

I heard them moving around in the bedroom, so I figured they'd be coming into the kitchen soon. I sat at the table, and Mr. Shoes came running from their room and jumped up on my lap. I tried to snuggle with him, but all he wanted was to lick my face a few times and be let out. I followed him to the front door and onto the porch.

It was one of those spring mornings when everything outside feels just about perfect. Bakers Mountain was starting to turn green with leaves on the trees and the birds were having a regular choir practice in our yard. Down below the garden the wisteria was blooming all over the pine trees. There was a gentle breeze blowing which brought the smell of those purple flowers up to the house.

But still, something was missing. It took me a minute or two to realize what it was. Daddy's truck wasn't in the lane!

I went back into the house and right to Momma and Daddy's door. It was half open, so I pushed it the rest of the way. Momma was down on her knees digging pasteboard boxes out from under the bed. The mattress was bare and the sheets were on a pile by the door. She had pushed her dressing table into the middle of the room. And her cedar chest too.

"Momma, is everything okay?"

My momma's baby belly was dragging on the wood floor, preventing her from getting any closer to whatever she was after. She pulled her head out from under the bed and the look on her face told me not to ask questions. But I did.

"Whatcha looking for?"

"I'm just making changes."

"Changes?"

Momma reached behind her for the broom, which was laying on the floor. She used it to push a box out to the other side of the bed.

"Where's Daddy?"

She grabbed the iron bedpost and pulled herself up. Just watching her so slow and clumsy made me want to give her a hand. But when I started toward her, she waved me off. "I don't need your help," she said. "Go eat your breakfast."

"But Momma, what are you doing? Where's Daddy?"

She sat on the edge of the bed to catch her breath. "Probably in South Carolina by now."

"South Carolina? Where's he...?" And then I figured it out. To Georgia. To Mamaw and Papaw's.

Momma got up and started pushing the bed across the room. Every so often one of its posts would catch on the edge of a floorboard. But she didn't let that stop her.

I started toward her. "You shouldn't be—"

"Don't tell me what I shouldn't be doing." She shoved the bed again and stopped to catch her breath.

"What about the baby?"

"Well, what *about* the baby? He needs a change too."

Something was different about my momma. She had some sort of plan and there wasn't anybody going to interfere.

I helped her push the bed into place with the head of it against the back wall.

"Thanks," she said. "Now go wake the girls up and get yourselves off to school."

So I did. But of course the twins were full of questions. "Where's Daddy?" asked Ellie.

Momma came out of the bedroom just then. "He's gone," she said. "And he won't be back for a while." She poured herself a cup of coffee and sat at the table with us. "We don't have to keep living like this. I am *not* bringing a baby into the middle of a war zone."

That's when it hit me what my momma was saying. She had run my daddy off! She explained to the twins that Daddy was probably halfway to Georgia. And that she hoped being with his momma and daddy would make him feel safe again. "He hasn't figured out that the war is over," she said. She rubbed both hands over her belly. "And it's not right for his wife and children to be his enemy."

Ida didn't ask any questions. For once she let Ellie do the talking for her. "When's he coming back?"

Momma sighed. "I guess we don't know. But don't you worry. We survived by ourselves before. We can do it again."

I had no idea how Momma thought we could survive without Daddy and his paycheck.

Peggy Sue's father had been real good to him at that hosiery job. I got to thinking how wrong it was for Daddy to up and leave him without any warning. Especially after Mr. Rhinehart paid my way to Warm Springs and everything.

When I saw Peggy Sue at school I told her about it. "So your daddy just lost a worker," I said.

But she didn't seem concerned. "Daddy's got men and women both, standing in line for work," she said. She was probably right about that because plenty of people had lost their jobs right after the war.

And I figured I had just lost my job too, since I didn't have a way to get there. On the bus that afternoon, I told Jean Whitener to please tell her mother that I probably wouldn't make it to work the next day.

All of a sudden our family had gone from two people working to none.

At least that's what I thought. But boy, was I in for a surprise! On Saturday morning I woke up the same time as always and let Mr. Shoes out to do his business. When I did, there was my daddy sitting on the front porch.

I didn't know whether to be happy or worried. Did this mean the war had come home again? I hadn't heard anything unusual during the night, and as far as I could tell, Momma was still sleeping. It was probably the best sleep she'd had in a long time.

Maybe I should've hugged my daddy's neck. Or acted the least bit glad to see him. But to be honest, I didn't know if I was.

"I thought you were in Georgia."

"Is that what your momma told you?"

"She figured you went..."

"Running home to *my* momma?" Daddy didn't look at

me. He just stared at his truck in the lane and said, "I come to take you to work, Ann Fay. Are you going to get ready or not?"

Well, I sure didn't expect that. I had a lot of questions, but I figured I could ask them later. I went inside to get dressed and the girls woke up and found out Daddy was there. While I was eating cereal they came running back in the house hollering for Momma. I heard Ellie telling her that Daddy was not at Mamaw and Papaw Honeycutt's house.

Momma sent the girls out of her room and she stayed inside. So I went to her door and told her that Daddy was taking me to Whitener's Store.

"I'll see you tonight," she said. And that was the end of the conversation.

I went outside and climbed in the truck. I didn't take a cane because I never had to walk that far, after all—only from the porch to the truck and then from the truck to the store. I could handle it easy, and I liked looking like a normal person for a change.

There was a pasteboard box on the truck seat. A blue shirtsleeve was hanging out of a top corner. And Daddy's lunchbox and garden shoes were on the floorboard. There was a pine needle stuck to the box. I picked it up and put it between my teeth. I liked how sharp it tasted. Almost like lemon. It put me in mind of Warm Springs.

Ellie followed Daddy to the truck. She wanted to know if he was coming back soon. "Don't worry," he said. He climbed in and looked out the window at her. "I'm not going far."

On the way to the store I asked him if he was going back to work for Mr. Rhinehart.

"I never left."

"But where are you staying?" I asked.

"Don't you worry. I'm a big boy and I've slept in worse places."

Worse than what? Where could he possibly be sleeping? But Daddy wasn't saying much. Just that he would pick me up and take me home again at the end of the day.

As far as everyone at the store was concerned, it was an ordinary Saturday. Only Mrs. Whitener raised her eyebrows when I went in. Evidently Jean had told her I might not be coming.

At eleven o'clock Otis came in and had his dill pickle same as usual. Then he sat on a straight-backed chair and joined two farmers talking about raising chickens and selling eggs. One of them was a war veteran named Joe. You'd think Otis would've learned by this time that Joe wasn't interested in talking about the war. But something about eggs got Otis on the subject of starvation and concentration camps.

"Forget it!" snapped Joe. "Leave it be! There ain't no good in carrying it around on you the rest of your life!"

Otis just lifted his hat and scratched the top of his head. Then he stood and walked to the door. I thought Joe had shut him up. But before he left, Otis turned to Joe. "The way I figure it," he said, "a body can carry it around the rest of his life if that's what he wants. Or he can get it off his chest. Which one are *you* doing?"

And just like that, he went out the door.

Nobody said a word. Except Otis's words were still there. And what he said made a lot of sense to me.

"I'll be right back," I said to Mrs. Whitener. She was sitting at her sewing machine in the corner, but she was so interested in Joe and Otis that she'd forgot about the dress she was working on. I went as fast as I could toward the door.

And right when I went out the door I heard Mrs. Whitener saying to those men, "Well, look at that—our little polio girl is running."

"Otis! Otis!" I started to run toward the highway.

Otis turned and looked at me, and then he ran back. He grabbed my arm. "Crazy girl!" I guess he thought I was fixing to run into the traffic. He pulled me toward the store building.

But I didn't want to be near the window where the people in there could hear us.

"Let's go across the road," I said. We waited for a car to pass and he helped me across. I sat in the grass next to a barbed-wire fence. Otis sat too.

"What?" he asked. "What do you want?"

"You. I want you to talk to my daddy. He needs someone who's been through the war. It keeps following him around and it's scaring my momma and us kids real bad."

I told Otis about Momma's black eye and about Daddy slamming Ida up against the wall and Momma kicking my daddy out of the house. And how our home wasn't a safe place anymore.

"I don't know where he is right now," I said. "And I don't know where he slept last night either." But then, right when I said that, I had an idea. "Wait a minute," I said. "There were pine needles on his box of clothes. That's it! He slept in Wisteria Mansion."

Well, you should've seen the look on Otis's face—I could see that my daddy sleeping in a mansion didn't make sense to him. So I explained everything I could about Daddy and the playhouse we built in there and how he was a real good man before the war but now he wasn't the same. And could Otis please do something about it.

"All you gotta do is come back this afternoon," I said. "And ride home with me and Daddy. Then I don't care what you do. Go somewhere and talk. You can talk about concentration camps and people getting their heads blowed off, for all I care. I know it will help. I just know it. Because I went to Warm Springs and it done wonders for me being there with people who understood exactly what I'd been through. And some of them was much worse off than me."

The words came pouring out of me like water from a wide-open spigot. I didn't know what I was going to say before I even said it. But I knew it was true, and I knew if anyone in the world could help my daddy it was Otis.

Somehow I convinced him to give it a try. Maybe he just needed to talk as much as my daddy did. Because that afternoon he was back at Whitener's Store a whole fifteen minutes before Daddy got there.

35

Otis

April 1946

When Daddy got to the store, I didn't wait for him to come in and get me. Instead Otis helped me carry the groceries that Mrs. Whitener was paying me with. A loaf of light bread, a bag of dried pinto beans, and a MoonPie each for Ida and Ellie.

Otis opened the door of Daddy's truck and that's when I remembered the pasteboard box full of clothes. "Daddy," I said, "I invited Otis to ride along with us, but I forgot about this box. Do you reckon we can put it in the bed of the truck?"

Daddy squinted at me and then at Otis. He wasn't going to be rude and refuse to give him a ride, but I could see I had some explaining to do. He gave Otis a little nod.

I just pushed on the box a little and started climbing in the truck. There wasn't much else my daddy could do, so he got out, shut the pasteboard flaps up tight, and put the box in the back. I noticed he had changed into his old garden shoes and they had fresh dirt on them. What was he doing all day?

I scooted myself to the middle of the seat and Otis climbed in too. He offered Daddy a cigarette. Just like that, I was riding toward home with Daddy on one side of me smoking and Otis on the other, doing the same thing.

I talked the whole two miles about who came in and out of the store that day. When our mailbox was in sight I told Daddy why Otis was with us. I told him about Otis wanting to talk about the war and Joe telling him to let it go.

"But Daddy," I said. "Maybe Otis *needs* to talk about it. And maybe you do too. You can't talk to somebody who doesn't want to hear it. But you can talk to each other. It'll do you a world of good. I know, on account of me being at Warm Springs. It was the best thing you could've done for me—sending me down there with other people who been through the same things as me. So Otis and you are going to talk. Okay? He's willing, aren't you, Otis?"

Otis lifted his hat and scratched his head. We were in our lane now and Daddy had stopped the truck. I was wishing Otis would open his door so I could get out.

Daddy turned off the engine and sat there staring at the dashboard while Mr. Shoes yapped outside. Finally he said, "Ann Fay, reckon what your momma and me ever done before you come along? I bet you're surprised we made it for two minutes without you there to fix things."

The sarcasm in his voice made me real nervous.

I started inching toward Otis, hoping he'd let me out of the truck. But then Daddy reached for the handle to his door and he got out and went around to Otis's side. I kept an eye on him while I slid under the steering wheel and climbed down on the driver's side. Daddy reached through the window, took the groceries from Otis, and carried them to the porch. Then he went back to the truck.

Mr. Shoes was yipping and trying to climb my leg, so I sat on the step and held him while Daddy and Otis drove out of there.

"Thank you!" I hollered. I didn't want Otis to think I didn't appreciate what he was doing for me. And I sure hoped he didn't regret it.

What in the world were the two of them going to say to each other? There was no telling. If I hadn't learned anything else from Whitener's Store, I had seen that the way men get along is a far sight different from how women do.

Ida and Ellie came out on the porch and Ellie sat down on the step beside me. "Daddy planted 'taters today," she said.

"Yeah," said Ida. "And Ellie took him iced tea and baloney sandwiches. And cake."

So that's why Daddy had garden dirt on his boots! He must have been trying to act like it was a normal Saturday. Trying to impress my momma. Hoping she'd take him back.

And then again, maybe he was just trying his best to be his true-blue self—the way he was before the war.

36

Mysteria Mansion
April 1946

I was dying to know if my daddy had slept in Wisteria Mansion. So after supper that night, when I thought the twins weren't watching, I took off in that direction. I just took my wooden cane. If I got tired, I just stopped and rested for a minute and then I went on again.

Evidently the girls were watching because when I was almost out of sight I heard Ellie calling my name. "Wait up," she called. "Me and Ida want to come with you."

So I waited. Wouldn't you know, they ran on past me and started to crawl in ahead of me.

"Ooooo," said Ida. "It's scary." She held back and waited for me to go first.

When we were all inside I said, "It's not scary. Just mysterious."

"Yeah," said Ellie. "Mysterious. Hey—we should call it Mysteria Mansion."

Mysteria Mansion? I couldn't believe Ellie had thought that up. "Very clever!" I said. "Why didn't I think of that?"

We were surrounded by pine trees and every one of them was draped with long vines that had clusters of purple-blue flowers hanging from them. And it smelled so sweet it just made a body want to lay down and breathe it all in.

As pretty as it was, I could see we had some work to do. "Okay," I said. "It can be *your* Mysteria Mansion if you want it. But these vines are taking over the place. You've got to cut them back. And don't worry—half the fun of having a mansion is fixing it up!"

The girls wanted to get started right that minute. But it would soon be getting dark. So I said, "You better wait for another day. By the time you get the tools out of the shed, we'll be fresh out of daylight."

The girls made plans while I snooped around. I didn't see anything Daddy had left behind, but I did think the pine needles looked a little stirred up, like someone had been moving around in there. And I couldn't imagine where else he would've gone.

I had a feeling he might even be back before long. Maybe once it was dark he would sneak past our mailbox and park his truck down the road where we wouldn't see it. That night I tried to keep my ears open for the sound of his truck, but I was tired and couldn't stay awake.

The next morning Junior came to the house and told Momma that Daddy had asked him to take us to church. Something about that gave me hope for my daddy. If he could swallow his pride and go ask Junior for a favor, then maybe things weren't as bad as I thought. So we went.

When people asked about Daddy, Momma told them he was sick. Some people might think my momma was lying, but the more I thought about it, the more I knew my daddy really *was* sick. Just not in the way most people would think.

After church and Sunday dinner my sisters wanted me to go to Mysteria Mansion with them. I did just to make sure they didn't hurt themselves with the hedge trimmers.

I took a tablet along, thinking I would write to my friends at Warm Springs, but for some reason I took a notion to write to Imogene. I hadn't heard from her for months and months.

Dear Imogene,

How are you? And how are things at your school? Do you have trouble getting around? I heard there is a place in Alabama where you can go and get therapy so maybe you can walk without crutches. But I don't remember what it's called. Maybe your doctor knows.

I went to Warm Springs, Georgia for more than two months. I only use canes now and sometimes I don't even need them. I still have my brace and I despise it! Before I went to Georgia a bully at school started calling me Click, but the brace maker at Warm Springs adjusted my brace so it doesn't make noise now. I guess that showed him a thing or two!

Is your daddy home from the army? Mine is home, but he is not himself anymore. It makes me wonder how many of our soldiers have problems that we don't even know about.

I sure wish I could see you. It would do me good. Whenever I have hard times I tell myself it mostly hurts at first. Your words comfort me when I get out of heart.

Your friend,

Ann Fay

I reckon I didn't exactly tell her the truth on account of I didn't mention that my daddy wasn't actually home right then. But it just seemed too complicated to get into with someone who might not even be my friend anymore.

I asked Momma about the baby. "Are you worried about it coming and Daddy not being here?" I asked.

Momma covered her tummy like she thought she could protect her baby from hearing what I'd just said. "Maybe he *will* be home," she said. "Maybe it won't be as long as we fear."

"But when?" I asked. "I mean, when are you expecting the baby?"

"Probably sometime in late July. Or maybe early August."

July or August. Blackberry time. Corn-on-the-cob and sticky-summer-nights time. And now a baby. And if we were lucky—Daddy at home again. Not the daddy that drove off in his truck with Otis but the one we sent off to war.

To tell the truth, I knew *that* was a daddy I'd never see again. Still, July was a month to start leaning toward. Almost four months away. But it seemed so far off. Somehow we were going to have to get by on our own until then.

In a way I hoped Daddy *would* go stay with Mamaw and Papaw Honeycutt. Because I knew what it was like down there. I figured if there was any place in the world that could make a sad person feel better, it was the state of Georgia.

We didn't hear a word from Daddy all week. And not from Mamaw and Papaw either. I had half a notion to go to the Hinkle sisters' house and call them. But on Thursday Peggy Sue told me he was still working for her daddy.

"Where's he staying?" I asked.

She shrugged. "Daddy told me it wasn't our business. As far as I can tell, he doesn't know."

On Friday evening, right when Momma was putting supper on the table, Daddy's truck pulled up in the driveway.

Momma gave out a huge sigh, rubbed at the small of her back, and straightened up her shoulders. She also pulled off her bib apron and run her fingers through her hair.

Daddy knocked on the front door and waited like a perfect stranger for someone to open it. Momma told us to stay at the table and she went to the door. They kept their voices low so I couldn't hear what either one of them was saying. From where I sat, I saw that Momma fastened the hook on the screen door. It seemed like she had her mind made up.

But after a minute she opened it and stuck her hand through the door, and when she pulled it back I saw she had some money. Evidently Daddy was turning his pay over to her the same as always.

Was he keeping some for himself? And if not, what was he eating? And where?

Momma came back and put the money inside the Hoosier cupboard in a baking-powder can by the flour bin. Then she sat at the table. Ida and Ellie were standing at the window watching Daddy drive away.

"Didn't Daddy want to come in and eat?" I asked. I thought feeding him was the least Momma could do if Daddy was giving her his pay.

"He didn't look hungry," said Momma. She was trying to sound strong. But I saw how her lip was trembling.

It rained that night. And thundered and lightninged too. I got up and went out on the porch and tried to see down past the garden. Was my daddy getting soaked? He said he'd slept in worse places. That got me to thinking about the war. And wondering if he had slept outside during thunderstorms while he was off fighting. What else had Daddy been through?

I sat on a rocking chair and listened to the rain on the

tin roof. Mr. Shoes had followed me out and now jumped up on my lap. He smelled damp and doggy, and for some reason that was comforting. I got to thinking that if Daddy was down in Mysteria Mansion tonight or any other night, Mr. Shoes would probably know it. And he'd be barking and scratching to go out the door.

More than likely Daddy was sleeping in his truck someplace. But that still didn't explain how he could get a bath or a shave or eat a good meal.

On Saturday morning he showed up again to take me to work. Momma didn't come out to talk to him, but Ellie did. Daddy sat on the step and pulled her onto his lap and put his face in her hair.

Ida was standing on the edge of the porch and hanging on to a post. Watching. She had changed since that scary time with Daddy. All of a sudden she wasn't the leader of the twins anymore. It was like she would let Ellie do things first, and then, if it looked safe, she would join in.

Daddy turned and jerked his head a little, inviting her to sit with him too. So she did. He pulled her in close and he was real gentle with her. "I guess you know there's something sweet hiding in my shirt pocket," he said. Ida was almost as quick as Ellie to go hunting for it. But Ellie got to it first. She pulled out a pack of LifeSavers and started dividing it up between the two of them.

I didn't talk to Daddy on the way to work because I couldn't think what to say. Even though I wanted to know where he was staying, I didn't feel up to any of his smart remarks.

When I got to the store, Mrs. Whitener was standing on a stool scrubbing shelves. "See why I need you, Ann Fay?" she said. She showed me how dirty her scrubbing rag was. "These shelves hadn't been wiped down for two years. With you waiting on customers I can get caught up on other things once in a while."

There was only one light bulb in the middle of the ceiling, so it's not as if anyone would know if there was dust on those top shelves. But she wiped them down anyhow. She reminded me of my momma in that way. She liked things to be clean.

I noticed her making a pile of canned foods at one end of the counter while she worked. And during a quiet spell when no one was in the store, she explained what it was for. "I want you to take these to your momma," she said.

"Why?" I asked. Somehow she must've heard that my daddy wasn't living at home.

"People talk. Especially when they come in here."

"Well," I said, "Daddy brought his pay to Momma on Friday evening. So maybe you should give that food to him. I'm more worried about him than the rest of us."

"Oh," said Mrs. Whitener. She added a couple of cans of black-eyed peas to the pile. "I'm not naming names, but someone said your daddy moved in with Otis Hickey and his mother."

All I can say is, it's a good thing Mrs. Whitener was the one standing on that stool and not me. Because I would've fallen right off when she said that. All that time I worried about Daddy sleeping in the rain or on the seat of his truck, it never crossed my mind that he would move in with Otis.

A customer came in then. He greeted me and struck up a conversation with Mrs. Whitener. While they were talking, I got to wondering why Mrs. Whitener, whose husband was dead, would be giving extra food to my momma. Didn't she need it just as bad? Or worse, even since she had more children than Momma did? I decided it just proved what a kind person she was.

I watched for Otis, and when I saw him coming, I asked Mrs. Whitener could I take a break. I got outside before Otis came into the store. Mrs. Whitener brought me a chair and sat it by the door. Then she brought Otis a dill pickle.

He squatted there beside me and munched on the pickle while I told him my daddy had brought his pay to my momma. Otis nodded.

"Mrs. Whitener said my daddy's living at your house."

He nodded again.

"That's real big of you," I said. "Your momma too."

Otis didn't say anything. He just ate his pickle. And when he was done he crumpled the wax paper and put it in his pocket.

"How's my daddy doing? Is he talking to you? About the war, I mean."

Otis stood up then. He used the edge of his shoe to scrape a bottle cap out of the dirt. He picked it up and pulled a toothpick out of his pocket and scraped the dirt out of that metal cap. He blew the loose dirt out and then he used the toothpick to clean out every little ripple around the edge. "Your daddy's a good man," he said finally.

"Well, I know that. He's always been a good man. But do you think he's going crazy?"

Otis laughed. "Some people think *I'm* crazy," he said. "So I reckon I'm not the one to judge. But I know one thing—if war won't make you crazy, nothing will."

37

Making Progress

May 1946

With Daddy gone, it seemed like we all settled down some. Momma didn't go around sighing as much as she did before. And she didn't scrub or organize things around the house as much either.

I started thinking more about Warm Springs, and not just as a place to escape to but about the good things that had happened there. About the way it changed my life and even the way I thought of myself.

Leaving it the way I did seemed like the right thing to do at the time, but it worried me that I had—as Mr. Botts would say—broke one thing while fixing another.

The people at Warm Springs would always be with me, in my mind anyway. I got to where I couldn't stand the bad feeling that came over me every time I thought of them.

So finally I wrote Mr. Botts a letter.

> *Dear Mr. Botts,*
>
> *I hope you are fine. I am writing to apologize for leaving Warm Springs the way I did. I feel terrible about disappointing you like that.*
>
> *At that time, I couldn't see any other way to handle my family's problems. Now I know that letting other people*

in on my family's shame is one way to get some help.

*Things are better here. They aren't exactly fixed, but
we keep praying and with help from neighbors and friends
I have a feeling that it will keep getting better.*

*Please forgive me for not listening to you. You were
always so kind to me and I will always remember singing
with you in Georgia Hall and talking to you about my
problems. I am so glad you are at Warm Springs because
you probably help more people than you can ever imagine.*

Someday I hope to see you again.

Yours truly,

Ann Fay Honeycutt

I didn't know how Mr. Botts would take the letter, but
it sure relieved my mind. I knew what a busy person he
was, so I never imagined he would write me back. But one
day when I came home from school Momma handed me
an envelope from Warm Springs with my name typed on
the front. Inside was a letter typed on special paper with the
Warm Springs name at the top.

Georgia Warm Springs Foundation
Office of the Registrar
Warm Springs, Georgia

Dear Ann Fay,

I want to thank you for writing to me.
Naturally I was disappointed about your
abrupt departure from the Foundation.
However, I accept your apology.

It is good to hear that things are

improving at your house. I join your
family in praying that the improvement
continues.

Your father served his country with
courage and fortitude during extraordinary
times. President Roosevelt had much love
and admiration for all of his men and
women who served, and he would honor your
father, as do I.

I hope your rehabilitation continues as
well and that your time at Warm Springs
will benefit you for the rest of your life.

Sincerely,

Fred Botts

I can't tell you how relieved I was to get that letter. And
the words about President Roosevelt warmed my heart. I
knew they would make Daddy feel good too, but I could
never show them to him because then he would know that
Mr. Botts knew all his problems. I would just hate to see
how mad he would get over that!

Even before I wrote to Mr. Botts, I sent a letter to Suzanne. I needed to know if she got in trouble for helping
me. She wrote me back.

Dear Ann Fay,

*I hope you are fine. I'm doing okay but I miss you.
Olivia finished her therapy and went home. That is the
hardest part about being here. I get attached to people and
then they leave me.*

*About me getting in trouble for helping you. For once
in my life, I did not get caught. Your escape is a great topic
of conversation around here. You should hear the rumors
flying. It is hard for me not to correct people—especially
Sam. For once, I know more than he does and I just hate
that I have to keep my mouth shut about it.*

*Gavin said to tell you hi. Olivia told him why you had
to leave.*

Please come back sometime. Don't wait too long.

Your friend,

Suzanne

I folded the letter and thought how lucky I was to have
good friends. It made me feel better about not hearing from
Imogene. But I was embarrassed just thinking that Gavin
had heard the truth about my daddy.

It wasn't easy letting people in on our shame, but I reckon we couldn't have made it on our own.

When they realized Daddy was gone, my neighbors
did their level best to look after us. Junior started coming
around again. And his momma had us over for supper every
couple of weeks.

The Hinkle sisters got to where they accidentally cooked
up too big a pot of stew or too many pieces of chicken on a
regular basis. Then Miss Dinah would drop it by our house
and catch some snuggle time with Mr. Shoes.

Even though people seemed real worried about us, Daddy
came by every Friday night to give Momma his pay. And
on Saturdays he'd come and do work around the house.
But of course I was never there on account of my job.

Every Saturday I'd ask Otis about his momma. I
thought maybe now that Daddy was at their house he'd say

something besides good days and bad days. Like how his momma was feeding my daddy or how Daddy was fixing things around their house.

But he never did. One day he said, "Your daddy just needs time to work things out in his mind. He ain't no different than any one of them men inside that store." He jerked his head in the direction of the wall behind me.

"Every veteran is carrying pictures around in his head," said Otis. "Not the kind you take out of your wallet and show off, but the kind you want to rip up and throw away. Only thing is, this ain't photographs we're dealing with here. This is moving pictures with sound and everything. And sometimes the sounds are worse than the pictures.

"You never know what's going to make one of them moving pictures show up, Ann Fay. You think it's erased and then a car backfires or a baby cries and all of a sudden your mind isn't staring at a blank screen anymore. And what it's seeing ain't the kind of thing you tell to your wife and young'uns."

What Otis was saying made a lot of sense. I wondered if he knew by now what things my daddy was seeing when he gave my momma that black eye. And on that night when he went crazy on Ida for jumping out at him and saying *Boo*!

But I didn't ask him. Maybe I thought my daddy wouldn't want me to know what-all he'd told to Otis. And then again, maybe it was because *I* didn't want to know.

I know one thing, though. I found out me and Momma did the right thing by not putting Daddy in that insane asylum. Because one day when I was in the library at school I found a story in *Life* magazine that scared the living daylights out of me.

It was all about mental hospitals. And how bad the

conditions were. It said the hospitals didn't have enough help, the food was terrible, and sometimes the people who worked there beat the patients. Or tied them up. Some patients had to go around naked. And there were rats in some places.

It didn't mention the North Carolina hospital, but still, I started bawling just thinking how I even considered putting my daddy in one of them places.

38

Muddy Water
May–June 1946

One morning in May when I was putting on my leg brace, one of the leather straps on it came loose. I fiddled with it just long enough to get aggravated.

"Oh, bother!" I said. "How come Daddy's not here when I need him? What in tarnation do I do now?" I was so frustrated that I threw the brace on my bed and went to the kitchen for breakfast.

Of course my momma asked about it.

"A strap broke," I said.

"Oh, dear! That's not good," Momma said.

"It sure does *feel* good. Like getting out of jail. I think I'll go to school without it."

"No," said Momma. "Not without talking to Dr. Gaul."

I showed Momma how I could put my weight on my left leg. "As long as I have my cane, I don't even need it. Just let me try it for one day," I begged.

Momma went into the bedroom and got my brace. When she came back out, she said, "Maybe your daddy can take care of it on the weekend. Or Junior."

"Why can't we just leave Junior out of it?" I said. I did not want to be beholden to that boy for one more thing. "Really, Momma, walking is easier without all that metal."

Momma sighed. "You best be careful," she said. It looked like she was done trying to convince me. So I went to school without it.

I *was* careful. Not having the brace meant I depended on my cane more and I hung on to walls and desks when I moved around the school. But I did just fine.

When I came home at the end of the day, Momma was waiting on the porch and I could tell she had spent the day worrying about me. She met me halfway out our lane. "How did it go?"

"Just swell," I said. "I won't ever need that miserable thing again."

But when I got in the house, the brace was right there on top of my bedspread. I didn't know what else to do with it, so I stuffed it under my bed, behind some pasteboard boxes. "Good riddance!" I said.

For some reason Momma didn't argue with me. She just shook her head and laughed a bit.

"Can you believe Suzanne wears two of those things?" I asked her. "And when she was little, she even had to sleep in them."

Honest, I didn't know how Suzanne could stand it. I felt like a new person without that brace. Going to school was getting easier all the time. I decided that, by the next school year, I was going to participate with everyone else in recess. Once school was out, I would have plenty of time to get my strength up.

And then, almost before I was ready, it was the last day of school. Mrs. Barkley had tears in her eyes when she hugged me goodbye. "Ann Fay, you've come a long way since last August."

I hated to leave Mrs. Barkley. On the first day of school

she predicted I would have a good year. And looking back on it now, I realized I had.

I could feel how much stronger I was. And not just from going to Warm Springs. Every hard thing I'd been through at home and school had toughened me up in one way or another.

After school let out, I had a lot more time on my hands. I practiced all the exercises I did every day at Warm Springs. But I sure did miss exercising in that pool!

And I missed everything else about the foundation. At least Suzanne kept me informed on what was going on.

Dear Ann Fay,

I'm sending you some photographs that my uncle took. You can keep them for your scrapbook. There are notes on the back explaining who is who.

Remember Leon? (Mrs. Trotter's son.) Guess what he did. He has a pistol—not a real one, of course. But it looks real. One day last week he covered his face with ketchup and laid the gun by his head. When the nurse came in she screamed! So the whole hospital staff came running! He got a good laugh out of that. We all did. Even Mrs. Trotter seemed to think her son had pulled a good one! What would we do without practical jokes to keep us going around here?

Don't wait too long to visit me. You can stay in my red room and we'll be scrapbook fiends together.

Your friend,
Suzanne

That crazy story about Leon and the pictures of my friends made me really homesick for Warm Springs. One picture was of Mrs. Trotter and Leon. There was one of Mr. Botts. And a picture of Suzanne and Gavin with someone named Carolyn who came back to visit.

I almost didn't recognize Gavin because he was on crutches and I'd never seen him when he wasn't in a wheelchair. It gave me goose bumps to look at him. Partly from thinking about the two of us holding hands at Magic Hill. But also because I realized how Warm Springs could change anyone who was lucky enough to go there.

At first I tucked the pictures in the frame around my mirror, where I could see them when I brushed my hair. But they made me smile one day and cry the next, so I finally decided to put them in the scrapbook Suzanne had sent home with me. I had fun writing little notes about each picture.

Of course I put the Franklin Roosevelt First Day of Issue stamps in the album. And Suzanne's letters. Gavin never wrote to me, and I sure didn't write to him. As far as I was concerned, he was like Warm Springs itself. Just a memory. He was a prince and I was Cinderella. Except I never even had a glass slipper.

There were more blank pages in the album, but I wasn't sure what I should put on them. A picture of Imogene would be real good. If only I had one.

Sometimes I thought my life wasn't much to put down on paper. Who would care anyway? But still, I figured maybe someday I would want to look back on this year and all I went through.

I even started dreaming about buying a camera for my family so I could take pictures of my own. I didn't have more than a few Roosevelt dimes saved, but at least it was a start.

The girls loved the peach bank Ma Harding gave me. If they found a penny on the ground, they would always drop it in there. That was another reason to regret leaving Warm Springs in such a hurry. I should have brought back some Georgia peach keepsakes for Ida and Ellie.

Ever since school was out, the twins spent lots of time in Mysteria Mansion. They were making up some play about bootleggers and they bugged me constantly with questions I didn't know how to answer. About moonshine and Junior's car and how fast would it go. And policemen.

Thinking about policemen just reminded me of my wrongdoings, and that made me feel crummy. So I usually told the girls to scram. One Wednesday evening when I got tired of the girls' questions I asked Momma would she mind if I went for a walk.

Of course I headed across the field to listen to the singing at the colored church. The field was planted in cotton, so I had to go around the edges. By the time I got across it I was dripping with sweat and plumb wore out. So I sat by the road with my feet in the side ditch and leaned against a fence post.

I loved how the singing of Imogene's people sounded so different from what I heard at my own church. It's not like I could actually hear the words. I'd catch a line here and there about the River Jordan, or Moses, or Mary, don't you weep. But mostly I just soaked up the sounds of voices going up and down.

I wasn't sitting on that side ditch for ten minutes before I saw Junior's car coming down the road. The next thing I knew, he was stopped in front of me.

"Ann Fay, are you okay? What in the world are you doing?"

"Of course I'm okay. I'm just listening to the singing."

"Singing?"

"From the church." I jerked my head in the direction of the building across the dirt road. Junior gave one glance in that direction and shook his head like he thought I was crazy or something.

"I think you better get in this car."

"No," I said. "I'm perfectly fine. Look what a beautiful night it is."

"Well, it's going to be dark soon, so let me drive you home. How long they going to be singing?"

I shrugged.

"The least you can do is sit in the car while you listen."

Well, I didn't mind sitting outside, but I was happy for a ride home, so I pulled myself up and started to climb through the side ditch. But Junior got out to help me. After I was in the front seat he pulled the car to the other side of the road, closer to the church. He turned off the engine. When he did, the sound of their singing was real clear.

"I can't believe you come across that field on canes to hear that," he said.

"Don't you like it?"

Junior shrugged. "It's okay. But Ann Fay, that's a hike!"

"Oh, it's not that bad," I said. "I'm getting used to it."

"You done this before?"

"Sometimes when I'm having a bad day those people singing is all that gets me through."

Junior just shook his head. "Ann Fay—honest to Pete!"

"What?" I asked. From the edge in my voice, Junior could probably tell I was fixing to fuss with him. "Is it all right if I want to hear colored people sing? They sing what I feel—*Fix me, Jesus* and songs about tribulation and sorrows. And not only that—those songs remind me of Imogene, who I'll probably never see again in my whole life! But you probably think I should forget about Imogene, don't you, Junior?"

"Did I say you should forget her?"

"I know you're thinking it."

He shook his head. "No, you don't," he said. "On account of I'm thinking you should just go see her and get it over with."

I was shocked when he said that. "Oh, well—that's easy for you to say. Imogene lives in Greensboro, you know."

"Well, if you told me, I forgot. Do you have her address?"

"Of course I do. She writes to me." That wasn't exactly true. I mean, I had got one letter from her soon after I got home from the hospital, but that was all. Still, I did have her address.

"Well then, let's go see her."

Was he saying he would take me? "Are you saying you'll take me?" I asked him.

"Well, sure," said Junior. "Why not?"

That's what I was asking myself. Why shouldn't I let Junior take me to Greensboro? But I knew why not. Mostly because I figured he was sick and tired of me always wanting a favor of some kind. And because I thought that he was a little bit mad ever since I'd hurt his feelings on the way home from Warm Springs. Part of me said I couldn't let him take me to see Imogene. I'd be using him if I did. I was starting to think I was real good at using people—especially Junior.

And another thing. Now that Junior was saying he'd drive me to Greensboro, all of a sudden it seemed real far away.

I thought how Imogene had said there was a muddy wide river between my people and hers. How many bridges would I have to cross to get there? It felt real complicated. I didn't see how I could do it without Momma finding out about it. And she wouldn't let me go.

"It's real big of you to offer," I said to Junior. "I'll be thinking about when's a good time."

I did think about it, too. I laid in bed that night and couldn't get to sleep for thinking about visiting Imogene. I thought about her momma too. And how Imogene said she didn't like white people.

I was holding on to my little wooden Comfort when I finally fell asleep that night. And it's a good thing, too, on account of I dreamed about bridges without guardrails on the side. Rivers swirled right up to the edges. Muddy water was everywhere.

39

Imogene

June 1946

The next Sunday, Junior announced on the way home from church that he could take me to see Imogene that afternoon. I expected Momma to argue, but she didn't.

Well, I was sure surprised. Momma hadn't acted much interested in me going to see Imogene, but maybe she was changing her mind about that. Or maybe she just couldn't say no to Junior. And that brought up another question. Why was *he* so interested?

But what I wondered about the most was why I felt the way I did. Why did I get the jitters after Junior first said he'd take me?

When Junior came, I said, "Maybe this isn't such a good idea. You don't have to take me if you don't want to."

"Ann Fay, what has got into you? Do you want to go or not?"

"I don't know," I said. "It's been almost a year since Imogene wrote. So how do I know if she even wants to see me?"

"Well, you're fixing to find out." Junior shut the car door. I watched him go around the front and get in his side. I couldn't help but notice how he'd grown lately. His shoulders were broader and he walked taller or something.

And he was acting mighty tough too—taking charge of

this little visit like he actually cared whether I saw Imogene or not. I fretted practically the whole way. "What if they aren't home?" I asked. "What if her daddy runs us off their property? What if Imogene doesn't remember me?"

Junior laughed when I said that. "Settle down," he said. "You're talking outta your head." I reckon he thought a song would calm me down. Because the next thing I knew he was singing, *"Oh, what a beautiful morning, Oh, what a beautiful day."*

"Junior," I said. "If you think your singing makes me feel better, you best think again."

"Help me out, then." Junior went back to the song. *"I've got a beautiful feeling, Everything's going my way."*

"That song is a big fat lie," I said. "If you insist on singing, maybe you ought to try, *Down in the valley, the valley so low.*"

He didn't pay me any mind. He just sang all three verses of his song. All the way to the end where it says, *An ol' weepin' willer is laughin' at me.*

It was pretty sad, actually. His singing was so bad I couldn't help but laugh.

"What do you know!" said Junior. "The weeping willow is laughing now."

I have to say he did cheer me up. Somehow he made me feel like this trip wasn't going to end in disaster.

When we got to Greensboro we had a little trouble finding Imogene's address. By this time it felt like my insides were doing the jitterbug all over again. So I said, "Can we just let it go?"

"Of course not. We come all this way." And then finally we found the street we were looking for. And the house with Imogene's number. There was a man and a woman sitting on the steps. The man was smoking cigarettes and the woman was flipping through a magazine. A couple of children were pushing each other on the porch swing.

I didn't see Imogene anywhere. But I saw how the woman looked up from the magazine and elbowed the man. He got up and started down the sidewalk.

Junior got out of the car then and went to greet him. He stopped at the end of the sidewalk and waited to see what the man would do. The man eyed him real cautious and nodded the least bit. "Can I help you?"

Junior handed him the envelope with Imogene's handwriting on it. "My friend is looking for Imogene Wilfong," he said. The woman stood then and come to stand by her husband. The children on the swing had left it and were crowding around too.

Junior came to my car door and opened it for me. "This is Ann Fay."

The man nodded. "Hello, missy," he said.

I started working on getting myself out of the car. "I don't see Imogene," I whispered to Junior. But he helped me out of the car anyway. And he got my canes for me while I hung on to the car door. But for some reason I didn't take it. Instead I hung on to his arm and walked without the canes. It made me feel a little stronger.

That's when I heard her momma say, "Jesse, get Imogene." So one of the boys went running into the house, yelling as he went.

"Imogene, there's some white folks out here looking for you!" He let the screen door slam behind him.

The man said, "Did y'all want to come up and sit a spell?" It wasn't exactly an invitation. Just a question. Like if we said yes, he would let us.

But that didn't mean the same thing as him wanting us to.

"If you don't mind," said Junior. So the man turned and the woman did too and we followed them up the sidewalk.

I noticed that some people at the house next door had come out on the porch. And I heard voices across the street. I knew without looking that everybody in the neighborhood had come out to see what the white folks was up to.

Junior helped me up the steps and onto the porch swing. "We can just sit out here," he said. I wished he hadn't said that. Imogene's daddy might get the impression we didn't want to go in their house. All of a sudden I was feeling really white. And analyzing every little thing Junior said and everything Imogene's family did and everything I didn't do.

"I'll get some lemonade," said Mrs. Wilfong, and she went inside.

Then I heard Imogene's voice. "Who's here, Momma?"

"Go on outside and see for yourself. I'll bring you some lemonade."

It was real quiet then, except for some whispers and giggles and Imogene's crutches in the hallway. And her braces clicking. And maybe the sound of my heart going extra fast. Then a girl came out and it wasn't Imogene either. She held the door and then I saw Imogene's face peering out.

I wish I could say it lit up like a candle, but it didn't. It might've even got a little darker for a second. Like she was thinking, *Uh-oh, I got a problem on my hands.* But then she smiled and said, "Ann Fay, I do declare. I never expected to see you today!"

She come through the door on her crutches and stood there and stared at me. I knew it was my turn to say something. "I just wanted to see if you're okay," I said. "You haven't written in a long time." It sounded like I was accusing her.

"I'm okay," said Imogene. Then she looked at the other girl, who was standing there watching the two of us. "This here is my friend Sue Etta."

"I'm happy to meet you," said Sue Etta.

"I'm glad to meet you too," I said. But I had a feeling Imogene was telling me she had her own friends now—colored ones—and she didn't need me anymore.

Just then I heard her momma's voice. "Jesse, can you please open the door for me?"

Jesse, who was busy staring at Junior, jumped up and did just that. Imogene and Sue Etta sat on chairs that Mr. Wilfong pulled up for them. And Mrs. Wilfong came through the open screen door with a tray of drinking glasses with orange and blue flowers painted on the side of them.

Mr. Wilfong took the tray from her, and she handed me a glass and then gave one to Junior and then Imogene and her friend.

Jesse wanted to know could he have some lemonade. "Come inside and I'll get you a cup," said Imogene's mother. "That goes for the rest of you too," she said to the other children. "How do you expect these girls to get reacquainted with you sitting there staring?"

So Mr. Wilfong rounded up all of Imogene's brothers and sisters and took them inside. But I wouldn't exactly say that me and Imogene got reacquainted. We tried. I asked her about school and what she was doing this summer. And I told her about Warm Springs.

"I'm sorry I didn't write," said Imogene. "But I did save your letters. Every last one of them."

I nodded. "I have yours, too."

"I still got the rose. Do you want to see it?"

She was talking about the yellow rose the Lion's Club

gave me at the Charlotte hospital. That's where they took us when Hickory's emergency hospital shut down. They had put the roses in the train station to honor President Roosevelt the night his funeral train came through. After the train passed, they brought them to us polios. At least to the white patients.

I gave my rose to Imogene.

Junior held the screen door, and Imogene and Sue Etta led us into the house. It was hot in there and darker too. It took a minute for my eyes to adjust to the darkness in the front room. There were two couches in the room and some other furniture, but I didn't pay them much mind. I was busy watching my step on their pretty flowered rug.

Imogene took me to the corner cupboard, and sure enough, there was the faded yellow rose laying behind the glass on a lace doily. And beside the rose was the letter I wrote her to go with it.

Dear Imogene,

I reckon you heard the sad news. I reckon everyone has heard. They give us each a rose that was bought just to honor the president when his train come through town. I want you to have mine. Yellow roses always dry real nice, so I know it will keep for a long time. Keep it forever and always think of me and the best president this country ever had.

Your friend,
Ann Fay Honeycutt

I stood there and read that letter and I had the hardest time holding back the tears. Did Imogene think about me anymore? Maybe it was for nothing that I gave up my precious rose. Maybe it didn't even mean a thing to her.

Then she spoke up. "I ain't forgot what you did for me," she said. "And I never will."

I looked at her and I knew that everything we'd talked about in the polio hospital was real. That, in an emergency, they could break the rules and put blacks and whites side by side in the same hospital. And we could even become best friends—for a little while.

But maybe other people weren't ready for blacks and whites to become good friends. And maybe we weren't ready either. All of a sudden I knew it was true what Imogene had told me in the hospital. There was a muddy wide river between her people and mine. And it would take more than a polio epidemic to get us across it.

But who wanted another emergency?

By now I knew I could overcome just about any obstacle I bumped up against. So maybe the real problem was that we all just liked being comfortable. Maybe making changes was too scary as long as things were running along smooth. Who wanted to go stirring up trouble where there wasn't any?

I bit my lip to keep from crying, and Imogene must've noticed. "Do you want the rose back?" she asked.

"No!" I said.

It wasn't true. I did want that rose. But I didn't want Imogene to think I was asking for it. I for sure didn't want her to give it to me. On account of that would be like taking away everything we had between us. And even if we couldn't be friends in the future, there was no way I was going to take my chances on losing what we had in the past.

After all, she was the one who helped me see that even something that hurts can make us stronger. You just have to face it, and after a while it starts to get better.

40

Pure Comfort
July 1946

By the middle of July, when Daddy came by the house he would even come inside. But he always knocked first.

I noticed Momma made sure there was always a fresh batch of iced tea on Saturday mornings. The twins told me she'd send them out to the garden with cold drinks a couple of times during the day. And she'd set sandwiches on the porch and he'd come and eat on the steps with them. One time the girls even talked him into a picnic in Mysteria Mansion.

Part of me wanted to be home on the days that Daddy was there. But at least I had my ride to work and back again in the truck with him. From all I could tell, my daddy was more at peace with himself.

One Friday evening he came by the house earlier than usual. Otis was with him. Momma was taking clothes off the line, so Daddy went out back to help her. I invited Otis inside for a glass of tea. I told him I couldn't believe how my momma and daddy were getting along.

I knew Otis wasn't a doctor or a preacher or anyone who might really know—but still I believed him when he said my daddy would be all right.

"I reckon a man is just born for guilt," he said. "Guilt for leaving his family in time of war. And guilt for what he does to other people's families. Then he finds himself in danger of ruining the family he wanted to stay home with in the first place. It's a terrible thing, living with all that guilt."

Otis shook his head. It seemed like he was trying to shake some sadness out. "It's a good thing I don't have me a family to ruin," he said.

"Tell me the truth, Otis. Is he getting better?"

Otis looked at me. "I'm not going to sit here and act like I'm a fancy doctor," he said. "But if you're asking for my humble opinion, I think he's making progress. For one thing, he don't seem to have nightmares so much any-more."

I didn't tell Otis what I read in *Life* magazine about mental hospitals. It scared me too bad to even mention it. But I said, "You know what, Otis? I think you might be do-ing him more good than any doctor ever could."

Momma and Daddy come up on the porch then. Daddy had the basket with the clothes in it. He held the door for Momma to go in first. He stood outside their bedroom door and waited to see what she wanted him to do with the bas-ket. She gave a little nod and he took the clothes in there and put them on the bed.

Did he notice how she changed the room around—like she was getting a fresh start without him? I figured he must be seeing lots of differences in Momma. It seemed like the bigger she got with that baby, the more sure of herself she was.

I could see Daddy in their room folding the clothes just like he belonged in that house. And all of a sudden I wished in the worst way that he didn't have to go back to Otis and his mother's.

276

Momma invited both of them to stay for supper. Daddy put on an apron and peeled the potatoes while the twins set the table and Otis poured the water. Momma made cornbread and heated up some leftover pintos. I chopped the onions for the beans, and they made the tears run down my cheeks. But I felt like having a good cry anyway. And it wasn't on account of being sad. It was because my family was all in the kitchen together and no one was yelling or tiptoeing around in fear.

Otis told us stories while we ate. The girls giggled and Momma smiled.

"Comfort," said Daddy. "Pure comfort, that's what this meal is." But from the way he looked at us sitting around the table and how his eyes landed on Momma's big belly, I had a feeling he was talking about a lot more than food.

41

Getting to Normal

July 1946

The next Friday Daddy moved back in. I looked into his blue eyes and tried to see how much of the old daddy was still there. He was grinning real big, but his eyes seemed like they had questions in them. Like he wasn't so sure how it was going to go.

In no time his arms were around me. And it felt so natural and so surprising at the same time, like when he picked me up at the Charlotte hospital the year before. It was the exact same moment I found out he was home from the war. But of course he had brought a lot of that war home with him. How much did he bring this time?

I didn't want to go to work the next morning, but Mrs. Whitener was expecting me. So Daddy drove me there. He even parked the truck, which made me think he was coming inside with me. But he wasn't. Instead he joined the men sitting on the bench outside the door.

I went inside and started wiping down the countertop and straightening things up the way I knew Mrs. Whitener liked them. But I kept my eye on Daddy through the window. Every now and again I would see his head nod. I was real curious about what they were saying. I could hear them but not enough to make out the words.

Daddy left before Otis showed up at his usual time. There were two other customers when Otis came in, so while I fished him out a dill pickle I didn't mention my daddy. Instead I asked, "How's your momma doing?" Of course I already knew his momma had good days and bad days, she did. But for some reason I wanted to hear him say it. I had got to where I was real fond of Otis and his strange ways.

While I collected money from the next customer, I saw that Otis was watching me. His left eye twitched a little and I thought how sweet he looked, even if his eyes didn't work together. Would I have noticed that sweet look of his before all the bad things happened? At least polio taught me to see people for more than just the parts that didn't work right.

I had a feeling Otis missed my daddy now that he had come home. The next afternoon Otis showed up at our house. I was reading on the front porch when he got there. Momma and Daddy were taking their Sunday afternoon nap just like they always did, which made things seem almost back to normal.

"I'll go get Daddy," I said. "He'll be waking up any minute now anyhow."

"No," said Otis. "Don't disturb them. Whatcha reading?"

I held up the book.

"Well," he said, "why don't you read out loud? I like a story as much as the next person."

So I did. I finished the chapter I was on and had started in to the next one when Daddy came out onto the porch, tucking his shirttail in his pants and pushing his hair back with his hand. "Well, look who's here," he said. He pulled up a rocking chair for himself and pushed one toward Otis.

"Nah," said Otis. "I don't mind the floor. Your daughter's a mighty fine reader."

"Yeah," said Daddy. "But there's something wrong when the children turn out smarter than their parents." Then he winked at me. "That's my opinion and it's worth two cents." He pulled his knife and a stick of wood from his pocket and started to whittling. "Go on and read, Ann Fay," he said.

Well, I almost couldn't read for the feeling that come over me then. I knew from Daddy winking that he was actually proud of me this time. And the other thing that made me feel so good was how he said that about his opinion being worth two cents. My whole life I'd heard my daddy use that expression—until he went off to the war. I was pretty sure I hadn't heard him say it since.

And hearing it now—well, it made me feel like maybe my daddy really was getting back to his old self.

Otis had a knife and a whittling project in his pocket too. I wanted to just sit there and soak up the look of those two men chipping away at their pieces of wood. But I read to them instead because they seemed to like it.

After a while Otis got up to leave, but Daddy wouldn't hear of it. "Don't rush off," he said. "It's time for biscuits and gravy." So Otis stayed for supper. While he ate lots of Momma's mashed potatoes he teased the girls and told stories about when he was a little boy.

I decided I knew why he talked so much. He was lonely. Even if he did live with his mother, she had probably heard all his stories already—maybe a dozen times.

Just a few evenings later Peggy Sue and her parents came by the house too. The whole family—except for Momma, who had got so big she could barely get down the front steps—was working in the garden. When Daddy looked up and saw the Rhineharts drive in, he said we could pick the rest of the squash and cucumbers later.

So we all went to sit on the front porch, and Momma poured iced tea. After we drank it, Ellie wanted me and Peggy Sue to go with her and Ida to Mysteria Mansion.

I hadn't told Peggy Sue about giving our mansion to the girls, so I started explaining. "The twins have taken over Wisteria Mansion since we never go there anymore. I hope you don't mind. Wanna go see it?"

I filled her in on the details while we went. "Forget about that place where nothing bad ever happens," I said. "Ever since the twins got ahold of our mansion, nothing good goes on down there."

Once we were inside, Ida and Ellie made us sit and the two of them disappeared for a minute. Then Ida reappeared all dramatic, like she was Shirley Temple herself. "And now," she said, "Mysteria Mansion presents 'The Mystery of the Deep Pine Woods.'"

Ellie came out and said in a creepy voice, "It was a dark night in the deep pine woods, and a little girl named Lula was lost—real bad lost. And there were bootleggers in the woods too."

Then Ida pretended to be a bootlegger and Ellie turned into the lost girl. Somehow the two of them acted out a whole play in which Lula found a moonshine still and the bootleggers caught her and stuffed her in the trunk of their car with bottles of whiskey. Policemen chased them around curvy roads, but the moonshiners had real fast cars. A boy named Junior had an even faster car. So he cornered the bootleggers on a dead-end road and rescued Lula. And of course he drove her straight home.

"That was good!" I said when they finished. "You

should've told Daddy and Momma and Peggy Sue's parents to come watch it."

"No," said Ida. "We need more practice. And we need to get some bottles together for the moonshine and find us an old car seat for the car."

"Well," I said, "if you need an old car seat, talk to Otis. He collects a lot of junk around his house."

So Ida and Ellie got to thinking of all the things they could ask Otis for the next time he came over. When we got back to the house they went inside to make a list.

A few days later Otis showed up at the house and they pulled out the list. "Do you have an old car seat?" asked Ellie. "On account of we need one for our play."

"Yeah," said Ida. "And we need some whiskey bottles too. And an old barrel for our moonshine still."

"Moonshine!" said Otis. "When did the two of you take up with the bad guys?"

Ellie giggled. "It's just pretend," she said.

Daddy came out of the house just then, and the girls started begging to go to Otis's house to look for an old car seat. Before Daddy could say no, Otis spoke up. "I don't mind," he said.

So after supper Daddy took him home and let the girls ride along. From the sound of their voices when they came home later, I could tell the twins had had a good time.

"Momma!" hollered Ellie.

"Ann Fay!" yelled Ida. "Come and look what we got."

It was getting dark by this time, so we could barely make out what was on the back of Daddy's truck. The car seat the girls wanted was there, but another seat was there too—shining in the dark. It was a toilet! And a sink too. And some pipes and a pile of boards.

Daddy put his arm around Momma. "Looks like our dream is coming true," he said. "All this time we've been hankering after a bathroom and Otis had one in his backyard."

Momma's mouth was open so wide you could've practically filled it with that bathroom sink. "Did you pay for it?" she asked.

Daddy shook his head. "Otis wouldn't hear of it. He said this is his way of thanking you for that good home cooking. And in case you think he hasn't eaten enough mashed potatoes to pay for it, I expect he'll be back for more."

And that's how it happened that on Saturday, Daddy and Otis started closing in the back porch to turn it into a bathroom. But first they went to town and bought a kitchen sink and a pump. And Junior Bledsoe helped them pick a heavy old bathtub with fancy feet on it out of the weeds at Otis's place and unload it off the truck at our house.

"A body just can never tell when a dream might come true," said Momma. She was rubbing her big tummy, so it was hard to know which dream she was talking about.

42

Nothing Finer!

July 1946

Bessie Bledsoe gave us about two weeks with Daddy back at home. Then she started making plans for the whole family to come to her house for supper. "And she wants the Hinkle sisters to be there too," said Junior. He'd come down special to inform us.

Then all of a sudden the plans changed. Miss Dinah dropped in to invite us to their house instead. "I've already talked to Bessie," she said. "She and Junior will join us. And Bessie will make fresh peach pie from those trees in her yard." Somehow she managed to get her words out between kisses from Mr. Shoes.

Daddy told Miss Dinah that he would be working on our bathroom that Saturday. "So Otis Hickey will be here too," he explained.

"Sure," said Miss Dinah. "Bring Otis along. The more the merrier! When supper is over you men can all go back to work while the women visit."

So that's what we did.

When I came home from working at the store on Saturday I just couldn't believe how much of that bathroom was done. The pump wasn't hooked up yet and the pipes weren't in place, but the room was closed in and there was a commode, sink, and bathtub all set in place.

My family was actually going to have a real bathroom! We could get rid of the chamber pot for good, and even though the outhouse was still in the backyard, we wouldn't have to go out there. "Unless," said Daddy, "we start missing old johnny!"

Daddy and Otis were fixing to put the pump into the well when Junior had to leave to take his momma and the food she cooked up to the Hinkle sisters'.

"Well, that's our cue," said Daddy. "Time for us to get ready for supper." So they put their work aside for a while, which almost made me want to skip the supper altogether.

Momma felt the same way. "It would be so easy to stay home," she said, and she gave out a big sigh. It seemed almost like she was in pain or something. But she hadn't been comfortable for the last couple of weeks, so I figured she was just ready to get the baby out of there.

Well, I didn't have any idea just how ready she was, or how quick something like that could happen! It seemed like it wasn't more than five minutes after we sat down at the Hinkle sisters' table when I noticed that Momma had only taken a tiny spoonful of each thing and was just pushing it all around on her plate.

Beads of sweat was standing out on her forehead. That wasn't surprising, considering how hot it was and how every last one of us was sweating. But it was more than just the sweating I was worrying about—it was the twitches in her face. And the way she would bite her lip and suck in her breath so loud I thought everyone at the table could hear it.

But Otis was telling a story about how when he was a child he got separated from his parents at the Old Soldiers

Reunion. And how the mayor of Newton found him and took him up to the stage and made an announcement to everyone at the parade that this child's parents were lost. And how he boo-hoo'd into the megaphone. So right when a group of clowns was going down the street handing out candy and trying to make little children laugh, he, Otis, was crying louder than any other noise at the parade.

Of course everyone at the table was laughing too, just listening to the story—except Momma, who looked like she was fixing to bust into tears.

You would think that I was the one with a megaphone. On account of all of a sudden I interrupted Otis and said, "Can't y'all see this is no laughing matter? Momma isn't feeling good. Are you, Momma?"

That's when Momma put down her fork and gave up on pretending to eat. She just gave up on good manners altogether. "Leroy," she said, "take me home this instant. I'm about to have our baby."

Well, just like that, my daddy jumped up. "Yes, ma'am!" he said. He looked scared. "Someone call Dr. Johnson. Ask him to come to our house quick!"

But Miss Pauline wouldn't hear of sending Momma home. "What if that baby decides to come on the way?" she said. "No sirree, I'm not about to let you have that baby in a pickup truck. And what if you get home but Dr. Johnson doesn't get there in time?"

"You can use my bed," said Miss Dinah. She jumped up and headed in there to get it ready.

But Miss Pauline wouldn't hear of that either. "Dinah, that dog has been on your bed. It is not a fit place for a baby to be born. Myrtle will use *my* room."

She went back to her bedroom door and opened it,

but of course, the minute she did, Mr. Shoes ran inside.

Well, you should've seen Miss Pauline then. She reached for the nearest thing, which was the telephone directory that Bessie was using to look up Dr. Johnson's number, and ran after Mr. Shoes. She must have swatted him with that directory, too, on account of he yelped and ran back out.

Miss Pauline took Momma by the arm and told Bessie to boil some water, and then she shooed all the men out of the house. "Go back to work on that bathroom," she said.

"Maybe I should wait until the doctor gets here," said Daddy.

"Don't be ridiculous," said Miss Pauline. "Leave the babies to us women. You've got men's work to do. Now go do it! You're going to need that bathroom more than ever. And take that dog with you!" She gave Daddy a little push and Otis pulled him the rest of the way out the door.

Junior shrugged and then he followed Daddy and Otis. They acted reluctant, but I had a feeling all three of them were relieved to be leaving the baby-delivering to us women. The next thing I knew, they were driving out the lane in Junior's car. But they forgot to take Mr. Shoes with them.

I don't know how Miss Pauline knew so much about delivering babies, but you would've thought she'd done it before. The truth is, she used to be a schoolteacher and it seemed like her natural bossiness just kicked in.

"You girls go outside," she said to Ida and Ellie. She looked at me then and jerked her head a little in the direction of the back door.

So I said, "Come on. Let's go wait for Dr. Johnson. Y'all can stand at the end of the driveway and flag him down so he doesn't miss it." I led the way out to the back steps. When I passed the dining room table I thought what a shame it was that most of that good food was still there filling up our plates. But I don't suppose any of us was in a mood to eat just then.

I sat on the steps and sent up prayers for Momma. And I prayed Dr. Johnson would get there soon.

Which he did. All of a sudden I heard the girls yelling and saw them waving. Dr. Johnson turned into the Hinkle sisters' lane and stopped his car. He jumped out and shut the door and then reached back inside the open window for his black bag.

The girls started to follow him into the house. "Ida and Ellie, you sit down here," I said. "He doesn't need your help."

But then I heard a baby cry and knew it had gotten there ahead of the doctor. So I didn't bother making the twins stay outside. In fact, I let go of Mr. Shoes and got up to follow them. Mr. Shoes ran in—right between Dr. Johnson's feet. I saw that he went straight into Miss Pauline's room.

By the time I got in there he was snuggled in next to Momma. Miss Pauline hadn't even noticed on account of she was busy telling the doctor how it all happened.

Dr. Johnson let me and the girls go in and look at the baby. He was all wrinkly, and he had a head of brown curly hair that put me in mind of my momma and my brother Bobby both. And I thought how nice it was of him to come out a boy instead of another girl. I didn't think I could handle one more girl in this family, and I had a feeling a boy would do Daddy proud.

When Miss Pauline saw Mr. Shoes there on the bed, she swatted him with a coat hanger. "Take that dog home, would you please?" she said to Miss Dinah. But it wasn't really a question. More like a schoolteacher telling a class to get quiet *right now*! So Miss Dinah and me and the girls all climbed into her car and we took Mr. Shoes with us.

The girls were out of the car practically before it came to a stop in front of our house. "It's a boy," they shouted together. They went running into the house yelling at the top of their lungs, and by the time I made it to the porch my daddy was coming out the front door.

I doubt he had time to put one pipe in place since he got back there. And now he was leaving again—to see his new baby boy.

I went through the kitchen and out to the back porch. Otis and Junior was busy lowering the pump down into the well so we could get water into the new bathroom.

Maybe it was all the excitement of the new baby, but my nerves were just on edge. Every time I watched Junior leaning into that well, I got a real dizzy feeling. In my mind I kept seeing him going headfirst into the dark water. So I started fussing at him the way Momma does at Daddy when he climbs up on the roof to clean out the chimney and she thinks he's going to fall.

"Junior," I said. "Would you be careful? You're fixing to fall right in that well."

But of course he just ignored me. I know he heard me, though, because he leaned in a little more. Showing off! I couldn't hardly stand to look. Finally I said, "Junior Bledsoe, if you fall in that well, I promise I will never speak to you again."

So he pulled his head out and gave me a big old grin. "No point in talking to a dead man. What I wanna know is, would you fish me back out or just leave me there?"

I made a face at him. "I couldn't just leave you on account of the water wouldn't be fit to drink after that."

Junior gave me a big wink then and said, "Who knows—

it might taste better than ever." And then he disappeared into the new bathroom to work on the plumbing on that end.

I sat on the porch and watched the stars pop up into the sky one by one. And the lightning bugs blinking on and off. Like they couldn't make up their mind what they wanted to do. Shine or not shine.

I felt that way myself sometimes. Like I didn't know what I wanted either. Sometimes I wanted in the worst way to go back to Warm Springs. To have myself a life that was finer and more interesting than this one right here. But then there were moments like this when the people I loved most were nearby and life wasn't boring at all. It was wild and crazy and filled with good food and new things to do and talk about and laugh over.

I thought about Imogene and how, if we couldn't be friends, at least I could listen to the songs of her people any Sunday or Wednesday night when I took a notion. And that was something to look forward to!

It got dark then. Too dark for Otis and Junior to get any more work done. I figured Momma would be sleeping in Miss Pauline's bed that night and wondered if Daddy would too. I just couldn't picture that. Where would Miss Pauline sleep? On the sofa? Or with her sister in that bed Mr. Shoes had been leaving his hairs on?

I laughed just thinking about it.

Junior told Otis he'd drive him home and he asked me to ride along. "The girls can come too," he said.

Well, the thought of being at home trying to get two excited little girls into bed was more than I could handle, so we all piled in. But by the time we were passing the Hinkle sisters' house, the twins were begging to go see their new brother again.

So we dropped them off. I almost went with them, but Junior talked me out of it. "That baby will be here when you get back," he said. He was right, of course, so I stayed in the car.

When we got to Otis's house, the headlights on Junior's car lit up the odd piles of junk in his backyard. It made me feel like getting out and walking through there to see what other treasures Otis had been storing up. But I just thanked him for hanging on to practically a whole bathroom just for us.

"Not a problem," he said. "Not a problem at all." And he got out of the car and went into his house.

As Junior backed out of the driveway, I watched him in the light of the dashboard, thinking how he looked so different to me now. It used to be that he was just an annoying neighbor boy who thought he was an expert on every little thing. I never knew whether to be glad he was there or wish he would go away.

But now it seemed like he had changed. Or maybe I was the one who was different. On account of now I realized that if he did go away—whether he fell into a well or just drove off in his car and never came back—I would not like it one bit.

Junior stepped on the gas until the air coming in the window whipped my hair into my face so that I couldn't see him so well anymore. The sounds of the crickets and tree frogs blurred into a song of sorts, and for some reason it put me in mind of Junior's singing.

I started singing myself. "*Nothing could be finer than to be in Carolina...*"

Junior joined in. And honestly? He really should've left the singing to me. But for once I didn't care that he couldn't carry a tune.

I just liked that the two of us were singing the same song.

Epilogue

I'm not saying my daddy was all the way better just on account of he and Otis talked about the war.

Or because Momma had him a baby boy.

I'm not saying he hopped out of bed every day singing, "*Oh, what a beautiful morning.*"

As Otis would say, "He has his good days and his bad days, he does."

And I reckon that's the way it should be.

The truth is, if my daddy had come home from war as cool as a slice of watermelon, I'd think he wasn't my daddy at all.

Someone with a heart like his can't watch people die (and take part in it too) without breaking right into pieces.

I reckon what happened to him is sort of like me getting polio. Only worse.

Disaster snuck up on both of us and after that nothing was the same ever again.

In that way, me and my daddy are still alike.

Sometimes we both think no one understands what we're going through.

And maybe they don't.

But with a little help from our friends, the two of us have more good days than bad ones, we do...

It mostly hurts at first.

After a while it starts to feel better...

Author's Note

I wrote *Comfort* because I needed to find out what happened to Ann Fay after *Blue* ended. I suspected that war had changed her relationship with her father, and I knew that polio would have created physical and emotional adjustments for her.

As an author, however, I don't simply decide what will happen to my characters. I have to read, interview, and listen to history in order to find my plot. In this case I was surprised to discover that my fictional character Ann Fay did not remain at home with her family but instead went to Warm Springs, Georgia, for rehabilitation. As I researched I began to feel that it was a special honor to tell the Warm Springs story.

When Franklin Roosevelt established the Georgia Warm Springs Foundation, he wanted to provide a place where "polios"—as people who had polio often call themselves—could rehabilitate physically and thrive emotionally. At Warm Springs, polios learned physical and life skills, and—perhaps even more important—they rediscovered themselves as people who were not defined by their disability. Many of them later brought their new awareness to the public arena.

Hugh Gallagher was one alumnus who did. He had been at Warm Springs in the 1950s. When he later worked for Senator Bob Bartlett in Washington, DC, he discovered that it was impossible for him to enter many government buildings without special assistance. With the support of Senator Bartlett, he wrote the Architectural Barriers Act. Its passage led to the installation of ramps, elevators, automatic doors, and other accessible features in public buildings across the nation.

In 1962, another polio, Ed Roberts, gained the right to attend college in an iron lung. His efforts to establish accessibility and fairness for people with many kinds of disabilities began at the University of California at Berkeley. From there, an independent-living movement spread across the nation, so that people with disabilities could have what they needed to live on their own, without special assistance.

Eventually, the efforts of Hugh Gallagher, Ed Roberts, and other polios brought about the passage of the ADA, the Americans with Disability Act, which condemned discrimination against people with disabilities. The ADA provided them with equal opportunities for jobs, housing, education, and public services.

Postwar Trauma

At about the same time that the disability-rights movement was gaining strength, soldiers were returning from the Vietnam War. Many were showing signs of postwar trauma. Vietnam veterans and their families began to ask for help, and as a result, war trauma began to be acknowledged as a serious problem.

Today we usually label the problem Post-Traumatic Stress Disorder (PTSD), a term that refers to various reactions people can have after *any* kind of traumatic experience. In the case of war trauma, soldiers' brains are programmed to respond to threats of danger. Sometimes vets cannot turn this response off when they return home. The smallest noise or unexpected movement can trigger a violent response. Vets often sleep lightly because they expect danger at any moment. In addition, some vets feel guilty for their wartime actions or simply for being alive when so many others died. Anger is a common symptom of PTSD.

Healing from war related trauma is difficult, but veterans can get help. Counselors encourage them to tell their stories. However, reliving war is painful. After World War II, many vets chose to be silent. They believed that putting it behind them would enable them to forget their terrible experiences.

It is possible that Ann Fay's father would struggle with memories of war for the rest of his life. Thousands did. In 2005 (sixty years after the end of World War II), more than twenty-five thousand WWII veterans were still receiving disability compensation for PTSD-related symptoms. In many cases, families paid the price of war by living with an angry or alcoholic vet.

In the wake of recent wars, thousands of families around the world are experiencing postwar trauma for the first time. Thankfully, in the United States today, military and veterans' organizations are better equipped to help returning vets than they were in the past. There are books, websites, and trained professionals available to help veterans and their families with PTSD.

Post-Polio Syndrome

Like war, polio has lingering effects. The polios I interviewed worked hard to overcome their disabilities. They danced, participated in sports, and took on jobs that used their good muscles. As they aged, however, many began to experience unexpected physical problems, and eventually they realized that these problems were related to their polio experience. Doctors now call these ailments Post-Polio Syndrome. Polios are banding together in support groups to share ideas for lifestyle tips, medical assistance, and emotional support.

People-First Language
Following the example of Franklin Roosevelt, many people who had polio call themselves polios instead of victims or survivors. Typically, however, individuals do not enjoy being defined by a disease or disability. Instead, they want to be known for what they can do well. Roosevelt did this by winning the country over with his smile, booming voice, and "can do" attitude.

Today, there is a move to name the person before the disability. For example, we say "He uses a wheelchair" instead of "He is wheelchair bound," or "She has autism" instead of "She is autistic."

For more information about People-First Language, visit www.disabilityisnatural.com/index.htm

Who Was Real? Who Was Not?
While writing *Comfort* I talked with people who had had polio and also with local citizens who remember the post-WWII era. Their experiences helped to shape Ann Fay's story.

Ann Fay's friend Suzanne, the girl with club feet, still lives in the village of Warm Springs, Georgia. She is a park ranger at the historic pools where Roosevelt used to swim. Suzanne has been in this community and at the Warm Springs Foundation for her entire life. She answered many questions for me. And oh, by the way, although Suzanne had a mischievous streak, she *never* helped anyone leave Warm Springs without permission!

The older girl named Martha who sometimes played games with Ann Fay was at Warm Springs in 1946 and even met and married Lou, a Navy man who came there for treatment. I interviewed her sister, read Martha's letters, and handled the items she made in occupational therapy.

Ed Frogge, the man who worked at the front desk in Georgia Hall, was a real person and apparently an unforgettable character. Dr. Pat (Raper), Dr. Bennett, and Ma Harding were all real people who worked at Warm Springs.

Ann Fay's attendant, Etta Mae Trotter, was the mother of a patient, Leon Trotter, who went to Warm Springs for multiple surgeries. She always found work at the foundation while her son was being treated. Leon is now one of my experts who reviewed the manuscript and helped me with accuracy. His practical joke using ketchup, recounted by Suzanne in one of her letters to Ann Fay, was one of many stories he shared with me. Carolyn Raville, mentioned briefly in *Comfort*, was at Warm Springs before Ann Fay's time. She also answered many questions and reviewed my manuscript.

Fred Botts was one of the first polios to show up at Warm Springs after Franklin Roosevelt expressed his vision for a rehabilitation center. He served as the foundation's registrar and stayed until his death. The story of his lost singing career and his travel by train in the baggage car are true.

Magic Hill was a real place. Several of my Warm Springs experts told me stories about it.

President Truman created the "National Employ the Handicapped Week" in October 1945. I felt that having Ann

Fay work at Whitener's Store was in keeping with a typical polio's experience. Many were "adopted" by local business people who sponsored their stay at Warm Springs or helped them acquire a job skill. The phrase "our little polio girl" came directly from Carolyn, one of the Warm Springs alumni I interviewed.

Ruth Whitener's store was a gathering place for farmers and other locals. Ruth's daughter Jean told me that her mother never hired anyone other than family to work in the store. The locals I interviewed all agreed, however, that reaching out to Ann Fay would have suited her character.

Jean's friend Beckie (Huffman) is a real person who helped me by answering many questions, sharing photographs, and reading the manuscript. Mrs. Barkley was an especially beloved teacher who taught eighth grade at Mountain View School during the 1940s.

And What About the Dog?
President Roosevelt did have a beloved Scottish terrier much like Mr. Shoes. Of course, Mr. Shoes—like Ann Fay, Junior Bledsoe, Otis Hickey, and most of the characters in Comfort—was fictional!

A Timeline of Disability Rights

1927 – Franklin D. Roosevelt establishes Georgia Warm Springs Foundation.

1932 – Franklin D. Roosevelt is elected president of the United States, the first and still the only president with a physical disability.

1945 – President Harry Truman signs a law calling for the creation of an annual "National Employ the Handicapped Week."

1952 – Hugh Gallagher (who later drafts the laws that make public buildings accessible to the handicapped) contracts polio.

1953 – Ed Roberts (who later becomes father of the "independent-living movement") contracts polio.

1962 – Ed Roberts, in an iron lung, becomes the first person with a severe disability to attend the University of California at Berkeley.

1968 – The Architectural Barriers Act (written by Hugh Gallagher) is passed. It mandates that federally funded buildings be accessible to people with physical disabilities.

1973 – First "handicap" parking stickers issued in Washington, D.C.

1974 – The Education for All Handicapped Children Act is passed. It establishes that children with disabilities have the right to attend regular public schools.

1976 – Ed Roberts establishes the Westside Center for Independent Living in Los Angeles, California.

1990 – The Americans with Disabilities Act is signed by President George H. W. Bush. It mandates that businesses, government programs, public buildings, communication, and transportation be accessible to people with disabilities.

1990 – The Individuals with Disabilities Education Act is passed, guaranteeing federal funding to schools for education of children with disabilities.

Resources

Books

Black Bird Fly Away, by Hugh Gregory Gallagher (Vandamere Press, 1998)

FDR's Splendid Deception: The Moving Story of Roosevelt's Massive Disability, by Hugh Gregory Gallagher (Dodd, Mead & Co., 1985)

The Greatest Generation Comes Home: The Veteran in American Society, by Michael D. Gambone (Texas A&M University Press, 2005)

Images of America: Warm Springs, by David M. Burke Jr. and Odie A. Burke (Arcadia Publishing, 2005)

A Nearly Normal Life, by Charles L. Mee (Little, Brown & Co., 1999)

Patenting the Sun: Polio and the Salk Vaccine, by Jane S. Smith (William Morrow & Co., 1990)

Polio's Legacy: An Oral History, by Edmund J. Sass with George Gottfried and Anthony Sorem (University Press of America, 1996)

Recovering From the War: A Woman's Guide to Helping Your Vietnam Vet, Your Family, and Yourself, by Robert C. Mason and Patience H. C. Mason (Viking, 1990)

A Summer Plague: Polio and Its Survivors, by Tony Gould (Yale University Press, 1995)

The Things They Carried, by Tim O'Brien (Broadway, 1999)

Through the Eyes of Innocents: Children Witness World War II, by Emmy E. Werner (Westview Press, 2000)

To Hear Only Thunder Again: America's World War II Veterans Come Home, by Mark D. Van Ells (Lexington Books, 2001)

Warm Springs: Traces of a Childhood at FDR's Polio Haven, by Susan Richards Shreve (Houghton Mifflin Co., 2007)

Books of Interest to Young People

Hero of Lesser Causes, by Julie Johnston (Joy St. Books, 1993)

A Paralyzing Fear: The Triumph Over Polio in America, by Nina Gilden Seavey, Jane S. Smith, and Paul Wagner (TV Books, 1998)

Sadako and the Thousand Paper Cranes, by Eleanor Coerr (Puffin Books, 2004)

Small Steps: The Year I Got Polio, by Peg Kehret (Albert Whitman & Co., 1996)

Soldier's Heart: Being the Story of the Enlistment and Due Service of the Boy Charley Goddard in the First Minnesota Volunteers, by Gary Paulsen (Laurel Leaf, 2000)

V Is for Victory: The American Home Front During World War II, by Sylvia Whitman (Lerner Publications Co., 1993)

Wilma Rudolph: A Biography, by Maureen M. Smith (Greenwood Press, 2006)

Wilma Rudolph: Olympic Runner, by Jo Harper (Aladdin, 2004)

Wilma Unlimited: How Wilma Rudolph Became the World's Fastest Woman, by Kathleen Krull and David Diaz (Voyager Books, 2000)

The Wonder Kid, by George Harrar (Houghton Mifflin, 2006)

Videos

All Quiet on the Western Front, by Delbert (Mann Lion's Gate, 1979)

In Search of the Polio Vaccine, by Modern Marvels (History Channel/A&E Home Entertainment, 2005)

Martha in Lattimore, by Mary M. Dalton (Mary M. Dalton, 2005)

A Paralyzing Fear, by Nina Gilden Seavey (First Run Features, 1998)

The War, by Jon Avnet (Universal Studios, 1994)

The War, by Ken Burns (PBS, 2007)

Warm Springs, by Joseph Sargent (HBO, 2005)

Wilma, by Bud Greenspan (S'More Entertainment, 2007)

Web Sites

www.americanhistory.si.edu/polio/ – Whatever Happened to Polio? – A Smithsonian Institution online exhibit about polio, the epidemics, and vaccines.

www.disabilityisnatural.com/index.htm – The Disability Is Natural website provides insight and resources for understanding how alike we all are and how disabilities do not define the individual.

www.kidstogether.org/kidstogether.htm – Site of Kids Together, Inc., an organization formed to provide resources for people with disabilities.

www.ncptsd.va.gov/ncmain/information/ – This Veterans
Administration site provides information about Post-Traumatic
Stress Disorder. This page contains links to Frequently Asked
Questions, a fact sheet about PTSD, and a video.

www.patiencepress.com – The website of Patience Mason, a
counselor who is married to a Vietnam veteran. Filled with
helpful resources on war-related and other kinds of Post-Traumatic Stress Disorder.

www.rooseveltrehab.org/ – The official website of the Roosevelt
Warm Springs Institute for Rehabilitation (formerly known as
the Georgia Warm Springs Foundation).

Thank You!

While writing *Comfort* I visited the Roosevelt Warm Springs Institute numerous times, where librarian Mike Shaddix answered my questions and generously gave me access to the archive. During a behind-the-scenes tour Linda Creekbaum handled my countless questions with grace and insight.

Steve Lane and David Burke of the Little White House also shared their expertise via phone interviews, and David M. Rose, archivist for the March of Dimes, welcomed my questions and provided me with 1940s photographs of the Georgia Warm Springs Foundation.

Suzanne Pike and Marion Dunn, who both had long-term experiences at Warm Springs, answered many questions and supplied me with rich details. Mary Ann Weston shared her sister's Warm Springs experiences, letters, and artifacts.

Both Carolyn Raville and Leon Trotter, Warm Springs alumni from the 1940s, were treasure troves of Warm Springs history and the polio experience. Leon and I swapped countless emails. He answered the smallest of questions about braces, surgeries, and the people, history, and daily schedule of Warm Springs. He read and reread my manuscript, made suggestions, and fearlessly challenged my "facts." Carolyn and Suzanne also submitted to multiple interviews, read the manuscript for accuracy, and inspired my story.

The following people shared their disability experiences with me, thus infusing Ann Fay's story with emotion and detail I wouldn't have known: Louise Lynch, Bobby Suggs, Jane Hewitt, John Myer, Shelby Duane, Kathryn Pennell, Sylvia Huffman, Dosia Carlson, Jackie Kimsey, and Dan Moury. Thanks!

Jean Whitener Frye, Rebecca Huffman, and Claude Wilson provided me with details about Whitener's Store as it was in the 1940s. Edgar Robinson, Rebecca Huffman, and Violet Barkley gave me valuable information about Mountain View School during that era.

My parents, and nearly every senior citizen I know, answered questions for me about life in the 1940s.

Librarians at the Catawba County Library and the Hickory Public Library dug for local history and borrowed materials through interlibrary loan. Thanks, Alex, Regina, Alice, April, Janey, Hannah, and Martin! Thanks also to Karen Gilliam, librarian at Broughton Hospital, and Jim Williams and Franklin DeJarnette at the VA Medical Center in Asheville, North Carolina, who helped me rule out hospitalization as a treatment for postwar trauma.

Carolyn Yoder, my most excellent editor, once again forced me to dig deeper into my character's motivations, analyze her relationships, and articulate her desires. Katya Rice, my copyeditor, enhanced the story by paying attention to details that I so easily missed.

My husband, Chuck, endured several research "vacations" and happily sent me on more of my own. Back home, when I slipped into another life in a different decade for months at a time, he waited patiently for me to resurface.